"An engaging novel with an unforgettable main character. Frances Delaney has lived a 'small' life, but as she responds to a devastating diagnosis, her rich and moving story unfolds. We learn the secrets of Frances's past and how she makes peace with those secrets, and we also see how that past shaped the woman she has become. By turns heartbreaking and hilarious, this is one of the most sensitive fictional portrayals of the end of life that I've ever read."
—TRUDY J. MORGAN-COLE, author of *By the Rivers of Brooklyn, Most Anything You Please, A Roll of the Bones*, and other Newfoundland historical fiction

"*The Good Women of Safe Harbour* will break your heart and mend it back together again. In this novel, set beside the changeable Newfoundland sea, Frances Delaney reckons with the question of how to make life worth living even as she nears the end of hers. With the help of her long-lost best friend, Annie, and the irrepressible teenager, Edie, Frances emerges from a self-imposed loneliness to learn that the only thing that truly endures is the abiding love they hold for each other. Bobbi French is a master storyteller as she gently leads us to Frances's final lesson with humour, compassion, and grace."
—CARRIANNE LEUNG, author of *That Time I Loved You*

"An absolutely soul-comforting meditation on what's possible when there's nothing left to lose. Rich, lively, surprising, warm, and wise, the voice of Frances Delaney won me wholly. I couldn't put this book down, and its message of embodied healing will stay with me. A cathartic and uplifting story about friendship, forgiveness, and healing."

—CARRIE SNYDER, author of *Girl Runner*

"Bobbi French brings an authentic eye to a tender truth: whatever our woes, it is never too late to lay down what we are carrying. A poignant, deeply arresting, and often funny portrayal of female friendships, even those that get lost for a time somewhere along the way."

—CHRISTINE HIGDON,
author of *The Very Marrow of Our Bones*

"Bobbi French has created an unforgettable character in Frances Delaney. Facing the premature end of her solitary life, Frances chooses to die on her own terms, assisted by two good women—her childhood friend Annie, with whom she has recently reconciled, and the savvy teenaged Edie. The final revelation in this deeply moving debut will leave you stunned, satisfied, and reaching for a box of tissues."

—DAMHNAIT MONAGHAN, internationally published
author of *New Girl in Little Cove*

"So vividly imagined, it was as if I carried the characters' worries and hopes in my own heart. Set in an unforgettable landscape, brimming with insights, Bobbi French's warm, honest prose makes even the most tragic secrets and events shimmer and lift."

—KELLY SIMMONS, international selling author
of six novels, including *One More Day*

"In turns moving and funny, *The Good Women of Safe Harbour* is a heartfelt story of a woman who is determined to live what life she has left as if it is only beginning. Whether for the tears or laughter, you'll want to keep a Kleenex box handy for this one. In lyrical prose and with a character voice that sings, Bobbi French offers a story that's all about forgiveness and the power of friendship between women. But this novel is also a call to reawaken the wonder found in the everyday world all around us. As Frances Delaney swims through her memories and surfaces reborn, she learns to make even the smallest experience count in her final days. In sharing that journey with her, you'll feel more alive and so much more *here*, in this precious, shining moment. This novel is a reminder to pay attention as we move through our day, to phone a friend or sister, to find connection and touch and meaning in our ordinary routines. Because life is made of these moments."

—GAIL ANDERSON-DARGATZ, author of *The Almost Wife*

"*The Good Women of Safe Harbour* lets you meet Frances Delaney gently, almost formally. That›s a kindness. None of that prepares you for a book that, as it quickly reaches take-off speed, quite simply won›t let you go."

—RUSSELL WANGERSKY,
author of *The Path of Most Resistance*

The Good Women
of Safe Harbour

The Good Women of Safe Harbour

A NOVEL

BOBBI FRENCH

HARPER**AVENUE**

Published by Harper Avenue, an imprint of HarperCollins Publishers Ltd

First edition

HarperCollins books may be purchased for educational, business or sales promotional use through our Special Markets Department.

HarperCollins Publishers Ltd
Bay Adelaide Centre, East Tower
22 Adelaide Street West, 41st Floor
Toronto, Ontario, Canada
M5H 4E3

www.harpercollins.ca

Library and Archives Canada Cataloguing in Publication

Title: The good women of Safe Harbour / Bobbi French.
Names: French, Bobbi, 1968- author.
Identifiers: Canadiana (print) 20210348798 |
Canadiana (ebook) 20210348968 | ISBN 9781443464048 (softcover) |
ISBN 9781443464055 (ebook)
Classification: LCC PS8611.R4425 G66 2022 | DDC C813/.6—dc23

Printed and bound in the United States of America
LSC/H 9 8 7 6 5 4 3 2 1

For the women of Newfoundland and Labrador—
good as gold, sharp as tacks, and tough as nails.

The Good Women
of Safe Harbour

Prologue

Late August 2019

I took a few halting steps, my feet slipping and sliding over the rounded rocks. The sea pushed against my knees, and slimy tendrils of seaweed wrapped around my ankles. I waded in up to my waist. Another step and a wave against my chest. A splash of salt against my lips. When the next wave rushed toward me, I inhaled deeply and surrendered. I tumbled under and over, limp and powerless until my body remembered the movements needed to propel me forward through the green murk, past the rocky shoal, and into the clear, deep water. I raised my arms above my head and sank down into the cool silence, waiting and listening until the last second of breath was spent, then burst up through the surface gasping for air. I faced the horizon, closed my eyes, and listened. I heard nothing but my panting breaths and the wailing gulls.

I was overcome with the beauty of it all—the bracing cold, the shimmering sunlight, the rhythmic rocking to and fro as I lay on my back smiling at the sky. All around me water quenching an unbelievable thirst I didn't even know I had. I'd faced it down and won, my prize this homecoming I now knew I deserved. I couldn't recall a moment in my life when I'd felt more alive—blissfully, intensely so. I was carefree and bound by nothing.

I drifted along until I felt the sun and salt burning my face, then I paddled toward the shore, where two women—one young and thin and fair-haired, the other older, shapely with dark curls—stood laughing and waving and calling my name. They looked happy, whoever they were.

1

Three months earlier

I woke with a start, disoriented and coated with sweat. The clock on my bedside table read a quarter to six. I lay wrapped in a tangle of damp sheets, my heart hammering, and knew any chance for more sleep was lost. I waited for my muddy head to clear, then rose to face the task ahead. A steaming bath and a mug of strong, sweet tea did little to calm my nerves. I opened the closet and unzipped a plastic garment bag that held a new grey jacket, matching trousers, and a filmy lavender blouse, all pulled from a clearance rack a week ago. My first snappy outfit in fifty-eight years of living. As I buttoned and zipped, it was as if I were trying on a better life. I imagined myself reborn, liberated from plainness at last. But the mirror set me straight. A scraggy little chicken with a few fine feathers added. What odds. Beauty would be of no use to me today. What I needed was a bit of backbone and all my wits at the ready. Now buck up, old bird.

I turned away from the mirror and looked down at my hands poking out through the cuffs of the jacket. Peasant hands, I always thought. Raw knuckles striped with fine bloody cracks and slashes. A permanent redness from fingertips to wrists, as if they'd been dipped in paint. I accepted them for what they were: my livelihood, the invaluable tools of a cleaning woman. But today they would have a well-earned rest under a slather of thick cream.

I skipped the bus in favour of a taxi—another rare splurge. The driver was mercifully quiet as he steered the car toward the older part of St. John's, along the narrow streets lined with brightly coloured row houses, then across Duckworth Street, heavy with traffic, past the shops and the cafés and the war memorial, a glimpse of the cold sun-sparkled sea just beyond, before stopping in front of a tower of metal and glass.

Inside the building, people dressed in stylish coats and holding briefcases were huddled in front of the elevators. The thought of squeezing myself in a steel box with strangers made my stomach roll and I opted for the stairs.

The office smelled of freshly brewed coffee. A spare, modern space with white walls and soft lighting where a young woman sat behind a curved desk, her fingers tapping loudly on a computer keyboard. She stopped typing and asked if I had an appointment.

"Frances Delaney. Nine o'clock."

"Right on time," she said. "Have a seat and I'll let her know you're here."

I passed my eyes over the magazines laid out on the low glass table in front of me, the usual dated fare except for one with a colourful drawing of a brain on the cover. I reached for it after spying a word I'd never seen before—*neurotransmitter*. I dug into my bag and wrote it in my little spiral notebook, filing it away for later, when I'd flip through my dog-eared dictionary as I did every time I came across a word I didn't know, a habit I'd acquired as a child. I'd look it up and underline it, rehearse saying it until I felt it was one of my own. I always put stars beside my favourites. Like *frippery* and *scintillate*. By now, I had collected too many to count. My head was chock-full of words, the majority of which I hadn't once uttered to another soul and probably never would. Still, they were like constant companions, popping up in my mind at every turn.

But this time, *neurotransmitter* and its mysteries weren't enough to distract me from the reason for my visit to this white-walled fortress. The air in the office seemed suddenly thin, and my chest grew tight. I eyed the door and started weighing the pros and cons of making a run for it.

"Frances? I'm Dr. Shirley Bell."

Her voice startled me. She was younger than I expected, probably not yet forty. She had smooth dark skin stretched over high cheekbones and black hair that was twisted into skinny braids that grazed the tops of her shoulders. She extended a hand with short lacquered nails.

"It's good to meet you," she said. "Shall we get started?"

She turned and strode down the carpeted hallway toward her office, where she poured two glasses of water from a pitcher on her desk and asked me to take a seat. She reached for a pen, a pad of writing paper, and a blue file folder, then settled herself in a chair facing me.

"Frances, your doctor has explained why she has referred you to a psychiatrist, yes?"

I nodded.

"You look nervous. Are you?"

"Maybe a little."

"Why is that?"

"Because I expect I'm the only Newfoundlander not keen on talking."

She smiled. "I'll try to make this as painless as possible. I already have a lot of information about you."

Dr. Bell opened the file folder and scanned the papers inside. I feared she would come to a swift opinion of me: a pitiful old halfwit, unhinged and in need of professional persuasion. She'd be dead wrong about that.

She closed the file. "So, Frances, tell me what you know about your diagnosis."

It had been exactly one month since another young doctor sat next to my hospital bed and gave me two new words for my notebook. I asked her to write them out for me on a scrap of paper after she'd offered her condolences. Her name was lost to me, but her face and voice were carved deep into my memory. The poor woman looked fully distraught, and I suspected she was fairly new to the game of breaking bad news. In the days that followed, I heard the words many times, but I had yet to say them aloud. I took a sip of water.

"Glioblastoma multiforme." I knew I'd pronounced them correctly, which pleased me.

"And what's your understanding about your prognosis?"

"It's an aggressive brain tumour. Ten to twelve months, best case."

She gave me a sympathetic look. "I'm very sorry that you've had such bad news." She waited a few beats. "Now, our issue is your refusal of the recommended treatment. Tell me about that."

I could have told her all about it—the burly surgeon I'd met a week before who wanted to cut my head open and dig out what he could, and the other doctor who wanted to pour poison into my veins to buy me a few months. Months that I would spend sick, terrified, alone, and maybe most important, unpaid. I imagined it wasn't easy to haul a vacuum cleaner around with one foot in the grave, which meant dying was within my budget, languishing was not. But I had decided the less said, the better. *Succinct*.

"It's just a delay in the inevitable," I said. "I'd like to spend what time I have left in a state fit enough to enjoy it." I was pleased with how calm and steady I sounded. Even better than when I'd spoken the lines to the mirror the night before.

"You understand that without treatment, your life expectancy will almost certainly be shortened?"

"I do."

She made a note on her yellow pad. "Frances, I have the results from your cognitive testing, and I have the report from the psychologist you saw at the hospital—all of which looks quite thorough to me. I see they've ruled out any major mental illness. Your file says that you have no previous psychiatric history, but I can't see much in here about your relatives. Anyone in your family ever have issues with their mental health?"

A rush of heat spread over me. My new blouse grew sticky on my back, and I wondered what it would cost to dry-clean it. "Not that I know of."

"Can you tell me a little about your past? Maybe a bit about your upbringing?"

I felt a sudden thrill at the prospect of telling someone about my small life. I also felt the dread of laying myself bare to a stranger, especially one with the power to derail my plans. I steadied my breaths and forced a smile that I hoped looked casual. "There's not much to tell, really."

"You prefer we stick to the present?"

"I do."

She ran through a series of questions that I was now familiar with. Tell me the date, the season, the name of this street. Spell the word *world* backwards. Remember these three words: *ball*, *pen*, *telephone*. Draw this, name that. Her pen scratched against the paper, tick, tick, tick.

"Have you ever had periods of feeling quite down or depressed?"

I pretended to reflect on it. "No."

"What about since your diagnosis?"

"No."

"Any changes in sleep, energy, appetite?"

"Not especially."

"Any experiences of hearing voices or seeing things that other people don't seem to see?"

"Certainly not."

"What about worries and fears?"

"The only worry I have is that they'll make me have that surgery."

"Nobody can make you. As long as you are mentally fit to do so, you have the right to refuse treatment."

"Which is where you come in."

"Exactly. Frances, I know you've answered this question more than once in recent days, but I have to ask again, have you ever had thoughts of suicide?"

On another day I would have asked her if being tired of living was the same thing, but I just shook my head.

She paused briefly and her expression softened. "You mentioned earlier that you live on your own, so I'm wondering about a support system for you. Do you have people who can help you through this?"

"Oh yes. All hands on deck."

She held my gaze for a few seconds. Something in her eyes registered doubt, and a sickly feeling came over me. By my tally, I'd told her at least three lies, and until then I believed myself to be entirely convincing, but suddenly I feared she had a clear view of every moment of my life, as if it were a film playing across my face. I looked down at my clenched hands, then looked back up and forced another smile.

She wrote a final note and then laid down her pen. "Well, you're clearly competent to refuse treatment, but you may change your mind, in which case your doctors are prepared to help you in any way they can, as am I. If you notice changes in your mood or anything else of concern, I'm more than happy to see you again. All right?"

I felt my body start to soften and cool down. The faint ringing in my ears fell silent, and I could feel my heart and lungs returning to their regular rhythms.

"So you're breaking out the sane stamp, are you?"

She laughed and thumped the folder with her fist. "Sane!"

We rose from our chairs and she walked me out. As she shook my hand, she asked, "So what now?"

"Oh, loose ends and all that."

"I know it won't be easy, but I wish you all the best."

As I watched her walk away, I realized she had never taken her eyes off me while we talked, not even when she was writing on her yellow paper. I wondered if she really cared. Maybe she'd just practised compassion in the mirror, honed it into a special skill, the same way she'd learned to write without looking down. I also wondered, if she and I had met years ago, would I have told her my truths and let her do her best to heal me?

I pushed through the glass doors and stepped onto the busy sidewalk. The bustle of downtown always rattled me—the crush of busy people, the traffic, the never-ending din of urban living. I'd never quite warmed to the whirl and twirl of the city. I was still a bay girl at heart. Sea and sky and craggy cliffs were more my speed. Room to roam and be at one with the beauty of the island. Standing in the shadow of that tall building, I may as well have been in the middle of Toronto.

I walked for two blocks, found a bench, and sat down so I could pry the stiff new shoes from my aching feet. I rubbed my soles and each one of my toes until I could feel the blood flowing again, then I pulled a pair of tattered white work sneakers from my bag.

It was the end of May, and the swollen buds had finally started to open on the tree branches. One of my first thoughts after the doctor broke the news to me was how lucky I was to have winter forever behind me. Never again would I huddle against the north wind at the bus stop, the blowing snow slicing my cheeks and ice crystals forming in my nose. My last days on this earth would be days of green grass and fresh breezes, cool drizzle and salty fog, and with any luck, a few bouts of sunshine in between. If there was an afterlife, which I doubted, let it be a state of perpetual spring.

My phone dinged, a reminder for my medication. My shield against another seizure, which was how this all began a few months back. The first indication that something was very wrong with me. The pills were large and chalky, and I had nothing to drink. I left the bench and walked toward a small grocery store at the end of the street. I stood in line behind an ancient man buying lottery tickets. He looked closer to death than I was. Now what was that fool going to do if his numbers came up? Maybe he had a brood of youngsters to leave it all to, or maybe it was just a habit he couldn't let go. The old man asked the clerk for two packs of Camels. I imagined the many years spent with a lit cigarette between his nicotine-stained fingers, and I envied him. I closed my eyes and I could hear the crack and hiss of the match, feel the hot pull of the first drag, see the white plume jetting up as I tilted my head back. It was over two decades since I'd given it up. People congratulated me on my commitment to healthy living, but truthfully, had the price of tobacco stayed within my reach, I'd have smoked two at a time until my last breath.

"Just the water for you, missus?"

"Yes. No, hang on. Give me a pack of Rothmans, please."

I walked back to the bench and removed the cellophane from the box. I pinched and pulled up a tightly rolled cylinder, placed the speckled orange tip between my lips, struck a match, and drew in the beautifully harsh smoke. It was like coming into a toasty firelit room after being locked out in the cold for twenty years. I sucked the cigarette down to my fingers, the buzz and spin from it as satisfying a sensation as I could ever hope to feel. My phone dinged again, and I dug out the pill bottle.

Another cigarette, then another taxi. I slouched down in the back seat. Through the window, I watched the tops of the buildings whiz past against the bright blue sky. I felt unburdened, almost energized. I asked the driver to stop two streets away from my place and walked the rest of the way.

My apartment was bathed in sunlight, and I realized I'd never seen it in the middle of a workday. It looked larger, edging toward spacious. Perhaps spacious was a stretch, no matter how lovely the light. It was nothing more than a few boxy rooms with a drafty window here and there, a tidy shelter behind a dented metal door at the top of a steep flight of stairs. A living room, a bedroom, a basic kitchen and bathroom, all done on the cheap, but still the best place I'd called home in my adult life. In comparison to the many shabby dwellings where I'd lived, this one was practically luxurious. As much heat and hot water as I pleased. A fridge and stove that worked without fail. A white tub surrounded by white tiles that I kept scrubbed to a sparkle. Tucked away on the top floor of a green clapboard house on a quiet street near the university, the low rent my reward for a decade spent scrubbing the massive Victorian house of my landlord's elderly mother, Mrs. Heneghan. She'd been dead now for almost five years.

I'd received many things from clients—well-worn clothes, cracked and mismatched dishes, faded sheets and blankets, boxes of books, even a television—all needed and most welcome. Particularly the books, my treasures. But this apartment was a kindness beyond compare for which I was immeasurably grateful to Mrs. Heneghan's well-raised son. For a year after he'd handed me the key, I lived in constant fear that he'd change his mind and toss me out. Every time I signed the rent check, my hand shook and I offered up a silent plea: please don't let this month be my last. Now I sent him his money by email using my phone, another hand-me-down. It was a useless relic to the teenage girl whose pigsty of a bedroom I dug my way through several times a week, but a marvel of technology to me.

I peeled off my rumpled clothes, showered, then stood by the open bedroom window wrapped in a towel, a cigarette in one hand and a tumbler of whisky in the other, the first drink I'd had in a very long time. The bottle was part of a Christmas cheer basket given to me by Mr. Heneghan a few years back, and it had been sitting unopened in my kitchen cupboard ever since. A rush of cool air passed over me. The skin on my scalp and chest tingled with it, and the hairs on my arms prickled. I stuck my head out the window, closed my eyes, and drew in a deep breath. I smelled the earth shifting into spring, then a waft of something cooking. Butter and onions. Sounds drifted up from the street below—a baby crying, a radio playing classical music, the idling motor of a parked car, and a siren blaring in the distance. It was almost overwhelming. Maybe this thing in my head had heightened my senses, or maybe I just hadn't paid attention before now. I wondered what else I'd been missing. I closed the window and stubbed out my cigarette on a chipped saucer.

I pulled on sweatpants and a soft T-shirt, then sat mindlessly in front of the television. How strange and unsettling it was to be so idle at this time of day. I poked around the apartment and found all kinds of chores that needed doing, but I was too tired to fix on any one in particular. Instead, I poured myself another drink and stretched out on the couch. My body was in favour of a nap, but my brain had other ideas about how best to while away an afternoon. Since the moment I was told about the tumour, I'd had little room for a single thought beyond how I would leave this world, but now I found my mind wandering back to how I came in, carefully cracking open the past like a spoon on an egg.

2

My life has been shaped by the sea—the frigid North Atlantic that surrounds Newfoundland. I was born here, and I'll die here too. In fact, I've never once set foot off the island.

I come from lines of fisherfolk that run six generations deep, right back to the early settlers of Safe Harbour, a small town on the southern shore. My father spent his days combing the ocean for cod, and my mother's hands were rarely free from silver scales and fish innards. It was Georgina and Patrick Delaney who taught me to appreciate the beauty of the ocean, to be grateful for its bounty, and to respect its power. I learned to fear and despise the ocean on my own.

My earliest memory is my mother's voice. For the first decade of my life, she sang more than she talked. Hymns and sea shanties, folk tunes and radio hits of the day. I begged her constantly for "Lukey's Boat," its rhythmic beat and repetitive chant of "Aha, me boys a-riddle-i-day" delighting me whether belted out as the call to supper or whispered as a lullaby when I was sick. She was the soloist at our church and the life of every gathering: baptisms and funerals, garden parties and weddings—including her own. My grandmother loved to talk about my parents' wedding, especially the part where my mother had sung her heart out while my father beamed at her over the bow of his fiddle. My grandmother also loved to talk about how it was music that first drew my parents together. In his childhood house, across the lane from my mother's, my father began scraping the strings when his small hands were barely able to hold the instrument, and once his fingers grew nimble, he would stand at the open window and play, drawing my mother to his door like a Siren.

They married when they were just eighteen—common for devout Catholics in 1960. But unlike their neighbours, all of whom had gaggles of youngsters, I was their only child. I never knew exactly why, but every time I pleaded for a sibling, I could see even with young eyes it was a pain they shared. One day they sat me down and told me there would never be other children. My mother's explanation was that it was God's will, and it was not to be questioned. Apart from a baby sister or brother, I was given everything any child could want. Fried bread dough dripping with butter for breakfast. Hand-knit mittens and socks in every colour of the rainbow. Fiddle lessons and a song before bed. Saturday afternoons on my father's boat. Undisturbed hours to poke about the tidal pools for seashells with my best friend, Annie Malone. I didn't know we were poor. How could I when there was fresh, sweet cod alongside potatoes and carrots pulled from our garden on my dinner plate, when there was wood burning in the black iron stove in the corner and a warm coat hanging on the hook by the door. It all seemed solid and sure, protected and permanent.

Two weeks after my eleventh birthday, my father drowned while fishing a stormy sea, him and his two brothers swallowed up by the icy black water. They were honoured with a ceremonial burial—three empty pine caskets lowered side by side into the rocky soil while my mother sang "The Parting Glass," my father's favourite. Her voice was low and strained with a raspy timbre. I fixed my gaze toward the ocean while she sang, hoping that her voice had the power to bring him back to us. After the funeral, she stood at the water's edge in the thick fog, her face taut and grim, and tossed his fiddle into the waves. She spent weeks in their bed, staring out the window and turning visitors away. I begged her to get up, to wash and eat, to walk with me to the shore, to sing to me, but she just laid her palm against my cheek and rolled away from me. When she finally emerged, I was frightened by this stooped, haggard stranger.

Before my father died, I'd rise every Christmas morning at dawn and tiptoe downstairs to dig into a red woollen sock filled with oranges and chocolates and hard peppermint candies. There was always a modest gift—a book and a deck of cards, hair barrettes and a trio of scented soaps. My mother would cook for days, pies and cakes and a golden turkey with silky gravy poured over turnip and soft cabbage. My teeth would ache from the sugar cookies and freshly baked bread sticky with molasses. At night, everyone in town who could carry a tune or play an instrument or tell a fine tale would squeeze in around our fire. That first Christmas without him, people still came, but only to bring plates of cold food wrapped in tea towels and hushed words of sympathy and encouragement. There was no music. The red sock was still filled and a gift from my mother (a pink scarf knitted by Mrs. Malone) still made its way to my hands, but there was no joy in it.

We didn't have any family beyond each other. Like me, my mother was an only child. She was born when her mother was in her early forties and her father was almost fifty. Her mother died of cancer when I was a baby, and her father suffered a fatal heart attack a few years after. My father's mother, also a widow, was consumed by her own grief and died less than a year after her sons were buried. The people of Safe Harbour stepped in to care for us. Hot suppers carried over by Mrs. Malone, clothes cast off by girls as they grew, bread and pies from other mothers, fish from other fathers, house repairs from other husbands. I mourned my father in private. I pressed his scratchy wool sweater to my face until it was soaked with tears and watched the sea every day, waiting for his fiddle to wash up on the shore. At night, I lay in my bed, sifting through my memories of him, always finding my way to the one I treasured above all others.

When I was five years old, I stood before the priest as he extended a thumb blackened with ashes and made the sign of the cross on my forehead. Then he said, "Remember that you are dust, and unto dust you shall return." Later that evening, I sat with my parents at the dinner table, each of us with the stain of our faith on our skin, and I asked them why Father O'Leary had called me dust. My mother said he was talking about the circle of life, which made no sense to me. I looked to my father, and he said it was about going to heaven. All I knew about heaven was that it was some far-off place where "good people" like my granny and grandpa went after they died.

"Will I go to heaven too?"

My father reached out and stroked my cheek. "Indeed you will. But not for ages and ages."

"Will it be dusty there?"

My father's booming laugh echoed around the kitchen. "No, sweet girl. It'll be exactly what you want it to be."

"How will I know what I want it to be?"

"Just think about the place that makes you happiest, and that's where you'll go."

After mulling it over, I landed on a day from the summer before, the day my father taught me to swim. Riding on his back just past the rocky shoal, then paddling back toward the shore, where my mother stood clapping and cheering me on. At bedtime, when my father came to my room to kiss me good-night, I told him that after I died, I would live in the ocean. He laughed and said I'd made a fine choice. Then I asked him what place made him happiest. "Anywhere you are," he said, and turned out the light.

My mother gradually returned to living, but she was unrecognizable to me. I waited for her to snap back into the woman she was, but she never did. She moved silently and slowly and kept to herself, and we lived in a house so muted and still that I often wished we'd both been lost with my father. I found some comfort in books. I'd race to the library van every Thursday afternoon and grab all old Mrs. McCarthy would let me carry, then lose myself over and over in the pages of *Anne of Green Gables* and *The Secret Garden*. But really it was school that carried me through. Kind and mindful teachers, gold stars and the letter A written in red pencil at the top of tests. School and Annie Malone.

Days after I learned about my tumour, Annie began to float up from the depths of my memory. Just a random flashback here (the two of us huddled together on a red toboggan as her brother Gordie pulled us through a Christmas snowfall), a vivid dream there (Annie as a teenager, blindfolded, wandering in a churchyard while calling my name). But over the last few weeks, she seemed to be stuck to me like a shadow. *Spectre*.

I reached for an old hardcover copy of *Little Women* on the side table next to the couch and found the small blue envelope I kept pressed between the pages. I pulled out the grainy black-and-white snapshot. I couldn't recall when I'd last seen it. Ten years ago, maybe longer. It was crinkled and faded, but the image was still plain to see. A wide expanse of choppy ocean, a pebbled shore, and two downy-headed toddlers hiding behind their mothers' knees. Faint blue handwriting across the back: "Frances and Annie, 1965." Clear evidence that my dear friend from long ago was not some figment. The undeniable proof that regardless of how it had turned out between us, we had a shared beginning. *Inextricable.*

I woke with the photograph still in my hand. The apartment was dark and quiet. My back ached from the sagging sofa, and my heart ached from dredging the past. I poured myself a drop of whisky and climbed into bed.

What now? Shirley Bell had asked me. What now indeed. The Cleary house would be waiting for me in the morning. They would be my last clients. I had to tell them something and soon, but what exactly I hadn't yet decided. Dr. Cleary was a shadow in that house and would hardly notice I was gone. Mrs. Cleary would find someone to step into my well-worn shoes easily enough. But then there was Edith. What a stark handle for such a merry girl. I was puzzled by how such a modern, vibrant mother had landed on it for her daughter until she gave me copies of *The House of Mirth* and *The Age of Innocence* for Christmas not long after I started working for her. Then I understood. Little Edie Cleary, now sixteen, under my watchful, admiring eye since she was eleven. Parting with her would be a different matter altogether.

By the time I got to work in the morning, I was twenty minutes late. I barrelled into the laundry room, threw in the first load, then marched to the kitchen. The remnants of breakfast were scattered about the room. Half-filled coffee cups on the island, two empty bowls and spoons on the table, crumbs on the counter in front of the toaster, but no signs of Edie's morning milkshake. "Smoothie, Frances, it's called a smoothie," she'd always say, rolling her eyes. I made quick order of the place, then boiled the kettle for tea. I sat at the table and helped myself to a muffin. I wasn't in the habit of making myself at home in the Cleary kitchen, but after the night I'd had and the frantic morning that followed, some liberty-taking was in order.

It had started in the wee hours, a dull throbbing in my head that quickly exploded into a searing pain, like someone had slammed a cleaver through my skull. I staggered to the bathroom, swallowed one of the pain pills they'd given me at the hospital—the ones I'd sworn up and down I didn't need—and pressed a cold facecloth against my eyes. I rested my head on the pillow and took deep breaths until the pain began to retreat. I drifted off, then snapped awake again at three thirty, soaked in sweat. It was as if I could feel the tumour pulsing and expanding, spreading out over my brain like a big ugly squid. I've made a huge mistake, I thought. I should have relented and told them to cut it out. I struggled to breathe, and I felt the dark room closing in. I was sure that death had come for me, and all I could think about was that I would die alone. I curled up into a ball in my bed, sobbing like a child, longing for my mother, and wishing I still believed in God.

Then I heard a bird singing. I opened my eyes. The room was bright, and I was right again. I put my late-night hysterics down to the whisky and those blasted pills, which I also blamed for my forgetting to set the alarm, a first for me. I bolted out of bed, steadied myself against the dizziness, showered, and tore out of the apartment without so much as a sip of water. It was a wonder I'd made it here at all.

I'd been cleaning the Cleary house for almost five years. It was the best gig I ever had. It was a huge house but an easy one, a bright, modern bungalow with large open spaces and sparse furniture. No fussy antiques or intricate chandeliers, and surfaces that shone with a single wipe. Everything sleek and streamlined. Even when it wasn't clean, it fooled you into thinking it was, and after I'd worked my magic, it glittered like Mrs. Cleary's diamond rings.

They paid me twice my usual fee, compensation for the added duties of getting dinner started, running errands, and minding their sweet-tempered daughter while they were clocking in their fifty and sixty hours a week or jetting off somewhere for the weekend. He was a plastic surgeon, facelifts and big breasts and such, and she was the head of marketing at a publishing house, promoting local authors who were lately on the rise. She had an office (she called it her reading room) off the kitchen. It was full of bookshelves packed from end to end, from which I was welcome to borrow whatever I liked.

I'd first met Mrs. Cleary at my library, the one on Allandale Road, where I spent almost every spare moment of my time. I was in line at the desk, waiting to check out my weekly stack, when a tall, lean, beautifully dressed woman passed in front of me and kissed my librarian, Hillary, on both cheeks. They talked long enough for me to grow fidgety, then Hillary motioned for me to join them. "I wonder if you'd consider taking on a new client?" she'd asked. *Client.* Oh, how I liked the sound of that word, and I decided to adopt it immediately. As for new ones, I was more than open at the time. I'd been slogging it out at Mrs. Heneghan's for nearly a decade. She'd had a massive stroke and had been silently staring at a hospital ceiling for a month, just waiting to stare at the ceiling in a care home. Poor woman. I'd been doing small day jobs while frantically looking for a full-time deal and was gearing up to start hitting the hotels again.

Hillary introduced me to her friend from university whose housekeeper had up and taken off for the mainland, leaving her desperate. "Positively desperate," Liz Cleary said. When I told her that I could come have a look at her house, she reached for my hand, gripped it, and gave it a brisk shake.

Her lips parted into a broad smile showing a set of big white teeth. *Ferocious*.

The visit with Mrs. Cleary was twenty minutes of her showing me around the house, my employment obviously a settled matter in her mind. She apologized several times for disarray apparent only to her. Apart from her daughter's room, it was the most orderly house I'd ever seen. We ended in the bright white kitchen, where I noticed there were two dishwashers. You and I are going to get on just fine, I said silently to the house. As for Mrs. Cleary, I held off on my judgment of her.

Many a time I'd started off beautifully with the women—and they were always women—who hired me, only to have it unravel with no hope of reeling it back in. Like Mrs. Whelan, whose husband—that greasy man—was forever giving me the lusty eye. One day, I was down on my hands and knees, scrubbing the kitchen floor, when she came in and found him hovering over me, staring at my raised rear end. I was fired on the spot—hustled out the back door, as if I were the dog defiling her home. I was mortified and furious. It wasn't until later that evening that I realized she hadn't paid me the forty dollars she owed me. I called her three times and left three polite messages, but I heard not a word from her. Six months of cleaning up after the two filthiest people I'd ever come across and that was the thanks I got. I saw her a few weeks later in the supermarket. As I stood behind her in the checkout line with two people between us, I fantasized about telling everyone within earshot about the revolting state of Mrs. Whelan's house. She was never in any danger of such an outburst from me, though—I was better than that, and I needed my money. She paid the cashier and headed for the exit. I abandoned my cart and followed her outside. When I approached her in the parking lot, she was loading her groceries into the back of her car. I was still working up the nerve to speak when she gave me a withering look, and I knew I wasn't steely enough to take her on. I held my tongue and walked away. If I saw her now, maybe I'd let my tongue wag however the hell it pleased.

THE TEA WAS MARVELLOUS. I held the cup with both hands, pretending this was my kitchen, my view of my manicured garden. The house was waiting, and time was wasting away, but the morning light was too lovely, the moment too precious to be hurried. Then my phone rang, and the moment was gone.

"Frances. Are you at the house yet?"

"Yes, Mrs. Cleary. I'm sorry to be a little late today. It won't happen again."

"Listen, I'm in a total bind. My boss has decided that I need to be in Halifax for a book event tonight, and Robert flew off to Vancouver for a conference this morning. Now I'm in a panic because Edie's not feeling well. She was still in bed when I left."

"Edie's here?" I said, startled to realize that she'd been in the house all this time without me knowing. "It's not anything serious, is it?"

"Between you and me, she's probably just hungover. I know it's ridiculously short notice, but is there any way you could stay over with her tonight and into tomorrow as well?"

"Yes, yes, of course I'll stay with her. No problem whatsoever."

"Frances, you're a lifesaver. I'll be back late tomorrow night. I'll keep my phone on in case you need me."

I hung up and quickly gulped down the last of my tea. I poured a glass of ginger ale, lined a bucket with a plastic bag, and headed toward Edie's room. Hungover. Not likely. Every other young one in town maybe, but not Edie. I knocked softly and pushed her door open a crack. The floor was littered with clothes, the nightstand covered with glasses and plates, a streak of something dark across the white duvet. She was a riddle that girl, with her endless showers and pressed T-shirts, her precise handwriting and meticulously prepared schoolwork. But that room, I'd given up on it long ago.

She was sleeping on her back, her limp, dirty-blond hair fanned across the pillow, and the air whistled softly as it moved in and out of her open mouth. True, she was no beauty, her features somehow at odds with one another, but who was I to talk? All I saw were her warm brown eyes and her charming lopsided grin. "She's just so plain," her gorgeous mother said to her handsome father one morning as I was clearing away the dishes. I was stunned by Mrs. Cleary's cruel assessment of Edie. The way I saw it, their beauty had somehow skipped over her skin and lodged somewhere deep inside of her, choosing to show itself in her intelligence and sharp wit, her kindness, her capacity for love and concern for others. What else mattered? Anyone with a beating heart could detect the uncommon goodness in that girl, but God forbid she be plain. Then Mrs. Cleary asked her husband what he thought could be done to "fix" Edie's nose. And what, pray tell, could be done to fix you, Mrs. Cleary?

I'd not seen Edie sleeping like this since she was a child. Now she was more woman than girl, and the sight of her both touched and alarmed me. I'd never know her any older than this. I'd never know how she turned out, and the thought of that made me once again want to call the surgeon and tell him to start scrubbing his hands.

I carefully replaced an empty glass on her nightstand with the ginger ale and her wastebasket with the bucket, then shut the door. Nothing but tissues and chocolate bar wrappers in the wastebasket. A good sign, I thought, as I emptied it into the bin in the garage. A clump of tissues fell to the floor and a blue-and-white pen clattered across the concrete. I reached for it and tossed it on the pile. The moment it left my hand, I realized it wasn't a pen at all. I'd seen the commercials often enough—the ones with the pretty young women laughing and celebrating. They never showed the weeping ones. I pulled it out of the bin and held it up to the light, that bold blue plus sign staring back at me. Ah, Edie, here's a right pickle. This careful, clever girl snared in the oldest trap there was. I was the eyes and ears of that house, as I'd been of every house I'd cleaned, and nothing came to mind that would have warned of this. There was no boy. Well, clearly there was a boy—just not one I'd ever seen. Beads of sweat began to form along my hairline.

I wrapped the test stick in a white plastic bag, then another for good measure, and stuffed it down under all the rest of the smelly trash. I went back to the kitchen, then thought better of it, returned to the garage, fished the bag out, and slipped out the back door. I walked down the street, over a block, and put it in the trash can outside the convenience store. When I got back, Edie was standing in front of the open fridge.

"Good morning, Edie. Feeling any better?"

"Hey, Frances. Yeah, must be something going around."

"Must be. Should I make you something to eat?"

"No, I'm not hungry."

She shuffled away from the fridge and slumped down on a stool at the island, the spirit gone out of her. A swell of hectic energy rose in me, an intense need to step in and somehow make this right. I suspected that if I intervened in even the slightest way, we would both be somehow changed by it. The notion intrigued and terrified me. *Precipice.*

I laid my hand on the back of her head. She reached up and placed her hand over mine, sending a ribbon of electricity up my arm. I rarely experienced the touch of another person, and contact with this creature was a joy so profound that it was almost painful. Not long after I'd first met her, Edie fell off her bicycle.

As I cleaned and bandaged her knee, mentally rehearsing what I'd say to her mother, she leaned forward and rested her little hands on my shoulders. My heart opened and leaked into my chest, and I feared I would burst into tears and scare the poor youngster to death. Now it was commonplace for her to wrap her arms around me whenever she felt like it, and for me to let her. If I had to choose only one thing I would truly miss about this life, it would be the embrace of young Edie Cleary.

I sent her back to her bed with toast and an orange, then made myself another cup of tea and took it outside. I started tallying the tasks for the day—laundry, dishes, grocery run—just to shift my thoughts away from that stick with the plus sign. Then I heard a voice, like a stranger mumbling in my ear. It had come and gone before I could make out exactly what was said.

I whipped my head around expecting to see Edie, but she wasn't there. Just me and my teacup and my cigarette burned down to the filter. I laid the cup on the grass and took another look around the yard. It was one of those mornings bursting with the promise of the season to come. A blue sky streaked with cottony clouds. Not a breath of wind. A single bird twittering. The scent of soil and the sulphur of the match I'd struck.

"Frances. Calling Frances. Earth to Frances."

I spun around, blinked, and brought Edie into focus.

"Are you okay?" she asked. "You look all spacey."

I picked up my cup and walked toward her. "I'm fine. Just off in my head somewhere. I need to get at the rest of that laundry."

She waved her hand in front of her face. "Oh my God. Were you smoking?"

"Never mind about me, worry about yourself." I shooed her back into the house. "Go on back to bed and I'll check on you shortly."

I took my morning pill and changed into my cleaning clothes. By noon, I was almost caught up. I was folding sheets in the laundry room when I heard the voice again. I didn't recognize it, but it was clear and unmistakable, as if it had come from a person standing beside me. Three breathy words: "Lay it down."

I felt a familiar pressure begin to rise in my chest, that old harbinger of the panic I'd lived with for most of my life. I pressed my hand against my breastbone to try to tamp it down, then stood like a statue, horrified by the thought that the squid in my head had developed the power of speech. I lowered myself to the floor and rested my back against the cool metal of the washing machine. I gently kneaded my scalp, to what end I wasn't sure, other than it felt good. I panted and waited for my chest to loosen. As I slowly found my breath, the pressure started to subside, and a morbid curiosity took its place. I'd heard of people with tumours like mine who developed special skills before their brains were entirely ravaged. Things like a photographic memory or clairvoyance. Perhaps the squid would bless me in a similar way. Or at least it might have the decency to tell me what to do next. "Lay what down?" I whispered to the empty room. I sat very still, listening intently for an answer, but I heard nothing. Well, now. Wasn't this just grand. A grown woman slumped on a laundry room floor, waiting for the knot of deranged cells in her head to offer up a bit of sage advice. The absurdity of it hit me and I started to laugh—deep belly laughter that made me cross my legs for fear of wetting myself. I couldn't remember the last time I'd laughed so hard. It left me feeling refreshed and oddly composed. If the squid had plans for driving me right round the bend today, then hard luck. I had a pregnant teenager on my hands, and losing my mind would just have to wait. I stood up, stuffed a load of towels in the dryer, then made my way toward Edie's room.

3

Her door was open, but I knocked softly.

"Come in," she said.

She was lying on her side with her back to me. I leaned against the door frame and took a few deep breaths. "So what are you going to do about it?"

She rolled over. "About what?"

"You know what."

Her face blanched white as paper before she started to cry. "How do you know?"

"Edie, there's not much gets past me. I'm like an old owl perched up in a tree, surveying all that goes on below. Plus, I found that test stick in your garbage can."

Her eyes widened in surprise.

"What?" I said. "You think the garbage cans empty themselves?"

"No," she said. "I just don't think I've ever heard you say that many words in a row before."

"Nonsense. What about when you had strep throat? How many of those books did I read to you, cover to cover? Harry the wizard, all day long. Nearly drove me mental."

She reached for a tissue and wiped her face. "That was years ago, and it's not the same."

"Well, desperate times and all that."

She sat up and leaned against her wicker headboard. "You have to promise you won't tell Mom. Please, you can't tell her—I'm begging you."

"No need to beg, child. I wouldn't dream of telling her, or anyone else, for that matter. Now what are you going to do?"

"I guess I don't really have much choice."

Oh, bless her. "Yes, you do, Edie. And you'd do well to remember all the women before you whose only choice was a baby or a coat hanger. And you'd also do well to roll your eyes back down before they pop right out of your head."

She laughed and blew her nose. "Jesus, Frances, take it easy. I know who Gloria Steinem is. What is up with you today?"

I sat on the end of her bed. "Who's the boy?"

She hesitated, and I could see she was unsure if this new ground we were treading on was solid enough for full disclosure.

"I give you my word. Whatever you say goes with me to the grave."

Her head flopped forward, and she blew out a long breath. "My friend Colin. He's this amazing guy, honestly. Incredibly smart, hilarious, ridiculously beautiful, but totally gay, so that's that."

I blinked at her. "Gay boys impregnating young women. All the rage now, is it?"

"He wasn't a hundred percent sure, so I offered to have sex with him, you know, so he could decide once and for all. Plus, I got to lose my virginity with someone I love. Win-win. But the results are in, and he is not a fan of the vagina."

I had to swallow a smile at the absurdity of the situation. I pictured the two of them hatching up this caper, and I thought it was as heartwarming as it was foolish.

"Anyway," she said, "the condom broke. Maybe we didn't use enough lube or maybe—"

"Okay, okay," I said. "Spare me the nitty-gritty. What does Colin have to say for himself?"

"I haven't told him. He's just come out to his parents, and I don't want to freak him out. Not now. I'm actually not sure I want to tell him at all, which is maybe kind of selfish, right?"

"Edie, you are many things, but selfish is not one of them. You do what's right for you and don't think twice about it."

But I knew full well that she'd already decided what was right for her. As soon as she'd said she hadn't told him, I knew she had this all worked out, the way she always had everything worked out.

"I'm going to the women's clinic this afternoon," she said. "Will you come with me?"

"Oh, I don't know. If your mother found out—"

"Please. You have to come."

She wrapped her fingers around my wrist, and I felt a rush of breath escape from my mouth.

"Oh no," she said. "You think it's a sin or something, don't you?"

The air in the room suddenly felt hot and close. I shook my head, stalling until my voice returned.

"Just let me think about it, okay? Get some rest while I tend to the house."

I stood outside in the backyard and waited until my hands were steady enough to light a match. I sucked in the smoke, and with it came a flash of annoyance. Annoyance toward that sweet, scared girl who had unknowingly opened a tunnel back in time and shoved me down in it with her words.

IT WAS A LATE spring afternoon and Annie and I were walking home from school. How different we were—me, thin as a rail, unlovely, reserved to a fault, and forever withering in the shadow of Annie, with her glossy black curls and rosy skin, her high spirits and easy way with people. Yet we were closer than any sisters we knew, inseparable for almost all the years we'd been alive. As young girls, on weekends and holidays and all through the summer, we'd tramp up and down the back lane between our houses clutching pillows and pyjamas, one night at her house, the next at mine. I'd lie with Annie nestled behind me, my cold feet against her warm ones, and drift off with her breath on my neck. Even at sixteen, we were still spending many nights like that, our growing bodies overlapping in our narrow beds. She'd bring her magazines and chatter away, and I'd bring my schoolbooks and listen. At that time, what I listened to was an awful lot about Donny Doyle. I had no interest in dull, gangly boys—I could barely imagine their purpose—but Annie was almost frenzied in her desire for the Donnys of the world.

I tugged at the sleeve of Annie's jacket. "Come on, walk faster. I want to get my homework done before supper."

"The eyes on him. I swear, one of these days I'm going to faint dead away when he looks at me," she said.

"Annie, I can't hear any more about Donny Doyle or that stupid bonfire."

"Oh, please. You have to come," she pleaded.

"I don't want to come."

"Honestly, if I left you on your own, you'd wind up a brittle old skeleton in an attic surrounded by dusty books. Your mother can do without you for one night."

"See, that's just it. You will leave me on my own. You'll be too busy making eyes at Donny to bother with me. I'll spend the whole night by myself, bored stiff."

"I won't leave your side. Not even for a minute."

"Yeah, right. Sometimes you forget how well I know you."

"Well, smart-arse, what you don't know is that my mother thinks I need you around to keep me on the straight and nar-row. She won't let me go unless you go too."

"Ah, now I see why my presence is required."

"All right, you got me there. But besides that, I really, really want you to come, and not just for my sake. It'll do you good to get out of the house for a change. You'll have a grand time, I promise."

I picked up my pace, knowing full well she'd natter at me until the sun set if she had to.

"Frances, stop walking and look at me. If I miss out on this, I may die of unhappiness. It will be all your fault, and I fear for your conscience and the fate of your soul."

I took on the voice of the principal of our school. "Miss Malone, two minutes in, you and Donny Doyle will disappear. And knowing what you and Mr. Doyle will get up to, I'd say it's the fate of your own soul that should concern you."

She laughed. "Bless me, Father, for I have sinned. It's been two weeks since I last got felt up."

We were only half joking. It was 1978, and beyond our shores the world was in great flux, but Safe Harbour lay fixed in the tight fist of the Catholic Church. It was as if there were a giant umbilical cord snaking along the ocean floor, tether-ing the whole island directly to the Vatican and feeding us a steady diet of guilt and shame. The priests and nuns warned us constantly about the dangers of "self-abuse" and "fornication," and then expected us to kneel and confess and beat back biology with a set of rosary beads. Everything the priests and nuns had to say about sex (and countless other subjects) was all a load of malarkey to me. I hadn't even contemplated a sin of the flesh, let alone committed one. But for Annie, it was like waging war with God himself every minute of the day.

"So are you coming or not?" she asked.

Whether I would do this for her was not the question. The only question was what wouldn't I do for her. Annie knew I didn't like to be around other kids our age outside of school. She thought me shy and bookish, but terrified is what I was. Terrified of saying the wrong thing, of doing something foolish, of being looked at and judged harshly. I longed to be one of them, to be welcomed and accepted and adored like Annie. And she was adored by no one more than me. No, *adored* wasn't the right word. That was a word for all the other people who knew her. My feelings ran toward worship, with only a trace of envy. Not the naked jealousy I saw in other girls when they caught the boys eyeing her blooming body. I just wanted to be more like her and less like me. She was all that I wasn't, the missing half that made me whole. The only person who could silence the constant grating noise in my head. And I had a deep need to be near her whenever possible. When we were together, I felt worthy, as if I was someone who existed beyond the shadow of my mother's misery, someone who could push herself toward a party at the water's edge on a chilly spring night.

"Oh, for God's sake. Yes, I'll come with you," I said, and she threw herself at me, wrapping her arms tightly around my waist. I stood with my face buried in her soft hair and wanted us to stay like that for the rest of our days.

I woke up that Friday morning soaked in sweat and unable to eat a thing. I suffered a headache all day at school, and my stomach turned over every time Annie mentioned the bonfire.

During math class, she passed me a note saying Donny had asked if they could walk down to the shore together, which she felt was a sure sign that it was a real date. I crumpled the note in my sweaty palm. The night hadn't even started and already I was on my own. On the way home from school, she asked if I minded meeting her at the party. I just smiled and told her I didn't mind at all.

At suppertime, I picked at a plate of food my mother had laid on the table. She sat across from me with a cup of tea. She was still in her robe and her hair needed washing, but she looked better than I had seen her in months. She'd gained a few pounds, and her colour was no longer as dull and sickly as it had been through the long winter.

My father had been dead for over five years, and in that time, I'd learned that my mother's well-being shifted with the seasons. As winter approached and the hours of daylight dwindled, her mood grew dark as well. She spent most of her days in bed, like a hibernating animal. Then, in the spring, she brightened and slowly rose back into the world, like the daffodils poking up through the soil in our yard. And when summer rolled around, I caught glimpses of the mother she used to be. Time in bed was traded for time in the kitchen, baking loaves of bread and stirring pots of partridgeberry jam. Mrs. Malone stopped by more often and would be asked to stay for lunch. Annie and I were permitted to have the radio on as long as we kept the volume low. On fine days, my mother and I strolled through town, to the grocery store or the pharmacy. People greeted her warmly and always asked when she planned to sing again. She just shrugged and changed the subject, the way she did when-ever I asked her the same question. At night, I read to her, from a book or the newspaper, or I found something on television for us to watch. In the early days of last summer, I persuaded her to help me clear the overgrown garden. We planted carrots and potatoes, then drank iced tea while we watched the sun go down. She seemed almost happy. But I knew it wouldn't stick, and in the fall, I pulled those vegetables from the ground alone.

The potato salad on my plate was made from the ones we had grown. I took a bite and tasted the diced green apple and paprika. She'd made it just how I liked it, and I took her effort as a sign that she was on the upswing.

My mother sat on my bed while I tried on almost every piece of clothing I owned. I settled on jeans and a powder-blue sweater that she said set off my hair and eyes. I stood in front of the mirror, trembling from head to toe.

"You know, I'm going only as a favour to Annie. If you'd rather me stay, we could do a puzzle or watch a movie."

She came and stood behind me and spoke to my reflection in the mirror. "Frances, I would far rather you go be with your friends. It'll be good for you."

I turned to face her. "That's what Annie said too. But what if it's not good for me? I'm so nervous, I feel like I'm going to keel over."

Her expression dimmed a little. "Oh, my darling, sometimes you remind me so much of myself when I was your age." She kissed me on the cheek. "Now go on and God bless. And don't stay out too late."

I made my way down the rocky beach until I spied Annie in the glow of the flames, already nestled in Donny Doyle's bandy arms. She was hoisting a stubby brown beer bottle to her lips, her eyes glassy and her cheeks ablaze. When she saw me, she hopped up and led me to a plastic cooler filled with beer. She opened one for me and promised that it would loosen me right up. She pointed to a boy I'd not seen before sitting next to Donny.

"That Donny's cousin Michael, over for the weekend from the mainland," she said. "When we go back, try to talk to him. And for the love of God, don't talk about books."

He looked like all the rest of them, a mop of unruly brown hair, a bland spotty face, and a skinny neck with a knobby Adam's apple that bobbed up and down when he talked. I ignored him and finished the beer, my first ever, and decided to have a second. By the time I'd started in on my third, it was as if all the nerves in my body had been washed clean, polished, and somehow tuned to a different frequency. I felt soft and fluid and normal. I was chatting easily with Michael about a book I was reading when Annie announced that the four of us were going for a walk down the shore. We ended up at a small wooden shack with a rusted wood stove, a couple of old lawn chairs, a card table, and wide benches covered with plaid sleeping bags against each wall. Donny and Michael made a fire from a pile of split logs in the corner. I felt groggy and the floor seemed uneven under my feet. Annie winked at me and joined Donny on one of the benches. He pulled a sleeping bag over their heads, leaving me alone with Michael, who took a flask of dark rum from the pocket of his jacket and offered it to me. It burned like a flame in my throat, disgusting and beautiful all at once. We passed the flask back and forth, then he kissed me, and everything grew hazy. I needed to sleep and stumbled toward the empty bench.

I opened my eyes to Michael's face hovering above mine. I could smell his yeasty breath and feel his cold hands rummaging around under my sweater and pulling at the zipper of my jeans. I twisted my head to the left and saw a blurred and distorted image of Annie, like I was looking at her through an old wavy window. I squinted until she sharpened into focus. She was lying on her back with her eyes closed. Donny was levered up on his bare arms, rocking back and forth above her. I saw the rounded side of her pale breast, the curve of her ribcage lifted by her arching back, a flash of her thigh and flexed knee. I could feel my heartbeat between my legs, a strong, hard pulse that I suddenly wanted to press my fingertips against. I could hear Michael's voice, far off and garbled. I felt him first poking at my flesh and in a moment thrusting into me, a jolt of stabbing pain. Only then was I able to pull my eyes away from Annie and back to Michael. He shuddered and moaned, the whole thing over before I even realized what was happening. He lay on top of me, a dead weight, panting into my ear while I watched the ceiling spin.

Three months later, I was put on a bus headed for a home for pregnant teenagers run by the Sisters of Mercy, a decision made by my mother and the priest without so much as a word to or from me. The two of them cooked up a story to tell everyone in town—a scholarship at a boarding school on the mainland. After the baby was born, I was to explain my early return by claiming crippling homesickness.

It was just how it was done back in the day, I'd told myself many times over the years, like it was some quaint tradition. A casual dismissal of events from my past that I found too painful to address any other way. But now, as I paced the perimeter of the backyard, trying to decide on the role I would play in Edie's pregnancy, all I could think about was the role I'd played in my own. About how I sat in my mother's kitchen, despondent and sick with shame, listening to her and Father O'Leary work it all out. Not once had it occurred to me to open my mouth and ask if there was another way. I simply nodded my head and packed a bag. *Stooge.*

So, little Miss Cleary, don't tell me again that you really don't have much choice. I stubbed out my cigarette against the sole of my shoe. And yes, Edie, my darling girl, I'll come with you.

WHEN THE TAXI PULLED up in front of the clinic, I glanced around nervously before we got out. Edie's parents were well-known people, and St. John's was nothing but a big wagging tongue. Edie bounced out and headed for the door. I followed behind, looking over my shoulder. And then there I was, sitting in the waiting room, cool as you please. As if Monday was garbage day, Wednesday was dusting, and Friday was laundry and ferrying clients' daughters about for abortions. I looked around at the clean, modern space, the posters on the walls, and the collection of pamphlets on display. Information, support, and options galore. I could tell it was a room made by women for women—a room where anything was possible. *Emancipation.*

Edie thanked me again for coming, then clasped her clammy hand on my forearm. "I don't think I could do this on my own. Could you imagine?"

A nurse appeared and said they were ready for her, and I went outside to smoke. I was bewildered as to why she'd chosen me as the hand-holder. Why turn to a nervous old fogey instead of a girlfriend from school? I decided I wouldn't ask.

I didn't know what I would have done had this place been on the menu in my day, but for sure Annie Malone would have been in the mix. She would have trotted into that clinic like she owned the place and had me sorted in no time.

It was Annie who'd dragged me to the doctor after she found me retching into the toilet at school for the third day in a row. Annie who'd held my hand at the doctor's office, and Annie again beside me the night before I was shipped off to the nuns. The two of us in that abandoned dory, which had been on the beach for as long as we could remember. We had staked our claim to it the summer after my father died. We'd sit and lick our ice cream cones, then raise our faces up toward the sun. Anytime other kids tried to climb on board, Annie would rise up and threaten to punch their faces off, and to my amazement, they'd simply back away. Once we were old enough to crave privacy, the dory became our refuge from the eyes and ears of Safe Harbour. It was the only place in town where we felt safe to talk about my pregnancy, or "the situation," as my mother called it. Annie shivered in the fog and cried in fits and starts. I was too numb to feel the cold or shed any tears.

"I could come with you," she said. "Explain the whole thing. Tell the Sisters it was all my doing."

"I doubt they'd believe it was you who got me pregnant, but thanks anyway." I rested my head on her shoulder.

"In six months, we'll be sitting right here like it never happened. Your mother will come around. My mom said she'd talk to her. It'll all settle down. You'll see."

"I don't know. You weren't there when I told her. You should have seen the state of her, sobbing like her life was over. Then not a word to me for three days. Not a single word. Now it's like she's just written me off as her daughter and can't wait to be rid of me. I know I'm breaking her heart, but she's breaking mine too."

Being pregnant at sixteen was hard enough, but getting cast out to face it alone was a cruelty I couldn't fathom. All that I knew and loved was in Safe Harbour. I'd never been anywhere else, not even for a day. I was half-crazy with worry over what was in store for me, but I was just as concerned about leaving my mother. At the best of times, I suffered a terrible, unrelenting fear that if I looked away from her for a moment too long, I'd turn back to find she'd disintegrated into a pile of rubble. And then there was the real crisis: being separated from Annie for six months. I'd had more than one nightmare about coming back to Safe Harbour to find that everyone in town could see me but her.

"Hey, Annie, I need to ask you something."

"Shoot."

"Think you'll miss me when I'm gone?"

"You know I will. I'm the one bawling my face off. Why would you even ask me that?"

"I don't know. I was thinking out of sight, out of mind."

"Well, stop thinking that."

"I guess I always wonder why you've stuck with me. Why you haven't gone off with someone more like you."

"Why would I want to spend all my time with someone just like me?"

"Because maybe that would be better than spending time with someone like me."

Annie shifted in the dory and turned to face me. "What are you getting on with at all? Nobody's better than you. You're probably the smartest person in town, which automatically makes me smarter. You're the best listener I know, which is perfect because I'm the best talker I know. I could tell you anything and you'd never say it to a soul."

"That's because I never talk to another soul."

She laughed. "That's true, but even if you did, you'd never tell any of my secrets. Like that time I stole the bottle of Communion wine from the church. Name one girl at our school who could keep that under wraps for more than an hour. You can't because there isn't one."

"I am very trustworthy."

"See? That's better. You're always so hard on yourself, but you're never hard on me. And if you lived with a houseful of brothers, you'd know what that's worth. Besides, you make me feel cozy."

"Cozy? Like I'm a blanket?"

"Christ, Frances, I don't know how to say things right. I just mean that you make me feel warm and happy and tucked away all nice."

"And at least once a week, I tell you how pretty you are."

"You could step that up a bit. Once a day wouldn't kill you."

"Plus, I do everything you ask me to do."

"Exactly. What more could anyone want from a best friend?"

She turned back toward the water and slung her arm around my shoulders. "We're like fish and chips, you and me. We just go together. And when you get back, I'll be right here waiting for you."

Annie and I sat together on the beach until it grew too cold to sit any longer, then we said goodbye at my front door. I had forbidden her to see me off at the bus, fearing I'd never get on it if she came. She hugged me tightly and said, "Don't worry about your mother. We'll see to her."

The next morning, my mother and I waited in silence at the bus stop. My legs felt weak, and my chest hurt. I asked her if she was ever going to forgive me. She pulled me into her arms and held me while I cried. "Frances," she said, "mothers and daughters can always find their way to forgiveness." But as the bus pulled away, I looked through the grimy back window at my mother's ashen face, her lips pressed into a thin line, her eyes dark and dry, and feared that neither one of us could go the distance.

4

Edie came through the clinic door. It was the first time I'd seen her resemble other kids I saw around town, those grumpy-looking youngsters who were always trying to show the world how pissed off they were.

"All done," she said. "Let's get out of here."

In the back of the taxi, she handed me a sheet of paper with a set of instructions. One pill now, another in six hours. Pills for everything nowadays, even this. The sheet warned of bleeding, cramping, nausea, vomiting, weakness, fatigue—all the things that would take place while that Colin was off skateboarding or doing whatever else he fancied.

I asked the driver to take us to the supermarket and made Edie wait in the car while I grabbed what we would need to get us through—overnight maxi-pads, a bottle of Advil, a heating pad, and ginger ale for her; a flask of whisky and two packs of Rothmans for me. Then to my place for a change of clothes and my pills. I raced around my apartment, every nerve firing at full tilt in anticipation of the two days ahead of me. What if she had some kind of reaction to the drugs? What if she bled to death in her bed? I wiped a trickle of sweat from the side of my face and settled myself. How mothers shouldered such burdens I hadn't a clue.

When we got home, I laid out the supplies on her dresser, then grabbed a garbage bag and placed it on the floor in front of her toilet. I wasn't about to add scrubbing blood and barf off that snow-white tile to this day, thank you very much. I tucked another garbage bag under her sheets and told her to wear old underwear and pyjamas, ones her mother wouldn't miss if we had to pitch them in the garbage.

Edie laughed. "I'm starting to think that maybe you used to work for the Mafia. Body-disposal division."

"I just don't want to have a conversation with your mother about a bloody mattress when she gets home." I took one last look around her room. "Okay, I dare say you're all set up."

"Frances, you look like you're going to have a heart attack. Go do what you need to do. I'll be fine, I swear."

I left her door half-open and started down the hallway, then stopped and went back. "Edie, your mother being suddenly called away today. That's some dumb luck, hey?"

"Sometimes the dice just roll your way," she said and closed her eyes.

I could feel my energy starting to flag as I walked to the kitchen to take stock of our food supply. There was enough to last us through any disaster. If she was hungry later, I'd make one of her favourites—grilled cheese or maybe chicken tacos. Three o'clock and I still wasn't through the laundry. I stood folding the plush towels and was suddenly so tired that I could barely keep myself upright. I dropped the last one in the basket and walked down the hall toward the guest room. I took off my clothes, slid between the cool sheets, and for the first time in my working life, slept away an afternoon.

It was almost seven when I woke up. Edie. I bolted out of bed and found her coming out of her bathroom. She walked across her room slowly, taking careful little steps, a sure sign to me that she was hurting.

"What can I do for you?"

She climbed into her bed, wincing with pain. "Could you rub my back a little?"

"Here, scooch over." I sat on the edge of the bed and placed the flat of my hand on her lower back, which was hot and damp from the heating pad. I rubbed the heel of my hand up and down the tight muscles and felt them give way. "Want something to eat?"

"Maybe."

"How about I make you some toast with peanut butter?"

"Okay."

I went to the kitchen intent on making toast but somehow wound up on the back patio. I puffed and sipped and realized this was the happiest day I'd had since I didn't know when— maybe since I was Edie's age. The chance to tend to a child I loved, to be the back rubber and toast maker, the keeper of secrets, the makeshift mother, felt like an unexpected gift.

The sun had set, and the evening was growing cold. I stepped back into the kitchen, then brought a tray to her room, where she was scrolling through her phone.

"Here, try this, and if that goes well, maybe some dinner."

"I don't feel that bad now, just a bit crampy. But the bleeding is well underway. It's like a horror movie down there." She nibbled at her toast, then gathered up her devices. "I'm making a move. All this time in bed is making me sad."

She wrapped herself in her duvet and shuffled off like a penguin. I started to pick up after her, then tossed the whole lot back on the floor and closed the door. When I got to the kitchen, she was frowning and wagging a pack of cigarettes at me. I ignored her and started in on our dinner.

Edie took a bite of the grilled cheese sandwich I'd made for her, then pushed it aside. She watched intently as I ate mine, washed down with sips of whisky.

"Good God, Frances," she said. "Smoking, drinking. Got any weed on you? Maybe we can score some crystal meth later."

"I don't know what crystal meth is. You better not either."

"I don't do drugs. I'm not that stupid. Well, stupid enough to get pregnant, I guess."

I took another bite of my delicious sandwich. Twelve-dollar cheese was indeed far better than the three-dollar blocks in my fridge. "Not stupid. Unlucky, maybe, but not stupid."

"Can I ask you something?"

"Sure."

"Do you think I did the right thing?"

"That's not for me to say, my love. It doesn't matter what I think or anyone else. Only you."

"But it matters to me what you think."

I stopped eating. "Why?"

She rolled her eyes. "Because. You're like my sweet aunt or something. If I didn't have you around, what would I do? Go to my bitch mother? I don't think so."

"Edie, she's not a bitch," I said, so earnestly that anyone would've thought I was telling the truth. "One day you might need her, so go a bit easy, hey?"

"Yeah, I hear you. I don't necessarily agree with you, but I hear you."

She gathered up the duvet and flopped on the couch in the adjoining family room—the great room, Mrs. Cleary called it.

"I didn't know you smoked," she said.

"Ah, yes. A woman of many mysteries, me."

"Like what?"

"Well, there's that stint with the Mafia you mentioned earlier."

She laughed. "You didn't answer my question."

I swallowed the last of my whisky and sat at her feet. "Edie, you've your whole life ahead of you. What good would come from having a baby now? For either of you. So yes, I think you absolutely did the right thing."

"How do you know?"

"I just do."

"Okay, but if it were you, what would you have done? Tell me."

Something in her face, something in the tone of her voice, made her seem older and me feel younger, as if we were meeting somewhere in the middle of time. I wanted to tell her everything, unload it all. About the day my child was born, that horrible day and the horrible days that came after. I'd ask her, "Do you think I did the right thing?" And I wanted to tell her that I was dying and what I was planning to do about it. I'd ask her what she would do if she were in my situation, as if we were two friends facing similar predicaments. Certainly, the alcohol and the pulsing squid in my head were giving me permission to speak freely. But as the words began to form in my mouth, Edie pressed her toes lightly against my leg, something she hadn't done since she was a little girl, an old signal for me to wrap my hands around her cold feet, and I let the words dissolve on my tongue.

"It's hard to know," I said. "We just didn't have many options when I was your age."

"Yeah, it must have been so hard back then. Much easier now, right?"

I reached for her feet. "Yes, Edie, everything's easier now."

She put on a movie that I tried to watch, but I was too distracted. There'd been a moment earlier in the day, in the taxi coming back from the clinic, when I feared we were undertaking something dark, like we were co-conspirators in some seedy venture. But looking at her lying on her side on the couch, as cozy as could be, laughing and having what appeared to be a grand old time, I wondered if half the girls in her class were at home doing the very same thing. The more I watched her, the more uneasy I felt. When she got up to go to bed, I was relieved to be free of her. I was irritated, almost angry. There she was, safe and snug in her beautiful bed, being watched over by someone who loved her, shaping her own fate while she slept just by swallowing a few magic beans. She'd asked me for help but hadn't asked permission from a single soul but herself. And tomorrow it would be business as usual, her future secured. *Entitled*.

I wiped down the kitchen and wiped it down all over again just to stop thinking about her, then went to bed. I turned out the light, but I was too stirred up to sleep. That time tunnel was open again, and there wasn't a thing I could do to stop myself from travelling through it.

BY THE TIME I arrived at the Sisters of Mercy Home, the heavy mist had turned to sheets of cold rain. I was green from the bus fumes, an added misery piled onto the relentless nausea I'd been suffering for two months. I banged the brass knocker three times. A wizened nun finally opened the door, but not until I was soaked through to the skin.

"Come in, child, and wipe your feet."

I stepped into the porch, shivering and dripping all over the floor, my eyes locked on the drops of water splashing down on the slate tiles. *Disgrace*.

The old nun wrung her hands and stepped away from me as if unwanted pregnancy were contagious, then led me to an office at the end of a dark, narrow hallway.

"Wait here," she said and closed the door.

A few minutes later, another nun came in, dismissing the first one with a flap of her hand.

"I'm Sister Bernadette," she said. "I was expecting you an hour ago."

She was a soft-bodied, hard-faced woman with lined paper-white skin and light blue irises, like a husky dog in a black veil. She stood in front of her desk, hands behind her back, and looked me over. She welcomed me with a curt speech about the grace of Almighty God, the charity of strangers, and my need to atone for carnal sins. I'd have my own room at the top of the house, and I was expected to keep it clean and tidy. I was also expected to be up at seven for morning prayers. Then she flapped her hand in my direction, and I picked up my bag and closed the door behind me.

As I climbed the stairs to my room, I realized this strange place was now my home. There was no turning back, and a nervous dread came over me. I changed into dry clothes and had a look around my small, spartan room. White walls, bare pine floorboards, a tiny window, and a black metal bed topped with a thin mattress with a set of folded sheets and a knitted blanket placed neatly at the end. There was a single wooden chair next to a low dresser coated in chipped white paint; a mottled oval mirror hung on the wall above it. I made the bed and sat on it, bone-tired and scared half to death. A woman appeared at the door, dark hair clipped short, dressed in a white shirt and jeans. A small gold cross dangled from a string of black leather wrapped around her neck. She was Sister Barb, and she welcomed me with a smile and a tray of food—a bowl of beef broth, dry crackers, and a glass of orange juice. "I know Sister Bernadette can be a bit stern at times," she said. "Just remember there's no shame in being human. Don't worry, Frances. We'll take very good care of you here." And I believed her.

The home sat in a meadow on the outskirts of a small inland town I'd never heard of. Nothing but flat land and boulders and the long gravel drive that led to the highway. At night I would stand under the blue-black sky, millions of stars scattered above me, not a sound to be heard, and long for the water—the rhythm of the pounding waves, the smell of the ribbons of kelp on the shore, the noise of the gulls wheeling over the dark schools of fish. But mostly I missed Annie.

There were four other girls at the home, each one as miserable as I was, but it seemed as if their shared predicament was a bonding force. They were warm and friendly and so at ease with one another—bickering and bantering and shoring up whenever the need arose. I did my best to be social, as much as my nerves allowed—smiling and nodding and giving brief polite answers to any questions that came my way.

Sister Bernadette had strict rules about contact with friends on the outside. "Now is the time for reflection and prayer, not for consorting with those whose influence likely landed you here in the first place," she said when I asked her to mail a letter to Annie the morning after I arrived. I was allowed use the phone in her office once a week, but only to call my mother. She would sit at her desk while my mother asked me about my health and if I was keeping up with my reading, then reach for the receiver once I'd said goodbye. Sister Bernadette would offer my mother an assessment of my progress. "Frances is quiet and obedient, I'll say that for her. And please God, she'll leave with better morals than what she came in with." Then Sister Bernadette would hang up the phone and command me to kneel and beg God's forgiveness. I loathed her.

Eventually I fell into the routine of the home. Sister Barb was one of those newfangled plain-clothes nuns we'd only heard about in Safe Harbour. She had a degree in social work from Memorial University, and it was her job to oversee all things related to pregnancy, from sickeningly detailed classes on child-birth to swift and discreet adoptions. Sister Bernadette, on the other hand, showed little interest in the baby side of things. She was on a quest for our souls. Daily prayers and catechism classes and an hour of silent kneeling before dinner. Lectures on moral hygiene and the joys of repentance and sacrifice, along with end-less "purifying tasks," as if bleaching a toilet would spare us from eternal damnation. The irony of it was that I found I liked the cleaning. A mop, a broom, a damp sponge, or whatever else was on hand had the power to turn chaos into order before my eyes, which I found unexpectedly satisfying. And it helped to pass the time. But mostly I liked the calming effect it had on me. As I worked, I was able to think of nothing but the task in front of me. One by one, any worries I had fell away until my head felt emptied out. Cleaning was like medicine for my troubled mind, and I volunteered for every chore going.

The other girls complained about the home non-stop. The eerie quiet, the early mornings, the isolation, the fire and brim-stone. As each pregnancy advanced, the complaints were more about swollen ankles, stretch marks, and aching, heavy breasts. I found my rapidly changing body horrifying. I was almost paralyzed by my fear of giving birth, and every time the baby moved, my heart banged wildly against my ribs and I'd start looking for something to scrub.

My labour began slowly, just a twinge in my lower back that went on for a day and a night, then went into full swing early on a Sunday morning. I was standing in the kitchen when I felt a warm sluice of fluid run down my leg and called out for Sister Barb. She loaded me into the car and sped down the highway to the cottage hospital.

In the delivery room, sweat-soaked and almost blind with the pain, I wailed over and over that I couldn't do it while Sister Barb rubbed a cold wet cloth over my face.

"Frances, look at me," she said. "This baby is coming, and you most certainly can do this. Women have been doing this since the beginning of time, and you will too."

The doctor was sitting on a stool at the end of the bed. I could see his scaly bald head as he peered and poked around between my legs.

"One more good push and this is over," he said. "There's a good girl."

I kept my eyes locked on Sister Barb's and drew in a huge breath. I bore down for all I was worth and felt my body split apart. Then it was over, the pain miraculously gone. My legs shook and I was dizzy with exhaustion. I looked at the slick, red-skinned creature dangling in the doctor's gloved hands. Two tiny feet with perfectly shaped toes and a round, hairy head matted with blood and gunk. The baby's sudden cries filled the room, and I turned away. Sister Barb laid her hand on my face and beamed at me.

"Well done, Frances. God bless you, you did it. Do you want to hold her?"

I shook my head and tasted the salty mix of sweat and tears streaming down my face.

"Do you at least want to give her a name?"

"Georgina," I said. "After my mother."

The nurse took the baby away, and two days later, I was back in the car heading toward the home one last time. We were barely through the door when Sister Bernadette came down the hall and beckoned Sister Barb toward her office. I climbed the stairs to my room and lay down. My muscles burned, my breasts ached and leaked, and my heart felt like it was cracking in two. And I could barely keep up with my feelings. One minute I was sobbing, the next I was bubbling with rage over everything that had happened. It was exhausting, and I was terrified that I might never feel normal again.

I realized I hadn't taken my aspirin and went downstairs for some juice. Sister Barb came into the kitchen, her face grave and slack.

"Frances, please come with me."

I followed her down the hall and into the office, where Sister Bernadette was sitting at her desk.

"Have a seat," she said and motioned toward the chair facing her.

I eyed the hard wooden seat, no place for my bruised flesh, and decided to remain standing. Sister Barb closed the door, then asked if I'd like a cup of tea or a glass of water, but I declined. I could tell something was up and I wanted to get right to it. Sister Barb stood in front of the window just to the right of the desk, arms crossed, eyes on the floor. Then Sister Bernadette cleared her throat and began to speak. She'd received a call from Father O'Leary. She paused and a flush of colour rose up in her white face.

"I'm sorry to tell you this, but your mother has passed away."

I turned to Sister Barb. "What does she mean, 'passed away'?"

"I'm so sorry."

"She's not passed anywhere," I said. "I talked to her two days ago." I looked back to Sister Bernadette.

"I can only tell you what was told to me by Father O'Leary. Your mother drowned. She was found on the beach at Safe Harbour early this morning."

There was no way my mother had drowned. Not in the water that had taken my father. She'd never go near it, not in a million years.

"Sister, I think there's been a mistake. My mother would never swim in the sea. She just wouldn't." My voice sounded foreign to me, too high and loud.

Sister Barb came to me and reached for my hand. "Your mother wasn't swimming. It appears that she took her own life."

53

Sister Bernadette made the sign of the cross. "May God show mercy on her and welcome her into his kingdom."

My legs started to tremble, and I eased myself down to the chair. I was completely baffled. For some reason, all I could focus on were the mechanics of what they were suggesting. Was I supposed to believe that my mother had somehow rowed a boat out past the shoal, then jumped over the side? Or that she'd leapt into the waves and swum out to the undertow? Most days she barely had enough energy to dress herself, let alone pull off something like this. And what about her faith? The Commandments and the deadly sins, the wrath of God and the fires of hell? Had she just cast all that into the water as well? No. Not possible. It was some other woman who'd taken her life. Some other woman lying on the beach. Just a dreadful mix-up that we needed to sort out. I was about to say so when I heard Sister Barb's voice, and my racing thoughts came to a grinding halt. She asked me if I understood what she had just said. I looked up at her stricken face, and suddenly I understood perfectly. My mother was gone.

Sister Barb started to speak again, but I cut her off.

"I need to go home."

"Frances, please don't make any decisions just now. You can stay here for a few days. Longer if you like."

I stood up. "No. I need to go home."

Sister Barb followed me to my room and helped me pack my things, then left me alone to rest. There was no bus until the next day, so I lay on the bed, straight and still, waiting for sadness to overtake me, but it didn't. Instead, what came was something that I couldn't quite put a word to, something like relief, a puzzling peace in the catastrophe I'd feared for so long.

The sun began to set and took my relief with it, leaving me in the grip of a cold fury. I was alone in the world, and it was my own mother who'd set me adrift. I finally fell asleep, cursing her and regretting giving the baby her name. But only hours later, I woke up with a tightness in my chest that I feared would kill me, a rising tide of guilt strong enough to satisfy even the good Sisters of Mercy. I opened the window and gasped at the night air. Suddenly, I could see it all through my mother's eyes. I'd disappointed her, shamed her, and left her no choice but to send me away. I knew that my mother's death was down to me, as surely as if I'd pushed her into the sea myself. I'd set this disaster in motion, and I saw a lifetime ahead carrying this on my back. I stood by the window, teeth chattering as the north wind blew in my face, wishing I could somehow shrivel down to nothing, slip through a crack in the floor and disappear.

In the morning, I faced Sister Bernadette for the last time. I refused the chair and stood sweating in my wool coat with my bag at my feet. I waited impatiently while she tidied some papers on her desk. Then I listened as she banged on—Jesus this, our heavenly Father that. Once again, she offered up a prayer for the pardon of my mother's mortal sin, something about her being cut off from God's sanctifying grace. I couldn't bear another word from her. It was out of my mouth before it had even fully formed as a thought.

"If you think God will let someone like you in heaven, then I'd say he'll find room for my mother."

Her chubby hand flew up and clutched the wooden cross that hung from her neck. "What did you say to me?"

I didn't answer.

She rose up out of her chair. "How dare you speak to me this way. When I think of the high hopes I had for you. Now I see you are no better than the others. Wanton ingrates, every one of you."

There I was, still bleeding from giving birth, my mother's body not yet in the ground, and she was calling me a thankless whore. It was the first time I'd ever had an urge to strike another human being, and we were both lucky I was too exhausted to even attempt it. But I had enough energy and anger to speak my mind.

"Sister, the word *wanton* has lots of meanings. Merciless. Inhumane. Malicious. It's not me who's wanton. It's you."

She took a step toward me, her pale eyes flashing, wild as a wolf. I picked up my bag and left her to sputter and seethe and turn to her God for comfort.

Sister Barb offered to ride with me to Safe Harbour, but I wanted no company. As I boarded the bus, she handed me a card with her name and number on it. "If you ever need anything, Frances. Anything at all."

The whole way home, I thought about the other grief Sister Barb had warned me I would suffer—the particular agony that comes when a child is taken from its mother. But mourning the loss of my child would come much later. At that time, I had room for only the loss of my mother.

I GOT OUT OF bed and went to Mrs. Cleary's office to look for a book. I'd had enough of my own story and wanted another to take its place in my head. I tried to find the book that Hillary had recommended the last time I was at the library, but no luck. I closed my eyes and picked one at random. On the way back to my room, I stopped at Edie's door and saw that she was sleeping soundly. I crept to her bed and watched her for a few minutes, my insides softening. Maybe being Edie wasn't as easy as it looked. Few things in this life ever were. Maybe there would be consequences she'd have to bear after all. Not like what I'd gone through, but an aftermath all the same. Perhaps regret would come to her somewhere down the line. I hoped not, as much for me as for her. I knew this day would be forever tangled up with her memories of me. Remember it, reflect on it, forget it, anything but regret it, I thought, and don't think ill of the dead. I kissed her clammy forehead and closed the door.

5

It was almost noon when Edie appeared in the kitchen. She looked puffy and pale, but once she started poking around in the fridge, I figured she was coming around. I'd been up since eight catching up on the work I'd missed the day before and was ready to resume the role of caretaker. I made a smoothie and a bowl of oatmeal for her and a cup of tea for myself. We sat in silence at the island, Edie tapping away at her phone while I flipped through the Saturday paper. Outside, the dark heavy clouds that had been hanging low in the sky all morning opened up. Fat drops of rain pattered against the window, and a sudden wind began to bluster. The kitchen grew dark and a great fork of blue lightning split the sky, followed by a loud boom of thunder. I went to the kitchen door and saw that the wind had upended two patio chairs and was threatening to make off with the table umbrella. Within minutes, torrents of rain lashed the glass. Edie came to my side.

"Not often you see wild spring storms like this," I said.

"See, this is what I'm talking about. This whole island may be underwater by the time I'm your age."

I'd listened many times as she talked at length about her fears for the planet and her many other concerns—refugees and racism, African and Indian girls who couldn't go to school because of their periods, disappearing elephants and whales, on and on. As the storm raged, I listened yet again as she warned about the warming planet. She tossed out facts and figures and gushed about young leaders with big ideas. Watching her animated face and listening to her passionate words, I felt the few remnants of my harsh thoughts from the night before finally wither away, leaving me with nothing but admiration for her.

"Maybe someday you'll be the one with all the big ideas," I said.

She clinked her glass against my teacup. "No maybe about it," she said and smiled.

There was another loud crack of thunder, then the house fell silent as the power went out.

"Oh my God, my phone," Edie whined. "My battery is already low."

"You'll survive a few hours unplugged from the world."

"I know, it's just that Colin has texted me twice to meet up for coffee and I haven't texted him back. I was thinking I'd tell him I have the flu."

"Tell him whatever you like."

"How do you do that?"

"Do what, exactly?"

"I don't know. Not tell me what to do or make a dig or judge like Mom does."

"Judge not, lest ye be judged, Edie."

I stepped away and refilled my cup, this time half tea, half whisky. Since the night my daughter was conceived, I rarely drank. I'd always thought of alcohol as a catalyst for disaster—because I was drunk, I got pregnant, which caused my mother's death, which upended my life—and fearing further calamity, I chose to abstain. But now, with death around the corner, I had no need for such caution. A power outage was enough to justify a lunchtime tipple. The whisky was warm and comforting, and I liked how it made me feel—steady and less fearful, verging toward confident. But I thought it bittersweet to find this new and improved version of myself with so little time left. Perhaps if I'd taken up drinking years ago, I might have been more outgoing and found a friend or two. I might even have found someone who loved me, or at least someone who would make me a grilled cheese sandwich or rub my back when I was low.

I sat at Edie's feet on the couch. "How are you feeling?"

She shrugged. "Crampy. Worn out. A bit regretful. I wish I hadn't fucked Colin. Sorry, had sexual intercourse with Colin. But I liked it, you know? Well, most of it. The touching part. Are you shocked?"

I made her wait for my answer, made her doubt for just a moment. But I wasn't shocked—I was envious. To be young with a lifetime of caresses and intimacy ahead of you. To feel your body react and rise under a hand that wasn't your own. I'd never known it and never would.

"I'm not shocked in the slightest. No shame in being human, child."

"Frances, what were you like when you were my age?"

"Much as I am now, I expect. Quiet, shy, tidy."

"What did you do for fun?"

"Well, I read a great deal, but I also spent time outdoors, unlike you lot. I'm amazed you all haven't come down with rickets."

"What were your friends like?"

"I had only one friend, really. A girl named Annie. Annie Malone."

"What was she like?"

"Nothing like me. Very lively. Sweet and caring. A lot like you."

"Do you still see her?"

All the time. In the girls who travelled in small packs at the mall, the girls who sometimes sat in the kitchen with Edie after school, working on their homework. In the girls who flirted with the boys on the bus, there was always one who brought the memory of Annie painfully close.

"I haven't seen her since I moved to St. John's, so that would be almost forty years."

"How come?"

"We just drifted apart, I guess."

Many times over the years I'd put pen to paper, to reach out and bridge the gap with a letter or a card, but I'd never been able to work out how and where to begin, how to stitch together something that had been so badly torn. I gulped down what was left in my cup, and the house suddenly whirred back to life.

I patted Edie's leg. "That's my cue," I said and went off to clear up the breakfast dishes.

Ten minutes later, she came into the kitchen holding her phone. "Hey, is this your friend?"

She turned the screen toward me, and I was face to face with Annie. I felt suddenly stiff and cold, frozen to the spot. Edie waved the phone at me, but I couldn't seem to raise my hand up to take it from her.

"So is it your friend or not?"

I leaned forward to get a closer look. It was Annie all right. Standing on a green lawn, smiling and holding a newborn baby in her arms. She was older, rounder, but the same girl I once knew as well as myself. How jarring it was to see her eyes and mouth set in this grandmother's face. In my mind, I'd always kept her suspended in time, safe from the ravages I'd suffered.

"Yes," I said. "That's my friend." I reached out and rubbed my finger lightly over the screen, and the photo disappeared and was instantly replaced by picture of a field of wildflowers. "Oh, she's gone. What did I do?"

Edie huffed and told me to go get my phone. She tapped on the screen for a minute or two, then passed my phone back to me.

"Okay, I set you up as Frances D. for now. Your friend doesn't seem to be too worried about privacy, which means you can just tap this button here to see her pictures. Go ahead, press it. Yep, that's it. Now just scroll through."

And there was Annie's whole life—a daughter and a grand-child, lunches with friends, a picture of her feet, red toenails on a beach with "Florida!" scrawled in the sand. We'd had far more years apart than we'd ever had together. All wasted and lost. I felt a surge of anger toward her for carrying on without me, and toward myself for letting her do it.

"Oh my God. Frances, is that you?" Edie pointed to a photo: two girls standing on a shore, laughing while the wind whipped their hair across their faces. "Me and my old friend Frances. Throwback Thursday!" was typed under it. I had no memory of that photo being taken, but there it was, and seeing it felt like a blow to my chest.

"It *is* you," Edie squealed. She yanked the phone from my hands and held it close to her face. "How cool. Oh my God, look at your clothes. Are there any more of you?" She jabbed at the screen, transfixed by her discovery.

"Okay, that's enough of memory lane today."

"Wow, Annie's hot. Look at this shot of her in a bikini."

"Come on, put that away now and go shower in case the power goes out again." She paid me no mind until I started snapping my fingers in front of her face. "Edie! For the love of Jesus, hand it over."

She dropped the phone in my open palm, then wrapped her arms around me and pressed the side of her face against mine. "Thanks for all this. For helping me through this. Sometimes I wish you were my mother."

A wave of heat surged through my body, and I felt an ache that I thought might crack me in two. I balled my hands into fists against her back to stop myself from clinging to her. Like she could save me.

She sniffed my hair. "You smell like an ashtray."

MRS. CLEARY MADE HER entrance at the scheduled time. The house was spotless. I stood in the kitchen smiling so hard that my lips felt about ready to split. Not a thing out of order, milady.

"Oh, Frances, the place looks great, as always. Thank you so much for staying. Edie's all right?"

"Back up to speed, I'd say. She's in her room."

Mrs. Cleary clicked down the hall, dragging her wheelie bag along the clean floor. I heard her calling Edie's name and then their mingled, muffled voices. Steady as she goes, young Edie. Keep the course and keep your secrets. I heard the heels coming back down the hall and started wiping down the spotless counter.

"I guess it's quitting time," she said. "Thanks again."

"Actually, Mrs. Cleary, there's something I need to talk to you about, if you have a moment."

"Sure, go ahead."

"It might take a few minutes. Could we sit?"

"Let's go to my reading room."

She sat at her desk and motioned for me to sit across from

64

her. "I think I know what you're going to say. I know staying over like this isn't our arrangement, but I really was desperate. Of course we'll pay you extra."

"No need. I was happy to do it. The thing is, I'm afraid it's time for me to retire."

She let out a strange sound, something between a squeak and a cough. "Is it your health? I thought you'd fully recovered from your episode."

Episode. Sweet Jesus. My stomach lurched at the mention of it. I'd been vacuuming about two months before when the sound of the machine became unbearably loud and a strange odour, like burned plastic, filled my nose. My last thought before everything went dark was that the vacuum was about to explode. I woke up in the hospital, every muscle in my body as hard as concrete and my pride deeply bruised once I realized it was Mrs. Cleary standing in the doorway telling the doctor how she'd found me foaming at the mouth and flopping around like a hooked codfish, a puddle of urine spreading across the polished hardwood. If only a stranger had found me half-dead in the gutter, anything other than what had happened. Since that day, I was too humiliated to even look her in the eye. And now this—a difficult conversation in the confines of her beloved sanctum. It took me a few moments to compose myself enough to continue.

"No," I said, "it's just time."

She rubbed the tips of her fingers up and down her forehead as I'd seen her do before when she was frustrated. "Perhaps I haven't told you enough how much I—how much all of us, I should say—rely on you. We can talk about a raise, if that would help matters."

"I'm not angling for more money, truly. What you pay me is more than a fair wage." I could feel my blood pressure steadily rising. Please, woman, for once don't make things harder than they have to be. "I have some names for you. All of them very good workers."

"Frances, please, I'm begging you."

She was on the verge of something. It would be either tears or rage. There was nothing in between with this one. I once saw her pitch a glass vase at Dr. Cleary's head as he walked away from her. He ducked in time and escaped without a scratch, but that shattered crystal was a right bugger to clean. I scanned her desk for projectiles.

She folded her arms across her chest. "So when are you leaving?"

"I'll stay until Edie finishes the school year."

"Two weeks? Come on, you know Robert and I are both crazy with work. I can't possibly break in a new housekeeper right now. Can't you delay until Edie finishes high school next year?"

"Mrs. Cleary, believe me when I say that's not possible. As I said, I have some names for you." I pulled a piece of paper from my pocket.

She shook her head and snapped the paper from my fingers. "Fine, but you need to tell Edie. I'm not having her think this has anything to do with me. I'm the bad guy around here enough as it is."

"I'll talk to her Monday after school, if that's all right with you," I said.

I left her there with her head in her hands. I waved at Edie, chatting on her phone in the kitchen, and slipped out through the back door. As soon as I turned the corner, I pulled my cigarettes from my bag. I stood and smoked and tried to figure out what I was feeling. Relief mostly, mingled with a strange giddiness. It was like what I'd always felt on the first day of school—the promise of something wonderful on the horizon.

As I ambled toward home, Liz Cleary's troubled expression came to me over and over. It was the first time I felt something other than contempt toward her. I wasn't at all happy with her talking about breaking in a new cleaner, as if we were wild horses that needed taming, but she was in a quandary now, to be sure. I was a tough act to follow and we both knew it. In my first moments of distance from her, my rigid view of her yielded ever so slightly. I saw that she was giving what she was able to give. She just had too many priorities; no wonder she couldn't organize them properly. She'd been given too many gifts, and somewhere along the way she'd lost sight of their value. Maybe I would've done the same.

I WENT TO BED early, strung out from the events of the past two days. The pain woke me from a deep and dreamless sleep. I swallowed the pills and endured the searing, splitting headache and the terror once again.

In the morning, my room was filled with blinding white light. Sunday. My thoughts started to gather speed. Clean the apartment. Pay the electric bill. Rent is due tomorrow. Books are due back at the library. Oh, for God's sake, I thought, what the bloody hell does it matter. Fretting is for the living. I got up, made a cup of tea, and burrowed back into the bed. I lit a cigarette and stared at the ceiling. I realized I had no plans for how I would spend my remaining days. Lounging a morning away seemed like a good start, but surely there were more inspired things to do. I wanted to learn how to cast off what only seemed important and keep what actually was. How to block out the clatter, slow down, and discover what was truly precious. But I also felt a frantic sense of urgency to attend to everything at once, to squeeze life for all it was worth and salvage what I could before time ran out. As for how or where to begin, I hadn't a clue.

I finished my tea and then I heard the voice again. "Tick-tock, check the clock." A phrase my elementary school teacher used to say as she herded dawdling children from the hallway into the classroom. The voice roused such fond memories of those days that I felt more charmed than frightened by its return. "Hello, squid," I said and pulled back the covers.

I showered and, as usual, fussed too long over what I would wear to the library. I walked past my full laundry hamper, left my dirty breakfast dishes in the sink, and grabbed my bag of books. I got off the bus four stops early and walked the rest of the way. When I arrived, Hillary was behind the desk talking on the phone. She gave me a cheery wave as I passed.

I settled in my usual spot, the prime real estate of the place, the armchair tucked behind the racks of DVDs, where few people wandered and where I had a clear view of the desk. I read and watched Hillary go about her work. I always marvelled at the obvious joy she took in her duties. I'd once heard her say that her love of books came second only to that of her family.

I always wondered how she came to this work. Every librarian I'd ever seen in movies or TV shows came off as either a stodgy spinster or a secret sex goddess in a matronly disguise. But Hillary was neither. She was an undeniably attractive woman, but one whose real beauty was revealed when I got close to her. There was no eye-grabbing flash, only radiant peachy skin over fine symmetrical bones. Wide blue eyes and a long delicate nose. Thick, straight hair—strawberry blond she called it when I'd once boldly complimented her—worn at shoulder length and parted on the left side. She was slight with thin, bony wrists and long skinny fingers. She had a surprisingly deep and rich voice, and a throaty laugh. She never wore dresses or the pencil-thin heels the young women were so partial to these days, always dark jeans and boots or flat shoes that reminded me of ballet slippers. And she was fond of scarves. One was always wrapped around her long neck— brightly coloured florals or jaunty polka dots.

I didn't know anyone who was as interested in words on a page as she was. Many times, I'd watched in awe as someone approached her and stammered through a scatty description of a book—"It's about a woman whose daughter drops out of college and begs for money on a street corner in Toronto"—only to have Hillary delight and amaze them by directing them to the title they sought. I'd never seen her miss, not once.

I was exhausted from the events of the night before and I kept losing the plot of my book. I pulled my phone from my bag and found the website Edie had shown me. I typed in "Hillary Bennett," but dozens of names appeared. I added "librarian," and like magic, there she was. Photo after photo of her with her chiselled husband, her three beautiful sons, her fashionable friends (Liz Cleary in the mix). I went back through her family photos and lingered on one of the three boys riding in the back of a speedboat. The oldest boy was fair like his mother. I had just zoomed in on his smiling face when suddenly Hillary was standing in front of me. I snapped my phone down against my leg.

"Frances, Liz tells me you're retiring?"

If only a team of experts could harness the speed and power of that woman's tongue. Enough energy to light Las Vegas, I thought. "Yes, that's right."

"Well, good for you. Any big plans? Maybe some travel?"

I was overcome with the desire to say something amusing or interesting. To ask her to join me for a coffee some afternoon. The same silly urges I had every time she spoke to me. Like always, I just breathed through it until it passed.

"Travel? Yes. Maybe."

"Let me know. I have some great travel book recommendations. Listen, I'm closing a bit early today, just by half an hour. It's my son's birthday and I haven't even made the cake yet."

I pictured Hillary in the white kitchen I'd seen in her photos, wearing an apron and holding a beater in her hand as the kids waited to lick it. "That's fine. I'm about to get on now anyway." I avoided looking at her as I gathered up my bag and books.

"Are you all right? You look a little delicate today."

"Oh yes, I'm fine. Just tired, I suppose. Thank you for asking. I hope your cake turns out." I smiled and left, my heart hammering. A block past the library I stopped to catch my breath and cursed my nature. Next time, I thought. Next time I'll find some words worth saying.

MONDAY AFTERNOON I WATCHED the clock for an hour straight before Edie walked through the door after school. I had a freshly baked banana bread and a pitcher of lemonade waiting for her.

"Well, hello," I said. "You look all rosy once again. Are you back to yourself?"

"I think so, although I kept falling asleep in class. The sheet from the clinic said that's normal." She clapped her hand over her mouth. "Oh shit," she whispered. "Mom isn't here, is she?"

I shook my head, cut her a slice of banana bread, and poured lemonade over a column of ice cubes. "Coast is clear."

"Ooh, it's still warm. Dee-licious. Aren't you having any?"

"Not just now."

I waited for her to finish, then asked her to join me on the back patio. The day was grey and cool—a small mercy, I thought. I didn't want this talk tied to the splendour of spring.

She sat down beside me on the cedar bench near the flower beds.

"Edie, I've decided to retire."

She stared at me, expressionless. "Like, today?"

"No, when you're finished school for the year."

"Why?"

"It's just time."

"Maybe you're working too hard. Maybe you just need a vacation, or you could try yoga. Mom swears by it, although I'm not sure it's working like it's supposed to." She looked down at her lap and picked at her nails. "Is it because of that seizure you had?"

I flinched. "How do you know about that?"

"I heard Mom talking to Dad about it."

I shuddered and hoped she hadn't also heard about the release of my bladder all over her mother's floor. "No, Edie. I'm just getting too old for cleaning a big house like this."

"I've only got one more year of school left. What if I helped you with your work? I could do the laundry and the vacuuming." Her lower lip began to tremble.

"It's schoolwork you need to be doing, not housework."

She nodded. "I get it, I do. It's just that I'll miss you. A lot. And we just got this whole new vibe going, you know?"

I held her small, cold hand in mine. It was soft as velvet against the chapped skin of my own. We sat quietly for a few minutes, and I was thankful for the peace of it.

"I forgot to tell you that the doctor and the missus are getting me a car for making the honour roll again," she said.

"And you with a brand-new licence burning a hole in your wallet. Lucky girl."

She smiled and wiped her wet eyes with her sleeve. "Maybe I could come visit you at your apartment sometime?"

"I wish you would." I kissed her hand and let it go. "Come on, back inside. You'll get a chill out here."

Two weeks later, I tucked my last paycheck into my bag, along with the parting gifts from Dr. and Mrs. Cleary—five hundred-dollar bills and a fussy silver charm bracelet—left my keys to the house on the counter, and quietly closed the front door.

6

"Frances, hold this over your left eye and see if you can read the letters in the last line."

"T-Z-C-O-F."

"Good. Cover your right eye and try this set."

"*B* at the beginning. *P*, I think, at the end. The middle is a mystery."

She turned on the lights and sat at her desk, the same desk I'd sat in front of a few times a year for almost ten years. She was a good doctor, the best GP I'd ever had. Smart, thorough, and not overly chatty, which suited me fine.

"Well," she said, "there's a deficit in your left eye, which is likely related to the larger problem. Any more seizures?"

"No, just the headaches."

"You're taking your pills?"

I nodded.

"I spoke with Dr. Bell. She's lovely, isn't she?"

"She is."

"So still a no-go on the surgery?"

"I want to move ahead with what we talked about."

She gave me a sad smile. "Frances, I want you to ask me one more time, just so we're absolutely clear on what you need from me."

I didn't need her, really. A fistful of painkillers and a bottle of whisky might well do the trick, but nothing was sure with that way of doing things, and the endgame was only part of what I was after. When I was a young woman, the law said I had no choice when it came to my own body. But now that I was older, the law was suddenly on my side. I would have my say. Death would come for me, as it had come for my father and my mother, but it would come for me on my terms. *Dominion.*

I stiffened my spine, then drew in a long breath and let it flow slowly out, just taking in the moment. "Dr. Langley, I would like a medically assisted death."

She opened a drawer in a filing cabinet and started pulling out papers. Perhaps she'd done this very thing for someone yesterday, and the day before. Maybe it was routine medical business these days. I'd seen the protests on television, the rants from those who deemed it murderous. They quoted scripture and stoked fears of doctors indiscriminately killing off old folks and disabled children. And I heard the cries from those who were in favour, the ones who wanted mercy for their loved ones and themselves. "Our dogs and cats have a better shot at ending their lives peacefully than cancer patients do," a tearful woman said on the news after nursing her mother through needless agony. Then two years ago, almost to the day, the politicians and the judges yielded to the will of the people—people like me, as it turned out.

Dr. Langley handed me the papers. "You'll need to make a formal request in writing, and you need an independent witness. Take some time to really think this over. You can always change your mind."

I took my papers and stepped out into the fresh June morning. I walked the six blocks home and found Edie parked in front of my house in her shiny new car, a jolly compact model the colour of a robin's egg. It looked good on her. I hadn't talked to her since leaving the house for the last time three days before. I'd meant to send her an email, then this business with my eye came up and I lost track of time. As soon as she spotted me, she waved through the window and tooted the horn. She hopped out of the car and spread her arms wide.

"Pretty snazzy, right? I was just about to leave. I came to see if you wanted to have lunch with me, celebrate the new wheels."

"I can make you some lunch if you like." I wondered if there was anything in my fridge fit to serve her.

"Frances, live a little. My treat. Anywhere you like."

I hadn't eaten in a restaurant since the grotty diners of my youth. "All right. But you choose the place."

WE SAT AT A table with a large piece of brown paper covering the white tablecloth, a fine idea, I thought. Heavy cutlery, fresh flowers on the table, servers who wore black aprons tied at their waists and moved quickly and precisely through the dining room like bees in a hive. Edie was at ease there. She belonged. She ordered a pasta dish—handmade ravioli filled with roasted chicken, wild mushrooms, and Cambozola (a kind of cheese, she assured me) in a sherry cream sauce—as did I, too confused by the menu to decide for myself.

My food was placed gently in front of me, an enormous white plate and in the centre a neat pile of yellow squares with scalloped edges covered in a cream sauce and sprinkled with little bits of green. It looked like a painting. I pressed the tines of my fork into the soft centre of the top square, sliced it in half with my knife, and raised it so I could see what was inside. I dipped it in the sauce and placed it in my mouth. It tasted of earth and milk, wine and woodsmoke.

"Oh my God, this is so good, right?" Edie said.

I couldn't speak and fought against weeping. I ate a second piece, even better than the first. As Edie talked, her words became muffled and distant, and the hubbub of the restaurant fell away. All I heard was the clack of my silverware, the sound of my teeth working. All I felt was the texture of the moist chicken and silky cream. There was nothing but that beautiful food. When the last bite was gone, I swiped a crusty piece of bread across the plate to sop up the sauce and suddenly the room roared to life.

When Edie stepped away to pay the bill, I grew cold, deep to the bone. The skin on my face tingled, and when I tried to stand, my legs buckled. I went down. I felt my head bang hard against the floor, and I saw Edie's frightened face above me shouting my name. Then blackness.

I came around in the emergency department with no memory of how I'd got there. My head throbbed and my mouth tasted of iron. I tried to roll on my side, but my muscles were locked, stiff as stone and burning with pain. Edie's voice was somewhere under the ringing in my ears.

"Frances. Frances."

I looked to my right and there she was, leaning on the bedrail, red-faced and tearful. I strained to put together what was happening. A young male doctor dressed in blue scrubs appeared at the other side of the bed.

"Mrs. Delaney, I'm Dr. Virani. I'm on call for neurosurgery today. How are you feeling?"

"Thirsty. Edie, could you . . ."

Edie slipped outside the curtain.

"You had a seizure at a restaurant today. Do you remember?"

"Not really."

"Your granddaughter called the ambulance and they brought you here. I've looked at your file. Have you been taking your medication?"

I nodded.

"The CT today shows significant growth of the tumour since your last scan. I know you've refused treatment for the glio, but your seizure meds need to be increased. Okay?" He examined me, then he sat on the end of the bed. "Mrs. Delaney—"

"Not missus. Just Frances."

"Frances. I highly recommend you reconsider the surgery."

"No, thank you."

"There's nothing I can say to change your mind?"

"No, thank you."

He shook his head, handed me a prescription, and left. Edie came back holding a bottle of water and a small plastic cup. She poured a little and offered it to me.

"Do you need me to hold it for you?" she asked.

I reached for the cup and took a small sip. Then another.

"I told them I was your granddaughter," she said. "They weren't going to let me come in, so I improvised. I hope you don't mind."

"I don't mind. Other than you think I look old enough to be your granny."

Edie stood by the side of the bed, her arms hung by her sides, nibbling her lower lip as she often did when she was nervous.

"You can go home now. I'll be fine."

"No way. I'm not leaving you in this dump." She tried to smile, but her lips were wobbling and trembling too much. "I don't know what to do."

She looked more distressed than I'd ever seen her, and I realized that she knew about the tumour.

"I'll tell you what to do—go find me a nurse. I want to get out of here."

She drove me home, helped me up the stairs, and sat on my bed as I fell asleep. When I woke up, she was lying next to me, reading a book.

"What are you still doing here? What time is it?"

"Almost seven thirty."

"Have you called your mother?"

"I told her I was at Colin's."

"I need a hot bath and you need to go home. Help me up." I hobbled behind her while she gathered up her things. "Listen, I can't tell you how sorry I am about today."

"You don't need to be sorry." She walked toward the door, then looked over her shoulder at me. "Frances, what's going to happen to you?"

"I'm going to die like everyone else on the planet."

"When?"

"I don't know, my love. A few months from now, I'd say. Possibly sooner. I'm sorry."

"Me too," she said and closed the door.

After a long soak in the bath, I lay my stiff and aching body on my bed and watched the twilight through my window, sick and sad about the way this day had turned out. I'd planned on telling her gently, with care. What a mess.

The sky grew dark, and the moon rose, bright and full. I felt the sudden crush of time bearing down on me and closing in fast. I'd yet to find my independent witness for the assisted death request, and it could wait no longer. I got up and found an old phone book, squinted at the page, and there it was, a name and number I thought would take me ages to find. I dialled and was amazed by how unchanged her voice was.

"Dear God. Frances Delaney," she said. "After all this time."

◇◇◇◇◇◇

THE NEXT MORNING, MY phone rang just as the bus pulled away from the curb. Edie, checking in and asking to come see me. "Tomorrow," I said. "I have something to do today." I checked for the third time that I had indeed taken my seizure pills. The fear of falling in a heap on the filthy floor of the bus was so strong I could barely breathe.

Half an hour later, I was within walking distance of the address Sister Barb had given me on the phone the night before.

I rang the bell and smoothed my hair. Then she was in front of me, an old woman but instantly recognizable. That same wide smile that took over her whole face, that same clipped haircut now like a silver cap on her head.

"Hello, Frances."

"Hello, Sister Barb."

She led me to her kitchen, a long tidy space with knotty pine cabinets and a well-used harvest table set in the middle. I sat quietly while she made a pot of tea and laid out a plate of sticky raisin buns.

"No one has called me Sister Barb in a long time," she said as she poured. "Milk?"

"Yes, please."

She still wore a small gold cross around her neck, this one dangling from a thin gold chain. She noticed me eyeing it as she spread a large pat of butter on a bun.

"I left the nuns, not God."

"When did you leave?"

"A few years after you left the home."

We sat and sipped tea together, as we had many times before in the kitchen at the home, and a wave of nostalgia swept over me. Being with her was surprisingly pleasant, almost easy, not at all tainted by the ghosts of grief and resentment as I had expected it would be. She asked me if I still carried around that old dictionary.

"Every time I hear the word *choreography*, I think of you," she said. "I can see you now, circling it and saying it out loud a few times after you heard it on the radio. I always thought it such a charming habit."

"Why did you leave the nuns?"

She blew out a long breath. "Oh, lots of reasons, I guess. Mostly because I found that I worked better without the restrictions of holy life."

I smiled. "Lots of things work better without the restrictions of holy life."

"So tell me about yourself. Did you marry or have any more children?"

"I did not. You?"

"No. I did a lot of travelling. Spent ten years with a children's charity in Vietnam. Then another ten in an orphanage in China. Now I'm happy to be a homebody. What did you end up doing workwise? I remember you saying you wanted to be a teacher."

"I was a housekeeper. Just retired, actually."

If she was disappointed, she hid it well.

"Have you been happy, Frances?"

"Here and there. You?"

"Here and there," she said and sighed. She pushed the plate with her half-eaten bun on it aside and swallowed some tea. "You know, we weren't allowed to have any involvement with the girls once they'd gone. But after you left us, I was concerned about how you were coping with your mother's death, and I called your priest. I remember using the pay phone in town so Sister Bernadette wouldn't find out. He told me you were well cared for, and I was so relieved. Then after I left the Church, I decided to get in touch with you and see how you were getting on, but I couldn't find you. Not a trace of you anywhere. I gave up when I realized that maybe you didn't want to be found."

Her expression darkened a little, like a cloud passing across her face.

"It's odd because I've thought a lot about you over the years, but then when you called, I wasn't sure if I was ready to see you or not."

The air had somehow shifted in the room, and I felt my nerves start to rev up. I reached for a bun and took a bite. My throat had gone dry, and the bun caught going down. I took a swig of tea to help it along.

"You know what?" she said. "I really believed I could make a difference. Change the system from the inside. I believed I was doing good work, helping you girls get through, placing those babies in deserving homes—that was the phrase of the time. Deserving homes. But now, when I think back on it, I feel ashamed of it." She paused and shook her head. "I didn't even ask if it was what you wanted."

"Nobody asked me what I wanted."

"I know, I know. My God, I was so naive. I wanted to become the new guard, oust all the Bernadettes. And believe me, I tried." She looked away, toward the open window. When she turned back, she reached for my hand. "Do you think you can forgive me?"

Look at you, asking me for absolution. And look at me, about to ask you to bear witness and secure my smooth passage to the grave. Two young women who'd been trapped by time, now two old women within spitting distance of death with not much to show for it but heartbreak and regret. I felt a powerful urge to embrace her, to say something that would make her see that we had been in it together all along. Don't you see, Sister? We were duped, you and me. Fooled by the guilt-mongers and the shame-brokers into believing that there was no other way. *Bamboozled.*

"Barb, I remember your kindness," I said. "I remember it very well." I gave her hand a couple of soft pats.

"And I remember your strength." She topped up our tea. "Now, tell me why you've come to see me."

I reached into my bag and pulled out my assisted death application. "I need your help with something."

She raised her hands. "Frances, I can't help you find your daughter. You'll need to go to child services and—"

"All I need is your signature." I slid the paper across the table.

She started looking around the room, and I pointed to her head, where her reading glasses were perched.

She read what I'd written, then looked up at me. "How old are you? Late fifties?"

I nodded. "Fifty-eight."

She laid her glasses on the table and rubbed her eyes. "Too young for this. I'm so very sorry. More than I can say. You've had a hard go in this life, haven't you?"

I shrugged. "Harder than some, easier than many."

"Are you in a lot of pain?"

"I'm managing. I just don't want any more than I can bear."

"Do you know when it will happen?"

"I'm not sure yet. I still have a few things to work out."

She tapped the paper with her index finger. "And this is what you want? What you really want for yourself?"

I nodded. "Thank you for asking."

She got up, rifled through a drawer, and came back with a thick black fountain pen.

I pulled the paper across the table and signed my name with her beautiful pen, then passed the pen and paper to her. She hesitated for a moment, then signed her name.

"And what will your God have to say about your part in this?" I asked.

"I don't know," she said, smiling. "I guess I'll ask when I see him."

We sat quietly for a minute or two, then chatted about her travels and her young nieces and a little about Edie, and when she opened the door for me to leave, she asked me why I had chosen her to be my witness.

"You said to call if I ever needed anything," I said. "And I figured maybe you owed me one."

She laid her hand on my forearm. "Frances, may I pray for you?"

I leaned in and kissed her cheek. "I'm hedging my bets these days. I'll take anything you got."

I thought about her on the bus ride home. I wondered if late at night she saw the faces of all the girls she'd known, the faces of all the infants offered up, the ones passed over willingly by sad, silent girls like me and the ones torn from girls who screeched and carried on and begged to keep them.

Go to child services, she said. As if I hadn't been there more times than I could count. The first day I walked into the run-down low-rise building, all hepped up on indignation and rage, I couldn't have been more than twenty-one, skinny, broke, almost mad with loneliness. I hadn't given a single thought to what I would have done had they handed me my child. All I knew was that I wanted what was mine. But before I uttered a word to anyone, I panicked and ran out.

A week later, I went back, and again the next week and the week after that, never finding the nerve to speak. I let a few weeks pass, then went back again. I was loitering in the hallway when a woman walked up to me, introduced herself as Judy, a social worker, then led me to her office. She made me coffee, then I sat while she wrote notes and filed papers and occasionally looked at me and smiled. Twenty minutes passed before I left, having not said a word. Six months later, I wandered in again and asked the receptionist if I could see someone named Judy, but by then she was off having a baby of her own. After another six months went by, I went back and found Judy at her desk. She looked at me and said, "How can I help you if you won't speak?"

"I just want to know if Georgina is all right," I said and burst into tears.

Judy took down all the details of the birth, then left me in her office. Twenty minutes later, she came back with a file. She told me a married couple had adopted my daughter, two professors at the university. They'd left a note on the file for me in case I came sniffing around someday. Judy said they were "open to their daughter exploring her heritage," whatever that meant, but they asked that I wait until she was at least twelve, the age they believed she'd be able to cope with my surfacing.

The whole time Judy talked, I cried. Looking back on it, I see now that I was likely depressed, but at least I was with it enough to know that my child was best left there in that room, safely tucked away in a beige file folder. I thanked Judy and went home to my freezing room in a boarding house at the bottom of Cochrane Street.

After that day, I'd think I saw my daughter every so often in a crowd. Or I'd wake in the night, sweaty and gasping for air, having dreamt she'd drowned or been abducted or contracted a deadly disease. I'd had a few jobs in houses with small children, and I spent far too much time cleaning their cribs and high chairs and wiping down all the toys and doodads required to keep a toddler entertained. Eventually, I started turning down jobs in houses with children, and professors.

By the time Georgina's twelfth birthday rolled around, I was a healthier person, but not a richer one, and not a more educated one. And every time I thought it might be the right moment to reach out, I imagined her greeting me in a well-appointed living room, with her wealthy, intellectual parents by her side while her "heritage" sat facing them—a penniless cleaning woman with bad nerves. I believed I had nothing to offer her, and also that she would twig that within five minutes in my company. I feared that she'd be disappointed at best, ashamed at worst, and that either way she'd be somehow harmed by me. I decided to let her be, and instead I wondered about her constantly. If her hair was gingery like mine and my mother's. If she liked books and did well at school. If she had a friend who loved her. If, if, if.

By now, my daughter had had forty-three birthdays. And I had had forty-three years of wondering and waiting for the right time to present myself to her. But now the window had closed. I knew there was a solid argument to be made for revealing myself, but there was an equally solid one against it. If she wanted no part of a relationship with me, then I'd carry that until my last breath. And one day she might suffer the guilt of rejecting a dying woman. If she wanted to know me, then she'd have found me only to have me snatched away. Either way, it was a burden she didn't deserve. Still, I wanted nothing more than to be known as her mother, just for a few minutes. Just long enough for her to tell me that it had all worked out for the best. I'd feel righteous, the wise and sacrificing mother. But I couldn't bring myself to risk hearing that it hadn't worked out, that the woman who'd raised her was vindictive and cruel, that her father had beaten her or worse. That I'd made a mistake of epic proportions and she'd spent her whole life blaming and hating me for what I had and hadn't done.

Barb had asked me for forgiveness. She'd looked so earnest— she'd so badly wanted me to grant it. I wasn't sure I had. I too wanted to be pardoned, to sit and have tea with my daughter in a cozy kitchen, to reach for her hand and beg forgiveness for not fighting to keep her.

I got off the bus near Dr. Langley's office, dropped off my witnessed paperwork, and then began walking toward home. I stopped at a restaurant that looked like somewhere Edie might eat. I sat at a table on a wooden patio set up to face the street and ordered a glass of champagne. The waiter recited the specials and I told him to bring me the one he thought was the best, a seafood soup followed by a seared breast of duck. I ate and drank and smoked a cigarette in the late afternoon sunshine as if my life were just beginning.

7

I'd had a rough night. The rich food and wine from the restaurant mixed with the new pills made for fitful dreams. But I was more than happy to pay the price for that beautiful evening. And with the morning light came a sense of peace. The manner of my death had been secured and the only task that remained was to live the life I had left. All I wanted now was to find a way to make every minute count.

I was still lounging in bed when Edie came knocking a little after nine. I was too tired to dress and settled on greeting her in my robe and slippers.

"Oh no, I woke you," she said. "Should I come back later?"

"No, no, it's fine. Come in."

She was carrying a cardboard tray with two cups and hoisted a greasy white paper bag. "I brought breakfast. Green tea and egg-and-cheese croissants." She set the food out on the table and dug in.

"So I've decided what I want to do this summer," she said.

"Ah, which lucky cause shall you be championing this time?"

"You. You're my cause. I'm offering to help you out or just hang, whatever. Now before you say no—"

"I accept."

She stopped chewing. Her lips were covered with flakes of pastry, and a stray bit of egg had lodged on her chin. "What?"

"I said I accept. Depending on your terms, of course."

"But I spent an hour working on a speech to convince you."

"Sorry. Go ahead."

"It's no good now. You're after throwing me all off-kilter."

"Stop pouting and tell me your plan."

As I watched her wolf down the last of her breakfast, hope rose up in me like never before and I could barely stand the wait for her to speak. Come on, Edie. Lay it all out. Show me how to make a life worth living.

"Okay, the first thing is to make a wish list. All the things you want to do or see and whatnot."

"Edie, have you told your mother about this?"

"Nope." She wiped her hands with a napkin and pulled a small red leather notebook from her bag. "I'm going old school, no digital footprint. Mom thinks I don't know that she checks my phone. Last week I did a whole text exchange with Colin about how I wanted eyelash extensions, as if. Two days later, she hands me a hundred-dollar bill, 'just because,' she said. Anyway, I gave her money to the food bank."

I sipped my tea. I was instantly sold on this idea of hers, and if her mother got wind of it, so be it. But how to take her up on it safely? How to have her around without scarring her as my body, and possibly my mind, began to fail? It would be tricky. She was so eager, all flushed and filled with purpose. I figured not taking her up on it was the bigger gamble.

She opened her red book, pen poised. "So," she said, "number one on the list is what? Think big."

I didn't know where to begin, but whatever I managed to come up with was bound to be disappointing to her. I had a grand total of five thousand dollars to my name, my emergency fund—not a bad haul for a cleaning woman, but the sixteen-year-old girl sitting across from me likely had twice that sitting in her spending money account. She knew nothing of what it meant to be thrifty. It was an acquired skill honed by necessity and discipline, not much different from a religion, the central tenet of which is "thou shall not want." Every dollar that had ever made its way to my hands was guarded like the treasure it was, and then cleverly—no, artfully—transformed from paper to elastic. If they gave out degrees for making the best of being strapped, I'd have a PhD. Dr. Delaney, specializing in self-denial and deprivation. Queen of the charity shops and blessed with a uniquely hardy constitution that allowed for maximum output on minimal input—a full day's work on a banana and water. I'd learned to see my frugality as a reflection of strength of body and mind, of solid character and strong will. I'd never once taken what wasn't mine, even during the leanest of times, a source of great pride for me. My lucky stumble upon Mrs. Heneghan and Mrs. Cleary had helped carry me this far, but I liked to think I would have made it with or without them, my integrity intact.

Still, I'd often fantasized about owning a home like the one the Cleary family lived in, or any home, for that matter, and I also wondered what I could've done with all the time I'd spent over the years scrubbing stains from used clothes and fretting over where my next job would come from. Often, I'd wished for an apartment full of new hardcover books and a fridge full of fine food, a trip to any place where I didn't speak the language, a university degree. The remedy for such folly was volunteering one Sunday evening a month at the homeless shelter, doling out ladles of canned soup and slices of stale white bread to the truly unfortunate. No matter how bad I thought I had it, there were always so many so much worse off. For me, those poor people served as both consolation and cautionary tale. Every time I passed one of them a tray of food, I'd think, There but for the grace of a few months' pay go I. Now my little stash felt like a windfall, and I was ready to rip through it, one modest treat at a time.

"All right," I said. "I'd like a pile of new clothes. Nothing fancy, just new."

She wrote it down with a flourish. "Next?"

"Give me some time. I'll get back to you."

"What about a swishy haircut to go with the new wardrobe?"

"Fine. Number two is a haircut. But clothes first."

THE NEXT DAY, EDIE drove me to the mall, where Colin was waiting for us. "Impeccable taste, that boy," she said. He was nothing like I'd imagined him to be, not at all pimply or awkward. Tall and sculpted, more man than boy, a Norse god made over for modern times with his shorn blond hair and smart clothes. He was smiley and gracious, and I immediately saw why Edie cared for him. I shook his strong hand and tried not to think about the two days that Edie and I had spent cleaning up after him.

They whisked me around the mall, chose pants and sweaters and shirts and a denim jacket. I asked for a scarf and Edie chose one that she said made my eyes pop, which apparently was a good thing. Each time I emerged from a dressing room, they clapped and told me I was "killing it." Then they fixed me up with sandals and sneakers that I was assured were all the rage. Against their advice, I also chose a pair of flat black shoes like the ones I'd seen Hillary wear. Edie said they were mom shoes, but I thought them the best purchase of the day. Colin loaded the bags in Edie's car, and I watched them hug and kiss in the rear-view mirror. Anyone would have thought them madly in love, and I reckoned in a way they were. They had a way of making me feel more alive than I'd felt in years.

When I got home, I laid all my purchases on my bed and tried on every outfit again. Then I poured a whisky and smoked out my window wearing clothes with the tags still dangling from them.

Two days later, Edie took me to a hair salon. We walked past a bank of elevated recliners where women sat drinking coffee and chatting while other women wearing surgical masks were cutting toenails and sloughing skin off rough heels. I followed Edie up a set of glass stairs to a bright white room with a row of black swivel chairs, each one set in front of a floor-to-ceiling mirror, reflecting the chic stylists and their clients. A tall, painfully thin woman with spiky platinum-blond hair sashayed toward us. She was dressed in a black tank top and shiny red pants, and her left arm was completely covered by a tattooed garden of colourful flowers.

"Frances, this is Debra, Colin's sister," Edie said.

"Oh yes," I said. "I've met Colin. He's a lovely young man."

"He's a sweetheart, isn't he? Now, Frances, have a seat and let's talk about this hair."

Edie stood behind me next to Debra, who began picking through my hair. Her fingers grazed the side of my neck and sent a thrill over my skin. She pursed her lips and made a face.

"It's really dry. What are you using for conditioner?"

But I couldn't answer. The sensation of her hands in my hair was too strong. Each time she lifted and moved the strands, I felt a flutter in my chest. Then she rested her hands on my shoulders and gave them a playful pat, and the fluttering stopped.

"Are we doing colour as well today?" she asked.

"Just a cut. Whatever you think would suit me best."

Edie wandered off and Debra led me to a chair in front of a sink. I leaned back and the warm water flowed over my scalp. I'd never been to a hair salon in my life. Why waste my hard-earned cash when I had two steady hands and a sharp pair of scissors? Before Debra, the only person who had ever washed my hair was my mother. I could see her raising the pink plastic cup she used for rinsing. I could feel the edge of her hand pressed against my forehead to shield my eyes from the soap. Then Debra began making small, deep circles with her fingertips, over my temples, behind my ears, at the base of my skull, and I imagined the squid smiling and flapping a tentacle, like the hind leg of a blissful dog getting a belly rub.

When she finished cutting and drying, my hair was no longer my own. It bounced and captured the light when I moved my head from side to side. I happily forked over the money for the bottles of goop that Debra assured me were essential to have from now on, and I laughed out loud at the look on Edie's face when she saw me.

"Pick up your jaw, little girl. Haven't you ever seen a beauty queen before?"

"You look so, I don't know, modern and sophisticated. It's really beautiful, Frances. Here, let me get a shot of you." She held up her phone and pressed the button.

She took another picture of me in the car when we stopped at a traffic light, and two more once she'd parked in front of the library. Then she spent five minutes editing the photos and deciding which one she should send to Colin.

"Edie, I'm getting out of the car now."

"Wait, wait. One more second." She tapped on her phone, then put it in her bag. "Why do you come all the way over here?

There's a bigger library about a five-minute walk from your apartment."

"It's quieter here. Not so many youngsters."

"Mom's friend Hillary runs this one. Do you know her?"

"Yes, I do. She's wonderful."

She leaned across the seat and hugged me. "You look great. You'll be driving all the men crazy."

"Thanks for today. You have a good night and be careful driving."

As I opened the library door, I heard Edie calling out to me from the car.

"Hey, Frances, number three on the list. Get on it." She tooted her horn and drove away.

I checked my reflection in the door before stepping inside. Hillary was sitting in front of her computer. I walked toward the desk, but her phone rang, and she got up and took it into the back office. I hung around for a few minutes, picking through the rack of tourist brochures I'd seen a thousand times until she reappeared.

"Hey, Frances. Wow, you look fantastic. Retirement really agrees with you, hey?"

She smiled and went back to her work. I went off to find my chair and decided the next time I came, I'd wear my denim jacket and the pretty scarf and see what she had to say about that.

Later, in bed, I picked up my phone and opened Hillary's life again. The pictures from her son's party were already there, the cake expertly piped and on top a candle in the shape of the number nine. Her husband was there too, smiling, looking well pleased with his family. He had the look of class and money about him. Edie had warned me about reading too much into people's lives as they were presented this way—that people often looked happier than they really were—but to my eyes, there was perfection in those images. Then I flipped through Annie's life again, long enough to feel her presence in the room. It suddenly occurred to me that maybe Hillary and Annie would be able to tell that someone was looking at their photos. Maybe they'd know I'd been lurking about, prying into their business like someone who didn't know how to behave properly in a world filled with people.

Many years ago, not long after I'd arrived in the city, I took a job as a housekeeper at a large hotel. One Christmas, a few of the other maids planned a night out, to have a few drinks, take in a local band. I was surprised to be invited along, and somehow worked up the nerve to go. They were a rowdy bunch, and they seemed to know each other well. I had no idea how to blend in with them, so I just sat and sipped a warm beer while watching them carefully for clues on how to act and what to say. With each passing minute, I grew more anxious. I drank a second beer thinking it would help me relax, but instead I felt bloated and queasy. I went to the bathroom to try to steady myself. I was still in the grimy stall when I heard the bathroom door open, then two women talking. I recognized Martha's voice. She was about my age and often on my shift. She reminded me of Annie, chatty and popular, with an edge to her that I found alluring. Every time she let fly a string of swears, it always made me smile.

"Jesus Christ, I'll be paying for this night in more ways than one tomorrow," Martha said. "If I'm too trashed, I'll have to ask Frances to double up."

The other woman spoke, but I couldn't place her. "Why did you ask her to come anyway? She just sits there like a lump on a log, staring at us like a retard."

"Oh, for fuck's sake, she's not retarded. She's just a bit off, that's all. I felt bad for her. But I dare say she's a bit creepier than usual tonight. Don't pay her no mind."

I waited until they left, then slipped out the back door of the bar into the freezing night and rode the bus home alone. The next day, I volunteered for the night shift and started looking for another job. I never saw Martha again, but the sting of her words was as fresh and sharp as if I'd heard them only moments ago. I turned off my phone and swore off looking at any more photos.

The next morning, I went to a neighbourhood café that I'd walked past many times but had never ventured inside. I chose a table near the window and watched the umbrella domes bounce up and down as people hurried along the sidewalk in the rain. I was meeting Edie for breakfast. She burst through the door half an hour late, plopped down in a chair, and caught her breath.

"Sorry, I overslept. Sometimes I feel like I could sleep for two days straight. Did you know that teenagers actually need more sleep than older people? So I'm not late exactly. I'm just exercising my biological rights. How are you feeling?"

"I'm fine. Now I want to exercise my biological right to breakfast."

Edie waved a waitress over and I took her suggestion for eggs Benedict with smoked salmon and fresh fruit on the side. I decided that if I did wind up in heaven, I might spend eternity eating eggs covered in that yellow sauce.

Edie pushed her empty plate to the side. "Okay, number three on the list. Thoughts?"

I leaned toward her. "That website you got me on. Can people tell if you're looking at their pictures?"

"Not generally, why?"

"Just curious. I don't know how any of this foolishness works."

"I'm pretty sure everybody creeps everybody else's page."

A dull ache began to form behind my eyes. "What do you mean, 'creeps'?"

"You know, just trolling around, checking people out. See, there's number three right there—getting you up on all the socials."

I shifted in the hard chair and dug my thumbs into my lower back. Ever since the last seizure, I was stiff and sore more often than not. I soaked in the bath, kneaded my calves and thighs, rubbed my shoulders until my hands were weak, and still I felt like a bag of knots. I had a sudden flash of memory, walking in on Mrs. Cleary laid out on a pop-up table in her bedroom while a young woman rubbed her feet with oil. Sweet Jesus, I'd thought at first, paying people good money to touch you, now there's the height of it. But then I saw Mrs. Cleary's face, the picture of peace, like a sleeping child. She hadn't even noticed I'd come into the room.

"I've got number three for you," I said. "What do you think a massage would cost?"

"Eighty bucks? Maybe a hundred? Mom has a woman who comes to the house. I can get her number for you."

I shook my head. "No, someone she doesn't know."

Edie pulled out her phone and within five minutes had found a guy named Oliver who specialized in people with cancer. Highly reviewed, she assured me. She called and booked an appointment for me, and she offered to get me there and home again. I was worried about having to strip off in front of a man, but the tingle produced by Debra's hands had set something off in me, like an itch I couldn't scratch, an ache I couldn't easily pinpoint. I wanted someone—anyone—to reach for me and work out the kinks.

"Frances? I'm Oliver. Come on back." He was a compact and well-muscled man with a shaved head and a pair of round silver glasses that seemed at odds with his tight blue T-shirt and stretchy fitness pants. I followed him to a dimly lit room that smelled of something fruity. He reached for the clipboard the girl at the front had given me and looked over the forms I'd filled out.

"So other than the brain tumour, do you have any health concerns?"

"No, that one is enough."

He nodded. "I see you've never had body work before, so I suggest we do some light massage today, just some gentle exploration so I can get a sense of your body and we'll see where to go from there. How does that sound?"

"Whatever you usually do is fine."

"I'll step out and let you get changed. Just take off whatever you're comfortable with."

I stripped down to my underwear and slid under the soft sheet. He knocked on the door and I asked for one more minute, then got up and took off my bra and underwear and stuffed them in the pocket of my pants. I scurried back to the table and lay fully unclothed between sheets for the first time in my life.

"Okay, I'm ready."

Oliver came into the room and I locked my eyes on the ceiling.

"Frances, I'm going to start at your head and work my way down your body. If at any time you need me to stop or change what I'm doing, just say the word."

I drew in a deep breath. He stood behind me, slid his hands over my hair and cupped the back of my skull with his palms. His fingertips pressed against the bones where my head met my neck. They circled and stroked, and I closed my eyes. There was music playing softly in the background, a meandering melody plucked out on a guitar. And as he made his way around my scalp, down the back of my neck, across my shoulders, I had the sensation of my body expanding in all directions, puffing up with air and floating above the table. His two hands slid down the centre of my chest, then drew apart, then back together and apart again. As my skin and muscles pulled away from my bones, my daughter came to me. I saw her newborn face, smushed and wet, and her tiny flexed body still attached to mine by the corkscrewed bluish cord. Then I saw her toddling across a kitchen floor for the first time and running around a grassy lawn on a hazy summer evening in yellow cotton pajamas, her hair wet and combed off to the side. A school uniform, a Christmas concert, a skipping rope, a skinned knee, braces on her teeth. I saw her walking arm in arm with another girl through town. A black hat with a tassel, her diploma held above her head while she grinned for the camera. A man by her side, a veil of white, a baptism. Glasses raised in honour of her new job. All of it passed before my closed eyes as if it were memory.

"Are you doing okay?" Oliver said.

The sound of his voice startled me back into the room. I nodded and he pumped his hands full of lotion from a bottle held in a pouch at his waist. He worked down the length of my right arm, then took my hand in his. The pressure against my palm flooded me with a pleasure I'd never imagined existed, wave after wave of heat coupled with a desire to laugh and waggle my shoulders just to cope with it. By the time he'd finished my left hand, the sensation had risen to such a fevered intensity that I feared my body would burst into flames.

He pulled the sheet and blanket up and over my left leg and tucked them carefully under my right, keeping my private parts private. He pushed and kneaded along my thigh and calf, and with each stroke of his hand I heard my mother's voice, her song high and clear. I could see her standing at the sink with her back to me, her body swaying as her tune flowed out through the open window toward the sea beyond. I could smell the bread baking in the oven and the sharp scent of the spruce boughs as they crackled and spit in the fire. She turned to face me and smiled.

Oliver did the same with my other leg, then asked me to roll onto my stomach. He pulled the pillow away and there was a hole cut in the table, a perfect fit for my face. More lotion, more laying of hands, across the expanse of my upper back, deep, almost painful pressure as the tension gave way. When he reached my lower back, I felt the hands of my father around my waist, hoisting me onto the deck of his boat. I could smell the sea and feel the mist on my face, taste the salt in my mouth. I saw the deep lines etched into the wind-burned skin around his blue eyes and his thick, calloused fingers wrapped around the wheel. I heard his booming laugh when I reeled in a toilet seat covered in seaweed. The sound of his fiddle came to me as Oliver worked down the backs of my legs. "Swallowtail Jig," a cheerful reel that had defined my childhood, rose up in my ears, and it was as if my father had been raised from the dead and was standing, playing, right next to me.

Oliver spoke and I opened my eyes. The carpet below my face was dotted with tears. I asked him to repeat what he said. He told me to turn over and passed me a tissue.

"Don't worry," he said. "This happens all the time. Massage can bring up all sorts of feelings."

I swept my face with my hands and lay back on the pillow. He flipped back the sheet and started working on my feet. I closed my eyes. It was the same pleasure I'd felt when he did my hands, only jacked up to an almost unbearable loveliness. And then I saw Annie, her smiling face shining through the thick fog at the shore.

"Frances, that's our time for today. Be sure to rest tonight and drink plenty of water over the next couple of days." He turned to leave.

"Oliver," I said and reached toward him.

He took my hand in his.

"Thank you."

He laid his other hand over mine and smiled. "You're most welcome."

I rose slowly from the table, not trusting my legs to support me. I dressed and paid for my hour and thought never was there money better spent. I booked another appointment and then stepped into the bright sunlight, where Edie was waiting for me in her little blue car.

"So how was it?"

Exquisite. "Very nice."

She smiled and pulled into traffic. As we turned the corner onto my street, I noticed the song playing on the radio, young men singing, an Irish drum and whistle, an accordion and a fiddle. A ramped-up, modern rendition, but there was no mistaking it.

"Turn that up."

"Dad loves this band. He went to high school with two of them." She pressed a button on her steering wheel and the car filled with "Lukey's Boat." She stopped in front of my place just as the song finished.

"Edie, I want to go home."

"You are home. Are you all right?"

"No, number four on the list. I want to go home."

8

Edie was thrilled when I said I wanted to go Safe Harbour. She thought I had finally landed on something substantial for the list, and I agreed. But later that evening, I feared that I'd spoken too soon. That I'd let the massage and the song on the radio carry me away, then made a hasty decision. Too much heart and not enough head. But once I'd said it out loud, it felt like a promise made to Edie, and to myself. One I couldn't break.

I soaked in a hot bath and tried to decide if there'd ever been any real truth in it, my long-held belief that I could never go home again. What I wanted was to blink and be transported to the town I'd resisted for so long, instantly set down by the sea before I could think of all the reasons not to go. No one wants to travel back to the time and place when they were at their worst, to revisit their most needy and tender selves. The day I took the bus from the Sisters of Mercy Home back to Safe

Harbour, my young heart was like an overripe fruit, bruised and on the verge of rotting away.

It was a cold January afternoon in 1979. The ride was hours longer than usual given the state of the roads. Mounds of slush had hardened to chunks of ice, and high winds forced the driver to pull us along at a snail's pace. When the bus finally slowed to a stop, I saw Father O'Leary's car, that Dodge Dart the colour of split pea soup, then spotted him behind the wheel, ramrod straight, staring into the distance. I watched through the window as he pulled a black wool hat over his grey curly hair, brought a set of rosary beads to his lips, and got out of the car. I walked to the front of the bus, the door opened, and Father O'Leary's eyes scanned me up and down, resting on my still-round belly. I buttoned my coat to cover it while he reached for my bag, then hustled me toward his car.

"Bad weather for a bus ride," he said, and started the engine.

We pulled out on to the main road.

"Frances, I'm so sorry about your mother. It must have been quite a shock for you."

I nodded.

"Now, because of how your mother died, it's the archbishop's position that she is not to have a Catholic funeral or burial, but I will say Mass—"

"Did she leave a letter?"

"No, she didn't."

"Then you can't be sure that she really meant to kill herself."

But he was sure. He told me that she'd tied a heavy rock to her leg with a thick length of rope. Everything he said after that faded into garbled noise. I didn't speak, and when the shore came into view, I turned away from it. He drove me to Annie's house, where it had been decided I would stay until a more permanent arrangement was worked out. Mrs. Malone met me at the door and pulled me into her arms. "This too shall pass," she whispered into my ear.

For six months, I'd thought of nothing but my reunion with Annie. Other than a few letters smuggled back and forth by Sister Barb, we hadn't communicated. Now there she was, standing behind her mother, eyes down and wringing her hands. She reached for my bag and Mrs. Malone went to the kitchen to fix me a plate. I followed Annie up the stairs.

I lay on her bed and she snuggled in behind me. I couldn't feel the warmth of her body. I couldn't feel anything. She placed the flat of her hand against my stomach.

"Did it hurt?" she asked.

"Yup."

"Mom told me not to talk about the baby. Or your mother."

"Then talk about something else."

"Like what?"

"Doesn't matter."

She told me how she'd broken up with Donny Doyle after she found him behind the school one day with his hand up Mary Simpson's skirt. "Mary bloody Simpson," she said. "Her with that hair and those teeth." She scoffed, then prattled on about everything I'd missed until I fell asleep.

The next day, Annie stood beside me while Father O'Leary said Mass for my mother. The church was cold and empty except for the Malone family and my mother lying in a plain coffin in front of the altar. No flowers, no music, just the priest's voice echoing off the whitewashed wooden walls. Then we stood in the freezing cold at the very back of the graveyard, as far from my father's grave as we could be. Father O'Leary said the blessing and flicked holy water down on my mother's coffin, loud splats against the wooden top. All I could think was she'd done everything he'd asked her to do. Never questioned him once when he'd come calling with a plot to cover my sin. But he wouldn't order the diggers to make a hole next to my father's grave and hadn't even rustled up a few wilted carnations for her. I couldn't look at him.

Beyond the gravesite lay the slate-grey water, whitecaps forming as the wind began to pick up. I watched as it shifted and rolled, its beauty and majesty gone and its motion taunting me. *Macabre.* I turned my back on the sea and made a silent vow never to go near it again for as long as I lived.

The next day, I told Mrs. Malone I wanted to go back to my house. She begged me to delay.

"I'll be all right," I said. "There's the bit of money my mother had saved. That'll be enough to get by on."

"Only just and not for long."

"I'm a week shy of seventeen. Sooner or later, I need to learn to live on my own."

Mrs. Malone shook her head and started filling a plastic grocery bag with food from her pantry.

"Frances, you come back any hour of the day or night. Do you hear me? I'll be over tomorrow to check on you," she said. She hugged me and closed the door.

The house was cold. There were no signs of my mother anywhere—no dishes on the table, no coat on the hook by the door—but I could see her standing in front of the sink peeling potatoes. I could hear her telling me it was time to put my schoolwork away and go to bed, and I could smell the flowery soap she used to rid her hands of any trace of fish. Upstairs her room was tidy, the bed smooth and undisturbed, but I noticed a layer of dust on the dresser and ran the tip of my finger through it. Then I wrote her name across the dark wood.

The air was stale. I opened the window and let in a blast of frigid wind. I lay down on her bed, my body fitting neatly in the impression left by hers. I waited for tears, squeezed my eyes shut as hard as I could, but they would not flow. I got up and wandered through the house room by room. In the kitchen, I followed a beam of sunlight from the window to the counter. Another thick layer of dust. As I blew it into the air and watched the motes scatter in the light, a clump of something heavier and browner than dust fell to the floor. I reached down, rubbed it between my fingers, and raised it up close to my face. Frayed ends of rope. I flung them into the kitchen sink and retched my breakfast over them, then I cleaned out the sink and just kept going.

All day and clear through to the next morning, I ignored the swelling and aching left behind by childbirth as I scrubbed and polished everything in sight. Then I stripped her bed and washed all the linens, bleached the bathroom, and swept the floors. As the sun began to rise, I folded my mother's clothes into neat piles and packed them into small garbage bags. I carried them one by one to the crawl space in the eaves, along with every photo I could find of her and all her songbooks. I put the lot in behind the boxes of Christmas decorations. Then I got into my bed, every part of my body screaming with pain, and shed enough tears to soak my pillow.

I was still asleep when Mrs. Malone knocked on the door with my lunch. I lumbered down the stairs and found her laying out a bowl of turkey soup and slicing a loaf of warm homemade bread.

"Sit down and get this into you, Frances. Baby or not, you look like those nuns were after starving you half to death."

She sipped a cup of tea and watched me as I took a few spoonfuls of soup and nibbled at a piece of bread. Then she explained to me that my parents' house had never been theirs. It was built on land owned by the Church and they had merely been caretakers. Mr. Malone had worked out a deal with Father O'Leary to look after the house for the time being. Mrs. Malone had planned for me to move in with them, but the thought of living full time in Annie's boisterous house made my head spin. I told her I wanted to live here, in my home. She made her own deal with me. She'd convince the priest to let me stay in the house, as long as I agreed that she could cast a motherly eye over me until I finished school. I had no idea how to return to school. The thought of it terrified me.

"I can't go back to school yet. I just can't," I said. "Everyone will be talking. 'There goes Frances. The one who got pregnant and killed her mother.'"

Her teacup clattered against the saucer. "Jesus, Mary, and Joseph. Now you listen to me, Frances. You've got enough on your mind without taking that on. Your mother's dying has nothing to do with you. Nothing. Sometimes people just have to lay it down, and that's all there is to it."

"Lay what down?"

"Whatever it is they're carrying."

I nodded and let her think I believed her.

ANNIE CAME TO SEE me every day after school. Her mother had tasked her with bringing me schoolwork and dragging me back home with her for supper. I did as I was told, mostly because I didn't have the strength to argue.

Every morning of that winter, I woke up convinced that some new disaster would come for me that day—a slip on the ice and a cracked skull, a raging blizzard that would split the house in two, a deadly virus intent on attacking my organs one by one. But each morning, I'd drag myself from my warm bed to find nothing at all amiss. Nothing but a world that didn't seem to notice or care what had happened. It was as if my mother had never existed, and it made me furious. Once a week, I stood by my father's grave, reaching for my rapidly fading memories of him. I wanted to walk to my mother's grave and sweep the snow away from the white wooden cross, just to prove to myself that she had indeed been here. But I didn't. Not once. My shame was like a second skin, and I just couldn't face her.

The only other time I left the house was to go out for food. I would go early in the morning, when the store was at its quietest and all the kids my age were in school. There were only ever a few people to contend with. They'd acknowledge me either by staring or by quickly looking away, and I could never work out which felt worse. By the time I'd filled my bag with cans of tomato soup and boxes of cereal, my body would be slick with sweat and my heart ready to muscle its way out of my chest.

I spent my days lying on the couch, the television on but the volume turned down low. I was always tired yet hardly slept. My arms and legs felt heavy and rubbery, and my joints ached. I had no appetite and forgot to eat for days at a time. My schoolbooks sat unopened on the kitchen table, my mind too woolly to concentrate on anything beyond just getting through the day. I had no interest in reading or anything else—not even Annie. She'd bounce through the door every day just after three o'clock, smiling and chatting and doing everything she could think of to perk me up, and I would become so irritated by her presence that I began to believe I hated her. Every evening I'd sit at the Malone dinner table and watch the clock, suffering them all until I could finally slip away. Then I would go home and clean the house until I felt calm enough to try to sleep.

When my clothes began to bag off my bony body, Mrs. Malone grew concerned enough to fetch the doctor. They both came unannounced to my door one morning. I listened while he talked about grief and my hormones being out of whack, about how I needed to eat more and get some fresh air into my lungs once a day. He and Mrs. Malone huddled in the front room whispering while I waited in the kitchen, wishing the floor would open up and swallow me. All I wanted was to be left alone, but Annie and her mother would have none of it. Mrs. Malone force-fed me fruity vitamin tablets and bread slathered in butter. Every day, Annie bundled me up and pushed me through the door to walk for miles with her no matter the weather. I agreed to go as long as we walked in silence and kept well away from the water.

Then one day in late April, as we walked, I unzipped my bulky parka. The snow had been whittled down to grey crust, and I felt the warmth of the sun against my face. I turned to Annie and asked her to talk to me.

"What should I say?" she said.

"Anything. Just talk."

She lunged forward and wrapped her arms around me, almost knocking both of us to the ground. "Thanks be to Jesus," she said. "You're back."

At the end of May, despite knowing that I'd failed the year, I walked back into school with Annie at my side. When Mary Simpson's jaw fell a couple of inches at the sight of me, Annie stepped toward her.

"Shut your gob, tart, or I'll shut it for you."

She linked her arm with mine and strutted down the hall, grinning like I was a prize she'd won. I was still carrying the weight of all that I'd lost, and I couldn't imagine ever feeling happy again, but in that moment, I believed as long as I had Annie to prop me up, anything was possible.

MY BATHWATER HAD GROWN cold. I stepped out of the tub and wrapped a towel tightly around my shoulders to fight off the chill. In the morning, Edie would be at my door. Together we'd travel back to where my life had begun. She'd begged me to take her with me, and whether it was wise or not, I'd said yes. I wanted as many minutes as possible with her, and I also needed her. The painkillers were now a nightly ritual. My failing eyesight seemed to have found its level, but I was off balance and unsteady on my feet at times, and I no longer moved about without thought or care. I also knew that she might provide a shield of sorts, a buffer between me and whatever would be waiting for me in a place where I'd known so much pain. I dried myself off and pushed down a pang of guilt about using Edie in this way before it got a chance to rise and reach full strength.

Edie wasn't licensed to drive on the highway, which left us on a crowded and very noisy bus. She'd told her mother that a trip to my hometown was a necessary part of her education. A chance to experience rural Newfoundland, which her mother decided was an inspired idea. Mrs. Cleary even called me to express her thanks for my role in expanding Edie's horizons.

It was the height of tourist season, and the only accommodation left was a slightly rundown vacation rental facing a rocky strip of shore two towns east of Safe Harbour. We arrived late evening, just as the cool fog began to drift in from the Grand Banks. Fog so thick you could lean on it, as my father used to say. Edie unpacked her gadgets, then laid my things neatly on the bed. She said nothing about the whisky or cigarettes, just placed them side by side on top of the dresser and set about checking for a signal for her phone.

I went outside and sat in a painted wooden armchair on the porch. The sea was calm and grey, the colour of a warship. A pungent mix of ocean brine and seaweed wafted in from the water. I breathed it in and I was a child again, combing the beach with Annie. Two pairs of tiny rubber boots, shiny mussel shells like jewels in our small hands. I closed my eyes and took shallow breaths to allow the past in just a little at a time.

The fog began to turn to fine mist. How well I remembered all this wetness. Rain and drizzle, sleet and snow, moisture always seeping into everything, under wool and through wood, every day a battle against the dampness. Water and wind. Howling gusts that picked off siding and toppled sheds every month of the year. The hard weather was an island-wide obsession worked into nearly every conversation, hated and feared yet secretly prized as evidence of our fortitude. And when the sun shone, strengthening bones and spirits alike, it was that much more radiant for its rarity, cherished above all other things in this part of the world and known to drive people out of doors half-dressed, even when the thermometer showed single digits. My island was a barren rock set upon by cruel weather, but it was never hard to find a reason to love it. Like this shore I was looking at now and that one I hadn't seen since I was nineteen. Had this stretch of coast not been the site of so much sorrow, I would have thought it a jewel of the earth.

I shivered and buttoned my sweater and thought about the day when I first asked Dr. Langley about how my exit would play out. She would come with her vials and syringes to the room I chose to be my last. I could invite whomever I wished to be present. She would explain to me and anyone else in the room what was about to happen, then ask me a final time if I was sure. Then she'd inject me with a drug that would bring about a gentle sleep, then two more drugs that would shut down my systems, the whole affair painless and brief, not more than ten or fifteen minutes from start to finish. *Deliverance.*

I imagined it would be just us two: doctor and patient. Who else was there? Edie was off limits. That room was no place for another woman's child, and I wasn't keen on my death being her last memory of me. But it gnawed at my heart, this thought of dying in a room without a friendly soul to bear witness. My solitary life had been carefully constructed, and on a few occasions, I was unable to find fault with it. I even found a small measure of pride in being a sole survivor, a woman making it all on her own. I'd convinced myself that there was nothing missing, and that I lived in circumstances of my own choosing. But more often than not, especially now, I could see what I'd made all too clearly—a life built on a foundation of faulty nerves, crippling shyness, and a battered heart that couldn't withstand another break. Walls built high and strong to keep everyone out. Annie had got in before all the bricks were laid, and Edie had seeped in through the cracks over time.

I used to wonder if people ever actually died of loneliness—if going for years without being talked to or touched could stop the human heart. I'd once had a bad bout of flu that kept me off work for a full week. For five days and nights, I didn't speak. I saw no other person, and no one saw me. When I finally managed to drag myself to the shop for food, the cashier's hand grazed mine and it burned hot from her touch. I wanted to beg her to tell me something about her life: where she lived, what she'd had for breakfast, what books she'd read. When I opened my mouth to say thank you, my voice was locked somewhere deep in my throat, immobilized by inactivity.

Maybe worse than being solitary was my paralyzing inability to step up and seize any opportunity to be otherwise. Many times, I'd resolved to join a book club or attend a free class or some such thing that gets posted on the corkboard of a public library, only to stand at my front door, gripping the doorknob in my sweaty palm until it was too late to go. I'd always feel utterly defeated, like I was a failure at living. Then again, I'd never had anyone show me how to go about it properly. About once a year, I'd become so desperate to be different that I'd think about finding a skilled person to help me. I knew people like that existed, but I was too nervous to venture out into the world to find someone to make me less nervous. Round and round it went, year after year, until the squid came knocking. If only I'd lowered my shield, reached out now and then, taken both the jabs and the caresses, or at least had the goddamn sense to ask for some help and accept any that was offered. But

I hadn't, and wishing it were different was about as useful as wishing the planet to stop spinning.

I jumped at the sound of Edie's voice. "Come in out of this weather," she said. I turned and looked at her standing in the doorway of the cottage. Forgive me, I thought. Later, when you're older and cursed with understanding, forgive me for needing you this much, for casting you in all these roles in my little drama—the girl I could have been, the friend I'd loved and lost, the daughter I'd cast aside, and now the strong, steady mother calling me in from the cold.

We ate fish and chips from the local takeout for dinner, then lay side by side in our twin beds. Edie put down her phone and drew the faded yellow chenille bedspread up to her face for a closer look.

"I wonder where they found all this vintage stuff."

I laughed. "In a 1975 Sears catalogue, I'd say."

"What's it like being back?"

"I'll tell you when we get there."

Edie's phone dinged and she squealed when she read the message. She hopped out of bed and did a little dance around the room, then plopped down on her knees beside me.

"Guess what we're doing tomorrow?"

I didn't have to guess. A quick poke about the town, a gander at my old house, and anything else my nerves were up for. Beyond that I hadn't the head to make any firm plans, and she knew it. She thrust her phone in my face, showing me a text message that I couldn't quite make out. I squinted at it and she yanked it away.

"It's from Annie Malone. She still lives there, and she knows we're coming tomorrow. You must be dying to see her." Her face froze. "Shit, I'm sorry. You know what I mean."

I sat up and stared at her. I saw her mouth moving, forming a string of words that made no sense to me. Her voice was a grating noise that flowed out of her and rose to a loud pitch, like a crow cawing in my ear.

"Edie, stop yammering for a minute and let me think."

She recoiled at the volume of my voice and fell silent. I raced back through the last few days, gripped by the fear that I'd somehow agreed to this and forgotten. No, I was certain I hadn't. Day before yesterday, on the phone, she'd asked me whether we'd visit Annie, and I told her there was no need to seek out someone I hadn't seen for so long. My words exactly. Good Christ, Edie, what have you done? I exhaled and asked her to pour me a shot of whisky. I took a sip and asked her to start at the beginning.

"It just made no sense to me," she said. "To come all this way and not meet up with her. I sent her a message online and asked if I could call her."

"You spoke to her? When?"

"Yesterday."

"You didn't tell her I was sick, did you?"

She shook her head. "I just said we were coming for a visit and did she want to meet up."

"What did she say?"

"Nothing much, really. She seemed sort of confused, but I think that might have been about who I was or whatever. Frances, you're white as a ghost. What's wrong?"

I left her kneeling by the bed and went to the bathroom. I had to lock myself away from her for a few minutes just to take in what she'd done. She knocked on the door, but I didn't answer. When she knocked a second time, I hollered at her to leave me be and immediately regretted it. I took off my pajamas and stood in the shower, hoping the spray of cool water would settle me down. I knew Annie was still living in Safe Harbour—I'd seen enough glimpses of the town in those photos Edie had found—but I also knew that without Edie's meddling, I'd have been in and out before Annie had even heard I was there. A long-forgotten Bible verse came to me: "Give thanks to the Lord, for he is good." I had no business with the Lord, but I leaned against the cold tile wall and spoke Edie Cleary's name like a prayer and offered her my endless thanks and praise.

When I came back in the room, she was sitting on the edge of my bed looking as morose as I'd ever seen her.

"I'm so sorry. Honestly, I just thought it would be an amazing surprise and—"

"No, *I'm* sorry. You did a good thing. I was just caught off guard by it. I should have reached out to Annie, but I didn't."

"Why not?"

"I don't know. Hard to keep anything straight with a squid swimming around in your head."

She narrowed her eyes. "What the hell are you talking about?"

"Nothing. Don't mind me. I'm just tired. Come on, back to bed. Big day tomorrow, then."

She prattled on for a bit, about the new housekeeper, Bernice, who apparently couldn't cook worth a damn and spent half her time trying to put some order to Edie's bedroom. Then she yawned, murmured another apology, and nodded off. I lay wide awake, listening to her steady breathing, still smarting from having raised my voice to her. Poor youngster. She had no idea what she'd stirred up with a single phone call. She was only just beginning to learn that good and beautiful things end. And she had yet to learn that good intentions were not always enough to right old wrongs. I thought about the bond she and Colin had forged. I bet they lived in the land of always and forever and believed they could weather anything. And maybe she and Colin would make it, live long, entwined lives, each the richer for doing so. But I'd learned something they hadn't: Any two people on the planet who professed to love each other were only one terrible conversation away from never speaking again. One reckless act from forsaking each other entirely. I knew it and Annie Malone knew it too.

9

Of the many images of Annie stored in my memory, there were two that took up the most space. One was of her tear-stained face, twisted with anger—the one I knew would materialize and take over my senses before the sun rose. It would come as it always did, unbidden and unwelcome, but as I sat in the living room of the dark cottage, blowing smoke through the open window while Edie slept, I willed the other to take shape—the one of her looking back over her left shoulder, winking at me as she strode across the stage at the parish hall to collect her high school diploma, a diploma that probably belonged as much to me as it did to her. Annie was a proper whiz with numbers, but anything to do with words both bored and frustrated her to no end, which is where I stepped in. I tried tutoring her but somehow always wound up doing her homework alongside my own. If our teachers saw my hand in her assignments, they never said. "For Jesus' sake, you could torch that school to the ground, and they'd give you an A plus in arson," was all Annie had to say when I expressed my fear of being caught.

But that rainy June day in the hall belonged to her alone. My own graduation would be delayed on account of the time I'd lost growing a baby and grieving my mother. She'd been dead for almost a year and a half. I'd pushed through the worst of it, but every time I thought of her, my body burned with shame and anger, so I tried not to think of her at all. On the anniversary of her death, Annie had asked me if I missed her. "Of course I do. What kind of freak wouldn't miss their mother?" I answered, with a snap in my tone that even I could hear. The truth was I liked my life better with her gone. The little things like the sound of the radio on blast while I showered, and the big things like being relieved of the burden of constantly worrying about her. I mourned my mother, but I did not miss her. Not like I missed my father. In the wake of my mother's death, I came to believe that had my father lived, he would have somehow prevented every misfortune that had come my way. That the things I remembered and cherished about him—his calm, steady demeanour and happy ways—would have rubbed off on me, making me a different girl altogether. I felt cheated twice over.

I hadn't spoken with Annie or anyone else about my mother since that day in the kitchen with Mrs. Malone. I hoped that people would eventually forget about her, but given the way I was still treated in Safe Harbour—the stares and awkward silences, the fawning and frantic efforts to be cheery—it seemed I was destined to become the face of tragedy in town, the orphan of the noble lost seaman and the village lunatic. I didn't know if folks were wise to the baby bit because that was also something never spoken of, not by me or Annie.

Annie's interest in boys had all but disappeared since my return from the home, and I wondered if it was my misfortune that had given her pause. Maybe she blamed herself for what had happened to me that night, or maybe she saw me as the embodiment of the hazards of lust. I was too afraid of the answers to ask her. All I knew was that I had her full attention, and that it was a kind of heaven. I suspected it was probably a mistake to need her as much as I did, to see her as the sole reason to leave my bed each morning, but I decided I didn't care. All I cared about was the grand adventure that was on the horizon.

It was six months before Annie's graduation when the plan first took shape. She'd decided to skip the New Year's Eve parties—both the one hosted by her parents and the one her parents knew nothing about—in favour of a quiet night in front of the fire with me. The clock struck midnight, the seventies were finally behind us, and Annie declared she'd had enough.

"Enough of what?" I said.

"This godforsaken place. Nothing to do, everyone's nose in your business. I mean, what's here for us anyway? No jobs, no money, no future."

"So what are you saying?"

"I'm saying that we're not spending the rest of our lives in this hole. We'll fuck off to St. John's and never look back." She began to speak in rapid bursts. "We'll get an apartment. Down by the harbour. You'll go to school and be a teacher. God knows what I'll do, but I'll think of something."

She banged on for ages—how we'd go out dancing every weekend, eat in restaurants and travel and meet gorgeous men in suits who'd treat us like queens. I listened in amazement as a whole lifetime beside her unspooled in my mind. I could see it all, and by the time she'd finished, I saw us as two old women laughing as we looked back on it all.

She leaned back on the sofa, breathless. "There'll be no stopping us, Frances. You and me against the world."

She guzzled down the last of her beer, turned the radio up as loud as it could go, and began to dance. I watched her twirl and bop around the living room of my dead parents' house. I imagined her cleansing it with every movement, smashing my legacy of misery with her unbridled joy. In that moment, I believed that she alone could chart a new course for me. I was overtaken by faith and hope, and decided to place every dream I'd ever held for myself in her hands and follow her wherever she led me. I popped up off the couch and she spun me around until I was dizzy.

The next morning, I woke with a sinking feeling that the talk of the night before was nothing more than a passing youthful fancy. Annie and I were still head to foot on the couch, covered by a knitted wool blanket. I could see my breath, and frost covered the windowpanes. I got up and moved quietly toward the wood stove, wondering how I'd manage to start the fire without waking her. I turned at the sound of her voice.

"You can stop tiptoeing around. I've been awake for hours hatching our escape plan. The first thing is money," she said. "We're going nowhere without money."

Cash quickly became our shared obsession, as neither of us had any to speak of. I'd taken to cleaning for a few old biddies in town who would hand me a five-dollar bill and a plate of dinner for my trouble. I was back at school, and even though I'd fallen behind, my teachers thought if I worked hard enough, I'd manage to snag a small scholarship. But we wouldn't get far on that. Annie pressed her parents for a loan to make the move, but they were tapped out at the end of every month like everyone else we knew. Annie fumed daily over the fact that there always seemed to be money for her brothers to play hockey but not a cent left over for what her parents felt was pure folly.

"A lark. That's what they said to me. And in front of those bloody fools too. Gordie laughing at me, telling me I'll be a townie harlot before my suitcase is unpacked. As if hockey isn't a goddamn lark. As if any one of those idiots will ever make a dime slapping a puck into a net. I'm telling you, Frances, he's lucky I don't take a hockey stick upside his head."

ALL THAT WINTER, THE weather bore down on us. Blizzard after blizzard blew in from the bay. Sleet storms raged, wiping out power for days. Enormous icicles hung from every eave for weeks on end, and the roads in every direction were encased in layers of treacherous ice. February was made darker and bleaker as Annie and I began to fear our bold vision would never be more than fantasy. By the time March rolled around, we'd pretty much succumbed to despair. Then one Saturday morning, Annie burst through my front door.

"It's a goddamn miracle," she said. "We're saved."

Our saviour's name was Ches Rideout.

"He's an old buddy of Dad's who left years ago to seek his fortune on the mainland, and apparently, he found it," Annie said. "Dad says he's dead clever. Made a pile of money, something to do with tractors. Or is it trucks? I can't remember now. Anyway, he's after getting tired of Toronto and he's coming back. Imagine trading Toronto for this mess."

"Sweet God, Annie. Get to the part about him saving us."

"Right. He's building a bloody big supermarket with a hardware store attached to it. And he's hiring all locals to work in it. His son is coming in May to start handing out jobs. They say it'll be up and running by the end of the summer."

My heart banged wildly, and sudden tears filled my eyes.

By mid-July, Annie had been hired as a cashier, and I'd applied for a part-time stockroom position. When I got the call to come for an interview, Annie came to my place to pick out my clothes and give me a pep talk before I left to meet Ches Rideout's son, Anthony, at the almost completed store.

"Just be yourself," she said. "Only more talkative, but not about books and stuff. And try to smile. Now, Frances, this is the most important thing: try to stay focused because Anthony Rideout is fair gorgeous. Wicked eyes on him, blue as the bay, and thick black hair all feathered back like Erik Estrada, but don't let that distract you."

"I think I'll manage."

Anthony met me in the gravel parking lot. Annie was right about his looks. He was the best-looking man I'd ever seen close up. I was expecting someone much older, but he didn't seem that far off from us in years. He smiled and shook my hand.

"Frances, good to meet you. I've heard a lot about you."

I nodded and pasted on a wide smile.

"Everyone I know with the last name Malone says if I don't hire you, I'm a fool. So part-time work is what you're after?"

"Yes, I missed some school last year. I still have six months left."

"Yeah, Annie told me about your mother. I'm sorry."

I was too preoccupied wondering how well he knew Annie to say anything sensible. He led me toward a black pickup truck and handed me an application form from a pile lying on the passenger seat.

"Just a formality," he said. "You can start right away."

A guy in a yellow hard hat called out to him from inside the store. Anthony asked if I could wait a minute and left me standing alone, somewhat bewildered by the ease with which I'd landed my first job. I wandered around the parking lot until he was done. He walked toward me, long confident strides, wide shoulders set back, a swagger if I ever saw one. He seemed to enjoy being in his own body more than anyone I knew, and he unnerved me beyond the usual agitations brought on by strangers.

"Hey, Frances," he said, "can I ask you something?"

I nodded.

"Annie. Does she have a boyfriend?"

I shrugged. "I expect you'll have to ask her."

"Fair enough," he said. "I might just do that."

He gave me a slow wink, and a cool little shiver rippled through me.

IT WAS LABOUR DAY weekend when the store finally opened. The whole town turned out to eat their fill of free grilled hot dogs and watch Ches and Anthony Rideout cut a big red ribbon in half. Annie worked one of the five cash registers while I was tucked away in the stockroom. At the end of the day we walked home together, exhausted but full of talk about how we'd soon be flush enough to make a break for town. Annie gushed about Anthony—his looks, his charming ways, his keen mind and helpful manner. She didn't mention if he'd asked her the question he'd asked me. I didn't mention it either. I didn't want to know. All I wanted to know was our good fortune.

My mother used to say that no good ever came without a balance of bad. Her words returned to me over and over that fall. School was almost unbearable for me without the steadying presence of Annie. I kept my focus on the lessons, ate my lunch alone in the empty classroom, and watched the clock tick away the minutes until I was free to run the half-mile to Rideout's, where Annie was always the first person I saw. She'd smile and buoy me enough to stock the shelves with cans of soup and bunches of bananas until six o'clock, when we'd walk home together and squeeze ourselves in at the rowdy Malone dinner table. I'd linger as long as I could, then trek back to my place, finish my schoolwork, and call Annie to say goodnight.

Then one night when I called, Gordie answered and told me she wasn't home. "She's off gallivanting with that Rideout quiff," he said and hung up. I lay in bed stewing over it for hours, then spent the rest of the night scrubbing the spotless kitchen. The next evening, she said nothing about it the whole walk home. I felt like my head was going to burst open, but I hung on until we got to the front door of her house.

"Why didn't you tell me about you and Anthony?"

She shrugged. "Because there's nothing to tell."

"How long has this been going on?"

"He showed up at the house and I went for a walk with him. That's it."

"He's your boss. And mine."

"So?"

"What if it goes south and he fires you?"

"There's nothing to go south, so give it up."

"And he's too old for you."

"He's twenty-two. Four years is nothing."

"I just think we need to focus. Eyes on the prize."

She pressed the palms of her hands against my cheeks. "Frances, you're gonna worry yourself to death. Trust me, my eyes are right where they need to be."

A month later, I let Annie talk me into going to the Rideout's Grocery Christmas party. The parish hall was hot and damp and tinselled beyond recognition. Annie danced and held court with our co-workers while I held up the wall and nursed a warm syrupy Coke until my nerves could take no more. I scanned the room for her but couldn't find her. I mumbled a few words of thanks to Ches Rideout and his wife, then jostled my way through the throng of merrymakers to the coatroom. I heard a rustling sound beyond the coat rack and peered into the dimly lit corner. I saw the back of Annie's red party dress and Anthony's hand cradling her mop of black curls while he planted soft kisses along the length of her neck, like I'd seen men in the movies do. He placed his other hand against the small of her back, drawing her toward him and away from me. I grabbed my coat and slipped out.

It was a clear night, cold and starry. I walked past wooden houses adorned with colourful lights, round wreaths of spruce boughs hung on their doors. Plumes of pungent woodsmoke billowed up from their chimneys, but the Christmas charm was lost on me. I was too preoccupied by what I had seen. Too busy trying to sum up what I felt about Anthony Rideout, addled by the search for a word that refused to rise. Sometime in the middle of the night it finally surfaced, and I woke myself speaking *interloper* into the dark.

I suppose I knew from the moment I met him that he would have her. People like that always got whatever they wanted. Sparkly folks from the mainland blessed with looks and charm and money, those come from aways as exotic as peacocks. She never stood a chance when faced with the likes of him. Neither did I. Within a month, Annie and Anthony had become the town's newest couple. Two or three times a week, I sat next to her empty chair at the Malone dinner table while Annie's mother piled too much food on my plate. Saturday nights were spent with my books. When I did have her to myself, she was distracted and restless and I could tell she was just biding her time with me until he was free.

On the first warm evening of spring, she appeared at my door trying to convince me to join a crowd from work down at the shore for a boil-up. She knew full well I couldn't go to that water, and I told her so. When she shook her head, exasperated, and said, "You can. You just won't," it was as if I were standing in front of a stranger. Through the window I watched her walk down the lane and toward the sea, feeling as if yet another part of me would be swept away.

THE LESS I SAW Annie, the more I retreated into myself. When it came time to collect my own diploma, I asked to be excused from the ceremony. My teachers were disappointed, but I was unable to steel myself enough for a crowded celebration. The only thing that had kept me going to that point was Annie's insistence that despite not having near enough money for me to go to school, we were still on track to leave at the end of the summer.

The day after I graduated, I started full time at Rideout's, where Annie was now head cashier. We ate lunch together almost every day and she carved out a night here and there to stay over at my place, and slowly the axis of my world began to right itself. I learned to be grateful for what little I got from her. Despite what I saw in Anthony—his winking, wandering eye for every girl who walked past, his lording himself above the local guys every chance he got—I decided that maybe he was neither the cock of the walk he thought himself nor the threat I'd worked him up to be. Maybe he was just another planet in Annie's orbit, spinning around the sun like everyone else. I convinced myself that Annie's dalliance with Anthony was just that, and I told myself that once the bright lights of town came into view, he'd be forgotten before she even got off the bus. I invested all my energy into making an uneasy peace with it all, and I was too busy just trying to stay afloat to feel the current shifting direction. Too focused on the horizon to notice that my boat was slowly sinking. Even when she came to my door that August night, pale and shaking, I didn't see it coming.

She'd come from a big talk with Anthony about our leaving and she was a wreck, rattled beyond anything I'd ever seen. I pulled her through the door and served her up a mug of tea. I sat beside her until she stopped sobbing.

"He said he couldn't see his life without me," she said. "He had it all worked out in his head. Training me up to be assistant manager. Me and him running Rideout's together someday."

I could barely draw breath enough to speak. "Annie, what are you getting on with? We're supposed to be leaving in a few weeks."

"I know, I know. But he said he loves me and I'm so confused. I can't go. Not yet. Not until I get this all sorted in my head."

"And how long will that take?"

She didn't answer and started crying again. "I know you must be raging at me, but what if I never get another chance like this?"

"There's a hundred boys as beautiful as him in town. You'll have your pick."

"No, I mean a job like that. Not everyone is as smart as you are. You have the brains to be anything you want. This is a chance for me to really make something of myself. And I don't want another boy. Anthony's not a boy, he's a man. And I want him." She reached out and held my hand between hers. "Listen, I'll give you all the money I've saved so you can start school in January just like you planned. You don't need me."

The sound of my heartbeat in my ears was deafening. I couldn't even hold a thought, let alone form a plan of how to talk her back around. I sat in stunned silence while a hot fury began to burn in my chest. That bastard had won, and I knew there wasn't a bloody thing I could do about it.

"I can't believe this is happening," I said. "What about us? What about all our plans? And what happens when he gets tired of you and runs off to the next one who'll let him put his hand up her dress?"

She recoiled as if I'd slapped her. "He loves me. Is that so hard to believe?"

"You're so blinded by his razzle-dazzle act that you can't see what's in front of your face. He loves himself too much to have any love left over for you."

"What the hell would you know about it anyway? You don't know what it's like to love someone. Who do you even know besides me? No one. You're holed up in this house with your books all the time, too afraid to walk through the door and speak to anyone. You're like a bloody hermit."

"I can't help that. It's just how I am."

"That's a load of shit and you know it."

"I don't even know who you are any more, talking to me like this. I believe this guy has you brainwashed."

"Oh, that's very nice. I can talk and think for myself, thank you very much. Stop being such a selfish bitch."

"Get out."

"What?"

"You heard me. Get out of this house right now."

"Like hell I'll get out. We're staying here until this is settled."

"Sounds like you already have it all settled, Judas."

She grabbed her purse off the table and stood up so fast that her chair fell over. "You know what, Frances? You're about as crazy as your mother, and if you don't get your shit together, you'll end up just like her."

"And if you and your sainted mother had seen to her like you promised, maybe she'd still be here."

We stood across from each other in my mother's kitchen with those ugly words wedged between us, our chests heaving and our eyes wet, and I knew we'd never be the same again. A wave of panic rose up inside me so hard and fast that it dropped me to my knees. I closed my eyes and panted through it. When I looked up, Annie was gone.

I got up from the floor and moved without thought or feeling up the stairs and into my room, where I packed a duffle bag with clothes and reached for the shoebox of money under my bed, just over four hundred dollars, and rolled it into a sock. I scrawled two words on a sheet of paper for Mrs. Malone: *Thank you.* I left the note on the kitchen table, closed the door, and started walking. All night I put one foot in front of the other, watching them move as if they belonged to someone else. Then I stopped walking. The night bled away into the morning light, and I sat on my duffle bag by the side of the highway. I had a sense of hovering high above the road, looking down at myself, like I was watching a scene on television. I saw a blue station wagon stop and an elderly woman wave me over, and I mindlessly got in the car. She and her husband lectured me on the evil that befell young girls nowadays and told me how lucky I was that God-fearing Catholics had come upon me instead a knife-wielding rapist.

They dropped me off at the Roadway Motel, a low red-brick building on the outskirts of St. John's, a place I chose simply because it was the first motel I saw. The woman at the desk smiled at me when I walked through the door. Her hair was wrapped around pink plastic rollers and she was wearing a blue windbreaker with "Martina" embroidered in white thread across the upper part of her arm. She pulled a key from a pegboard behind her. "Number 12—last one on the left side. Right quiet, that one is, and handy to the soft-drink machine," she said. It was twenty-one dollars a night plus an extra three for cleaning. I listened while she moaned about having to do all the rooms herself because her girl had quit three days before. "But you looks as clean as they come, so I don't expect you'll be needing me." I handed her some cash, trudged down the walkway, and flopped onto the musty-smelling bed.

It was dark when I awoke. I lay listening to the roar of traffic along the highway, the raised voices of the people in the room next door, the drip of the bathroom tap, and I longed for the safety and stillness of my bedroom. My body was stiff and sore, and I was suddenly full of regret about what I'd done. I reached for the phone and dialled Annie's number. She answered after a single ring.

"Hello?"

I swallowed hard and tried to speak, but nothing came.

"Hello? Anyone there?"

"Annie, it's me."

"Oh my God, Frances. Where are you? We're gone mad here looking for you."

"I'm at some motel near town."

"Cripes, Mom is here grabbing for the phone. Get away, Mother, you can talk to her in a minute. Listen to me, you have to—"

"Come now. Just get on the bus and come. Please. I can't do it without you."

I could hear her breathing into the receiver.

"No, you come back here," she said. "We'll work it all out. A whole new plan. I swear."

"I can't live there anymore. I just can't."

More silence, Annie breathing.

"Frances, listen to me. You have to come back."

"No, you have to come here."

"You don't understand. He said he wants to marry me someday."

I dropped the receiver in the cradle and slumped down to the grimy carpet. I felt like I'd spent the last year dangling from a cliff by my fingertips, desperately clinging to the only thing that made my life worthwhile. All that time I believed that Anthony and I were rivals. That he had slithered into my world intent on taking what was mine. It wasn't until that very moment that I understood Annie had never belonged to me. And now she was lost to me as surely as everyone else I'd ever loved. Our dream of building a bold new life together was mine and mine alone, and I felt broken beyond repair.

For three days I left the motel bed only to go to the bathroom. I didn't eat a morsel of food and took sips of water from the bathroom tap. I thought briefly about hanging myself or smashing a glass and opening my wrists, but I didn't have the energy to figure out how to go about it. I willed my heart to stop beating, but it ignored me and just pumped on. On the fourth morning, my stomach rumbled loud enough to wake me, and I wondered how long it would take to starve myself away.

Then I thought about my mother, holding herself under the waves, and for the first time, I realized the level of determination that must have required. Surely her body would have bucked and fought against the water seeping into her lungs, and still she held fast. That was how badly she wanted to die. Then I pictured her washed up on the shore, the Malones and my mother's neighbours gasping and weeping. I pictured Annie being told that my stiff, stinking body had been found in this crummy room. She would blame herself, and a small thrill passed through me at the thought of it. Yet it was the same vision of Annie's suffering that brought me around to living. And the need to prove her wrong. I would not end up like my mother. I would not return to her house and take up her role as the madwoman of Safe Harbour. And never again would I stand on that shore and risk feeling the pull of that water.

I eased out of bed, woozy and weak. I had to lean against the shower wall to keep upright. An image of a dead jellyfish I'd found on the shore when I was young popped up in my mind. A round white blob, pale and slack, all flesh and no backbone. I dressed and walked across the highway to a diner, picked at some toast and a greasy fried egg, and circled back to the motel office. I offered my services to Martina in exchange for a free room and a low hourly wage. Within three weeks, every surface in that motel was fit to eat off.

Six months later, Martina sold up to a developer looking to build a strip mall. She gave me a glowing reference letter and called her sister, who owned a boarding house in St. John's. "Nothing fancy," Martina said, "but it's clean and quiet and a good enough place to start."

When I got off the bus at the station downtown, I felt like I'd landed on another planet. The noise. The traffic. Strangers everywhere I looked. I was tired and jumpy and feared I might throw up. I sat on a bench and put my head between my knees. An older woman stopped and asked me if I was all right. I handed her a piece of paper with the address of the boarding house on it.

"Can you tell me how to get here?"

She squinted at the paper. "Sure you're not far at all, my love. Only ten minutes down the road," she said, and walked me right to the door.

I stayed in my small room, avoiding the city. I scanned the job postings in the newspaper for a week, then found one looking for maids at the Newfoundland Hotel. I stammered my way through an interview with a gruff, sweaty man called Harvey, and the next morning, I reported for duty as a junior chamber maid. The work suited me well. Slipping in and out of people's messy rooms while they were off living their busy lives. Moving through the world like a phantom, silent and invisible.

THE MORNING SUN WAS fully up, burning off the fog. I looked around the holiday cottage. It was not so different from my room at the Roadway Motel. Full circle, I thought. I heard Edie moving about the bedroom, then the shower running. I was still sitting by the window when she came out, fresh-faced and smiling and raring to go.

10

Cyril Strickland arrived at nine o'clock in his rust-
pocked gold Oldsmobile. The thought of being ferried
around in a rural taxi warmed me a little. For three
generations, Strickland men had been roaring along the back
roads and stretches of highway around Safe Harbour in whatever beater they managed to get their hands on. They were a
staple of life down here, and Cyril was the latest to take up the
mantle, which he told me when I called to book the car. I was
relieved that he seemed to have no idea who I was. As soon
as I got in the back seat, I knew why: he couldn't have been
more than thirty, born long after I'd left town. But I knew if he
mentioned my name to any of my contemporaries in town, he'd
quickly learn all there was to know about me.

"Off to see the lovely Mrs. Rideout, are ye?"

I nodded at Cyril, then Edie asked me who Mrs. Rideout was.

"Annie's married name," I said.

"Huh. You know she uses Malone online, right?"

I ignored her and busied myself with the search for a seatbelt.

Cyril regaled Edie with tall tales about sharks spotted just off the coast while I leaned back against the seat and closed my eyes. I was still under the spell of pills and no sleep, muddled and heavy-limbed, but my heart was beating so hard and so fast, I feared it would grind itself to a halt.

Just past the sign welcoming us to Safe Harbour, Cyril turned down a long asphalt driveway that led to a wide bungalow covered with pale yellow siding. It looked solid and well cared for. We parked next to a shiny black sedan. There was a sprawling green lawn, thick and freshly mowed, and a winding stone path to a wooden door set between high clay pots overflowing with flowers. *Prosperity.* Good for you, Mrs. Rideout.

Edie rang the doorbell. "Excited?"

Overwrought. Unstrung. Off my bloody head. Take your pick. "How do I look?"

"Nervous. Just try to relax." She reached out and combed my hair with her fingers. "There. That's better."

The door opened and nothing could have prepared me for it, the swell of sheer joy that rolled through me as Annie Malone tilted her head and smiled. I could not meet her eyes and kept my focus on her mouth as she spoke.

"Frances Delaney. After all these years. Sure I'd know you anywhere." She winked at Edie. "And I s'pose this is the young one who called me up the other day, is it?"

Edie stepped forward and offered Annie her hand. "Yes, I'm Edie Cleary. I'm very pleased to meet you."

"Well, come in off the step. I've got a pot of tea and a few biscuits ready. That's if you're fit to eat anything after racing around in Cyril's rickety boat. He's a wild man behind the wheel." She led us to the kitchen at the back of the house. "Sit,

sit, the two of you. I know Frances used to like milky tea. Do you still?"

I nodded and noticed that she, too, did not seem to want to bring her eyes to mine. My cheeks were starting to cramp from smiling, and I could feel trails of sweat trickling from my armpits toward the waistband of my new pants.

"Edie, I suppose you'll want a soft drink. I might have a drop of something fizzy in the fridge."

"Tea is fine for me as well. Thanks, Mrs. Rideout."

"Go on with your Mrs. Rideout. Annie to you. She's a polite one, Frances." She poured three cups of tea and raised hers. "To old friends," she said to no one in particular.

I raised my cup and faked a sip. I was too fascinated to be bothered with swallowing anything down. Annie Malone sitting on a kitchen chair, pouring tea and toasting the past. The sound of her voice, the texture of her hair and skin, the movement of her limbs, the very dimensions of her. An apparition materialized into body and bones before my eyes. Her hair was still glossy and black, helped along by a hairdresser, I assumed. She looked much younger than I did. Flushed and healthy, enviably so. Fit and stylish in her tight dark jeans and white linen shirt with a chunky silver bangle encasing her right wrist.

"Annie, may I use your washroom?" I asked.

"Down the hall, second door on the left. And don't be looking too close at that dusty floor."

I leaned against the sink to steady myself. I could hear them talking.

"Edie, you seem like a smart kid. Did Frances ever tell you what a whiz she was at school?"

"She never said, but I figured as much. She's always reading."

"Is she? Can't say I'm surprised. As I remember it, she always had her face stuck in some book. Don't let her fool you. If she's still the same old Frances, she's as quiet as a mouse, but with a mind like a razor."

My head was in a swirl and my legs were like wet noodles. Whether it was the effect of the squid moving about or what was happening in this house, I didn't know. I fished out my seizure pills and guzzled a mouthful of water from the tap. I checked my reflection, my face dewy with sweat, my hair gone limp. When I got back to the kitchen, Edie and Annie were flipping through a photo album.

"Christ, I'm after getting so fat over the years," Annie said. "Frances, you're not a pound over what you were when I last saw you. How do you do it?" she asked without looking up from the album.

"Cleaning keeps me fit, I guess."

Annie's head snapped up. "Cleaning?"

"She's the best in town," Edie piped in. "Everyone says so. And she's a great cook."

Annie gave Edie a quizzical look. "But she's a teacher."

I sat down and reached for my tea. "Housekeeper. That's how I met Edie. I worked for her mother."

And then Annie sought my gaze. She held it briefly, then closed the photo album. "Right. What's the plan, then? Stroll around the old stomping grounds? Show young Edie the sights? That should take all of five minutes. Still, it's a grand day for it."

We climbed into Annie's car. Edie filled the space with questions for Annie, while I watched my home slowly take shape through the window. The lichen-covered boulders along the side of the road, then the low, leaning picket fences in front of the wooden houses now all repainted in vibrant colours, then the white church gleaming in the sun. I shut my eyes until it was well behind us. And in the background, always in view, the big blue water, insistently moving and patiently waiting.

Annie parked at the top of the lane I once knew so well and then I was standing in front of the house where my life began. Gone was the dark green paint my mother had chosen, replaced by a turquoise glaze. Smart wooden flower boxes sat under the windows with perky pink geraniums waving in the wind. The glossy black door seemed better suited for a city house. I stood looking at it, trying to decide if the whole effect was hideous or beautiful.

"The colour is ridiculous, I know, but it's after growing on me," Annie said. "A couple of young fellas from town bought it years ago and spent three summers doing it up. They come out for their holidays. Made of money, those two. Anyway, Edie, that's where Frances and I first met, right there on that patch of grass. Still in diapers, the pair of us." She paused for a moment. "Feels like a long time ago."

"It feels like yesterday," I said and walked around to the back. My mother's garden had been gutted for a flagstone patio and neat raised beds of black earth sprouting fancy plants and tufts of high grass.

"It's pretty," Edie said over my shoulder. "Great for parties."

"My mother used to feed us from this garden. Potatoes and carrots and turnips and beets. But I suppose parties are good too."

We walked back to the front of the house, where Annie was chatting with an elderly woman.

"Frances, do you remember Mrs. Dillon?"

She was our neighbour three houses down, as I recalled it. She was a dour, religious woman, but also a woman who left casseroles and fruit pies on our doorstep for years after my father died. She peered at me with her watery eyes as I shook her hand.

"Hello, Mrs. Dillon, how are you?" I said.

"I'm above ground, so I expect I'm grand. You remind me of your mother, God rest her."

I looked at my feet and felt an unexpected wave of embarrassment as I waited for some sign of judgment.

"Oh, she was some singer, your mother. I can still hear her beautiful voice. What a lovely woman she was."

I almost wept from her words, words that made me suddenly hopeful that the world was kinder than I'd believed it to be. "Thank you, Mrs. Dillon. Thank you very much."

"Come on, Edie," Annie said. "The grand tour goes on."

We had lunch at a restaurant in the centre of town, a small café tarted up for the tourists. And we were tourists, Edie and I. Enough time had passed to make me feel like a stranger to Safe Harbour. Apart from Mrs. Dillon, I didn't see a soul I knew. And there wasn't a single remnant of the fishing life anywhere to be seen. Once the trawlers came along in the eighties, they dragged the ocean bare and I saw that Safe Harbour was like all the other towns that had no choice but to find their bounty elsewhere. Annie said that now it was all whale-watching excursions and holiday lets. She was playing the tour guide with an enthusiasm that felt forced to me, the strain between us still living just under the surface of the small talk about the town and its people. Edie's presence kept us well clear of any choppy waters, and I was content to drift about aimlessly in the small talk about the town and its people.

After dessert, Edie suggested we head to the beach. The path down to the shore was steeper than I remembered. I trailed behind, carefully planting one foot before the other. Edie doubled back and offered me her hand.

"How are you making out, Frances?"

"Fine, just a bit unsteady today. Now remember," I said, tapping my head, "not a word."

"Go slow. She'll just think you've got old and helpless."

I laughed. "Cheers, Edie."

I kept my eyes downward partly to avoid falling on my face, but mostly because I didn't trust myself to look at that water. I walked toward the sound of the waves until I saw the first glistening stones, then slowly raised my eyes up to the horizon. The sun's glare was blinding, and I was grateful for the seconds of adjustment it forced. I squinted and blinked and then Annie was beside me, her presence gracing me with the strength to focus. We stood in silence and faced the sea together, just as we had so many times before.

The dory was where it had always been, faded and splintered but still intact. Annie gave it a kick with the toe of her shoe.

"How this old thing has survived, I'll never know. Every year someone patches it up and gives it a lick of paint, but now I think they're finally going to let the elements have their way with it." She climbed over the edge and sat on the weathered seat. "Come on in, Frances. Old times' sake."

Edie helped me into the boat and went off toward the shore. She waded into the water, then jumped back from the shock of the cold and raced toward her shoes.

Annie laughed and said, "She'll know not to do that twice now. She's lovely, Frances."

"She is indeed."

"Christ, will you just look at her. She could be you or me back when."

Annie smiled but seemed to be growing restless, like she had somewhere else to be. We watched Edie for a bit, then Annie stood and hopped out onto the beach.

"I'm going by the cemetery if you want to come along."

"Yes, I do."

"Then let's get that fool away from the water before she freezes off a leg."

I called to Edie and she ran back toward us, her head back

and her arms spread wide. She was youth personified, and the sight of her brought a smile to Annie's face and to mine.

At the cemetery, I stood over my father's grave while Edie knelt beside me and placed a bunch of ragged wild daisies she'd yanked from the ground.

"Do you still miss him?" she asked.

"Every day."

She stood and looked around. "Where's your mother?"

"Over yonder."

"How come she's not buried next to your father?"

"Good question. It was a clerical error."

"Are you going to hers next?"

I turned toward the back of the cemetery, where she was laid. I could see the low white fence and the tall wild lupins bending in the breeze. "Wait here for me."

I started walking and felt a knot begin to form in my gut—a knot that tightened with every step I took. I made it about halfway, then stopped. I knew I'd find no peace in it. I'd managed to find a way to live without facing her again, and I'd have to find a way to die without facing her too. I turned my back on her and returned to Edie, who somehow knew better than to ask me any questions.

"Okay, I'm done," I said and pressed my hand against the warm grass that grew over my father's grave and walked away.

We found Annie by her mother's grave. I asked Edie to find me some flowers for Mrs. Malone. Then we followed Annie to another grave a few feet away. She straightened a vase of roses next to a black granite headstone, then backed away a few steps and closed her eyes. She appeared to be praying, and Edie and I stood behind her and waited quietly. A photograph was embedded in a small square of glass in the headstone, a boy on the cusp of manhood. He had Annie's curly black hair and rosy colouring. The stone read, "Stephen Rideout. Beloved son, brother, grandson, and friend." I leaned forward squinting at the dates—just eighteen when he died, and he'd been dead almost as long as he'd been alive.

"Annie, I'm so sorry," I said. "I had no idea."

She turned around, her face expressionless and unreadable. "How could you have?"

A sickly chill passed through me, and the pain in my head began to dig in. I gave Edie a look that told her we needed to get on, and she nodded and walked ahead. I waited a few moments before speaking.

"What happened?"

Annie kept walking, her eyes straight ahead. "Car accident. Rounded a corner too fast on the winter road."

"He looks just like you when you were young."

"I know. Everyone always said so, and it drove Anthony crazy. My daughter, Angela, is more like her father, in looks and personality."

"And how is Anthony?"

"Difficult. Although less so since I divorced him a few years ago."

"I'm sorry about that too."

"Well, don't be. I shoved him out the door and had a celebration drink poured for myself before he was out of the driveway."

I walked alongside her in silence.

"Go on, Frances, say your piece," she said. "Go ahead and say you told me so."

"I'll say nothing like it."

"He was never a great husband, but after Stephen died, he was a right bastard, and I had no more room for it. He's up in Toronto now, out to the bars whoring around every night of the week, or so I hear. Good luck and good riddance, I say."

"Do you have someone else now?"

"I have Angela and a new grandson, and my friends. A bit of money from Sobeys buying out the stores we owned. That's enough for now."

Annie offered to drive us back to the cottage and spare us another rumble in Cyril's car. We stopped to pick up some food to make a light supper, then parted with a promise to drop in the next day to see the baby. I watched her drive away and felt an ache in my chest like I hadn't felt for decades, the same ache I'd felt so deeply the last time I spoke to her. I could see the ugly green carpet of the motel room and feel the phone receiver in my hand. A wave of nausea rolled over me and I was suddenly soaked in sweat.

I lay on the bed at the cottage and woke with a start two hours later, having dreamt of tripping in the graveyard and falling into a deep, wide hole filled with water. The last thing I saw before I went under was Annie leaning over the edge yelling for me to grab her hand. I eased myself up off the bed and walked to the bathroom. I splashed some cold water on my face, then joined Edie on the front veranda. She was slouched in a wooden chair, a leg slung over the armrest. Her face had caught the sun, the pink rising underneath the sprinkling of light freckles across the bridge of her nose. Summertime Edie. *Poignant.*

"It's so peaceful here, isn't it?" she said.

I sat in the chair next to her and lit a cigarette, my first of the day. Peaceful was not a word I would connect to this place. Loss at every corner and all along that shore, a grave I still couldn't bear to face, and two women who could barely look each other in the eye. The fine weather offered an effective disguise, but as for seeing this part of the world as Edie did, I doubted we'd ever fully agree on it. How wonderful to be able to take a place as you found it, not to be influenced and encumbered by the history of what had happened to you there. I sat and smoked, wishing I had faith in a higher power, if only to put in a last-minute request for Edie to find peace wherever she wandered.

We ate a light supper and afterward sat watching the sun melt into the sea and then the stars, hundreds and hundreds of stars that Edie thought were the best celestial display she'd ever seen. My God, her happiness came easily. Where she'd got that from, I had no idea. Certainly not from her parents, who seemed to suffer from chronic unrequited desire. But this one, give her a plate of cut vegetables and a bit of cheese and crackers, a dying old maid for company, and a backwoods starry night, and she thought she was in paradise.

We stayed on the veranda and she talked about the colleges she was thinking of applying to, weighing the pros and cons of her many options. I grew gloomy as she prattled on about all the wondrous things she would do—all the wondrous things I would never see her do. I had to stop her mid-sentence and ask her to fetch me a glass of water, just to break from her for a few moments. When she returned, I was together enough to let her go on. She showed me funny videos of goats on her computer, then we went to bed. I took two pain pills and spent my night in and out of fitful dreams, watching my father swim alongside his boat while tossing strange and colourful sea creatures onto the deck, to my great amusement.

The morning was cool and overcast, like the summers I remembered. Once again, Cyril delivered us to Annie's house. She met us on the doorstep, holding her grandson. She passed him to me. It was the first time I'd ever held a baby in my arms. He'd been given the name of his dead uncle. Annie called him Stevie. He was impossibly fragile yet ingeniously made with all the working parts for survival—a flawless, firing brain; a heart pumping blood; lungs filling and releasing; a strong mouth that puckered and clamped around the tip of Annie's little finger. He was warm and surprisingly weighty in the crook of my arm. Annie stood by my side, cooing and rubbing his cheek. Edie hung back, unimpressed, and I wondered if it was a general lack of interest in babies or if this one was making an appearance too soon after her own brush with pregnancy. I handed Stevie back to Annie and we followed her into the house.

Angela was in the kitchen assembling a plate of sandwiches. She wiped her hands on a dishtowel. She was tall and thin, with no visible evidence of a genetic connection to her mother. Her hair was artificially blond, her skin coloured by something other than the sun. Her feet were bare, and her toenails were shaped and polished hot pink. She looked every bit the city girl and nothing at all what I expected.

"You must be the famous Frances," she said.

She approached, extended her hand, and smiled, but I could see it was an effort. Her tone was just shy of frosty, and there was something unnerving and unpleasant about her.

"I am," I said. "Although I can't imagine what would make me famous."

"Mom's been telling us stories about the two of you for as long as I can remember. Glory days, right, Mom?"

Annie was too busy adoring Stevie to catch what was said.

"Congratulations on your baby, Angela. He's just perfect." I introduced Edie.

Angela gave her a quick nod and returned to her food duties. Edie and I exchanged furtive frowns and sat at the kitchen table. Annie placed the baby in a motorized rotating contraption, and he promptly fell asleep.

"Will you just look at that machine," Annie said. "We'll have robots to mind them next."

"Mom, you sound like an old biddy when you say things like that," Angela said. She brought a knife down through a cucumber like a lumberjack splitting firewood.

"I think it's very cool, Angela," Edie said. "I was just thinking I wish they made them big enough for me."

"My mother thinks it's excessive." Chop, chop, chop. "Sit down and I'll make up a pot of tea."

"Marvellous," Annie said. "The old biddy could do with a bit of tending to."

We passed a pleasant enough hour over lunch despite the obvious friction between Annie and her daughter. Angela was gruff and snide, and with each passing minute in her company, I found it harder to see her as someone likeable. The way Annie let it roll off her led me to believe they'd been dancing to this tune for many years.

After dessert, I slipped away to the bathroom to take my seizure pill. I could no longer decipher the label with my wonky eyesight. I'd have to start taking measures to avoid mixing them up with the pain pills. My hands were weak, and it took me several tries to get the bottle open. Perhaps I had a touch of the old biddy myself, or perhaps the squid was staking its claim on yet another patch of brain.

When I came back to the kitchen, Angela was nursing Stevie. She looked softer and I decided she deserved a second chance. Edie reminded me that we had a bus to catch to town, and we took Annie up on her offer of a ride back to the cottage. When we got there, the sun was making an effort to shine, and the air had lost most of its chill. Edie went inside to pack up our things, leaving me with Annie on the veranda. She spied the pack of cigarettes on the arm of the deck chair.

"I'll be having one of those before I leave," she said.

"Help yourself."

She lit up and took a deep drag, moaning with pleasure as she blew out the smoke.

"Christ, I don't remember the last time I had a cigarette. Oh, it's bloody gorgeous."

We sat side by side on the veranda. I considered her in brief sideward glances while she kept her eyes on the water. I saw in her the beautiful girl she once was, but now there was a new depth, the allure of a story written on her face and carried in her body. I wanted to know every detail of it, and I wanted her to know every detail of mine. I wanted anything and everything she could give me. And I wanted to sit close to her and tell her that I was running out of time. I gripped the arm of the chair and readied myself to speak, but then I thought of her dead son, her hard husband, that scowling daughter. She was clearly stealing a moment of peace, and I let her have it. She stubbed out the butt of the cigarette on the sole of her shoe and laid it on the weathered railing.

"Frances," she said to the water, "I've no words for it, seeing you again." She stood and walked to her car with me trailing close behind. She opened the car door, then quickly closed it again and spoke with her back to me.

"You know what, I lied. I do have words for it." She turned to face me, and a deep and sudden flush coloured her cheeks. "What the hell happened to you?"

"What do you mean?"

"What do I mean? God bless her." She shook her head in frustration. "You just vanished. Like one of those poor youngsters on the milk cartons."

"It was"—I searched my pounding head for the word—"complicated."

"Christ, what isn't? That'll excuse precious little in this life."

"Annie, please." My voice sounded foreign, and the ground began to feel soft and yielding beneath my feet.

"That last phone call. It nearly did my head in. A week went by, then two, and so I thought, Well, she's good and gone now. Then not a word for years. Not a single thought for me left here in this goddamn fishbowl, guilty by association, the friend of that girl who got knocked up, the girl whose mother walked into the sea, the girl who up and disappeared. Not that I ever judged, mind you, but there were plenty who did. Half the time I think I got married just to rub the stain of you off me."

Her voice had been steadily rising. She glanced toward the open door of the cottage and dropped it down a level.

"You just cut me off, never to be heard from after. If you knew how many trips we made to town, trolling the streets looking for you. Mom even called the cops, who told us to go whistle, leaving us with no option but to fear the worst. For years, I carried it around, this sadness and anger, this . . . confusion, somewhere deep in my belly, always sitting there underneath anything good that happened. And then my children came along and I didn't have time for anything that wasn't about them. And like that"—she snapped her fingers—"I was rid of you. Oh, the relief of it." She drew in a deep breath and blew it out hard and fast. "But then when Stephen died, it was the oddest thing. I wanted nobody—not my husband, not my friends. It was only you I wanted to talk to. And I had to go through missing you all over again. And ever since, every now and then it rises up and worms its way back in. That old puzzle I could never solve, keeping me up half the night about once or twice a month. The disappearance of Frances Delaney. And now here you are, fucking resurrected, back home with that sweet girl in tow, doing your bidding and guarding all your secrets." Her voice caught and she looked away, her eyes flooded with tears.

Each word she spoke ignited a spark of shame for what I had done, for what I was doing, for being so wrapped up in how hard it would be for me to see her and not once thinking about how hard it would be for her to see me. Hot humiliation burned through my body like a brush fire, consuming me from the inside out. The skin on my neck and ears prickled. Bile burned in my throat. I swallowed and struggled to find enough air to power my voice.

"Annie, I'm sorry. I'd lost so much, and I felt so betrayed by you. I wasn't in my right mind. I'm not sure my mind has ever been right."

She heaved a shaky sigh and her lower lip began to tremble. "I know I let you down, terribly so. I know how much I hurt you. I've had a lifetime of regretting it, believe me. And I don't pretend to know what it is you suffered, but I suffered too." She tapped two fingers hard against the centre of her chest. "I lost too."

She turned and climbed in her car, started the engine, put the window down, and gripped the wheel until her knuckles blanched. Eyes forward, shoulders set. "Maybe someday you'll tell me why you came back. I'll be right here where I've always been, trying to decide if I care."

I closed my eyes as she pulled away, tires spinning on gravel and the piercing cries of gulls overhead. I walked to the cottage and picked up my bag, then boarded the bus and once more left it all behind.

11

I lay in the darkened room and surrendered my weary body to
Oliver's hands. Once again, every point of pressure released
memory—disjointed technicolour visuals that flickered
like a film, its soundtrack a continuous loop of Annie's cutting
words. It was both wondrous and gruesome, a bizarre state of
semi-consciousness that made me feel suspended somewhere
between life and death. When he spoke his soft words to let me
know he'd finished, it was as if I came crashing back into my
body with a loud and painful thud. I felt battered yet strangely
put to rights by it.

Two days had passed since Annie and I spoke, and I'd
thought of little else since, particularly what I could or should
do next. On the ride home from my massage, Edie seemed as
pensive as I was.

"What's on your mind, little girl?"

"Nothing."

"You know I read somewhere that it's a crime to lie to the terminally ill."

She said nothing until she parked in front of my place. "Okay. You haven't said a word about you and Annie."

"What about me and Annie?"

"Right before we left, I heard her talking outside the cottage."

"Ah, I see. How much did you hear?"

"I couldn't make out what she was saying, just that she sounded upset."

"She was. About me not staying in touch over the years."

"So you two haven't exactly drifted back together, then?"

"You could say that." I got out of the car and she followed me inside.

"Did you tell her you're sick?"

"I did not. Now begone, tiresome child. Thank you for the ride and I'll call you tomorrow."

I turned away and headed for the shower. She was lying on my bed when I came out of the bathroom. I nearly jumped out of my skin from the startle of seeing her there.

"I'd say we're both lucky I'm still wrapped in this towel. Get out and let me get some clothes on. Go on."

I dressed, then found her lingering in the kitchen.

"Frances, you need to tell her."

"Go off and do something fun. I'll call you tomorrow."

"I'm not leaving until you say you'll tell her."

"Why is this so important to you?"

"Because," she said and started to cry, "I just want you to be happy."

I took her into my arms. "You're a good girl, Edie Cleary."

She rested her head against my shoulder. "Why won't you tell her?"

"I don't know. It doesn't feel right, I guess."

"That sounds a bit flimsy to me."

She stepped out of my embrace and made for the door. She pulled her keys from her purse and looked back at me, a final plea for me to speak.

"Maybe I just don't want her pity, okay?"

"Yeah, I hear you," she said. "But maybe sometimes a little pity goes a long way."

My PHONE RANG JUST after midnight. I reached out and fumbled toward the sound. I said hello, but no one answered.

"Is that you, Edie?" My voice was hoarse, my head clouded by drugs and dreams.

"Shit. I woke you."

"Annie?"

"I assumed you turned the ringer off at night like a normal person. Hang up and I'll leave a message." Her voice was thick, her words a little slurred. I heard ice clinking against glass and a hard swallow.

I switched on the lamp. "No, no, it's fine. I'm awake."

"I'm coming to town next weekend. A bit of shopping and such. I was thinking about us meeting up for a drink or a bite to eat."

I sat up and swung my legs over the side of the bed. "I suppose we could."

I heard her take two full breaths, then another clink of ice and glass, another swallow. "Night, Frances."

"Night, Annie."

I checked the call history on my phone to make sure I hadn't dreamt it, then I lay back down and began to fret about her waking in the morning with no memory of her drunken dialling. Then I began to fret about dying in the night and not living to see the weekend. I pulled back the covers, opened the window, and lit a cigarette. It was after two when I spotted a young woman in a shimmery blue dress strolling along the sidewalk below. She teetered on her high heels and swung a dainty purse around in a circle as she walked. I wondered where she'd been. I pictured her swaying under flashing lights in a club with a man from whom she was now slipping away. He'd wake to find her gone and she'd be snoring in her own bed, her pretty dress in a small heap on the floor. I longed to call out to her, give her a wink and a wave, and wish her good luck. She turned the corner and I put the kettle on for tea.

The next day, Edie came for me at noon and drove me to the hospital for a battery of senseless tests—the "monitoring protocol," the doctors called it. Maybe they were hoping for a last-minute miracle. Maybe I was too. Blood was drawn, memory and nerves were tested, visual acuity was measured. Heart, lungs, and various other innards were evaluated. Then I lay in the CT scanner while a technician hid himself in a protective booth and unleashed a blast of radiation through my head. I pictured the squid basking in bright yellow light, splayed out on a sun lounger, wearing tiny sunglasses and sipping a fruity cocktail.

When the sum of information was gathered and reviewed, the conclusion was just the same. Death and I would likely meet on schedule, give or take whatever time units fell within the margin of human error. The doctor said he was so very sorry to tell me this difficult news, as if I couldn't feel the steady pressure of the Reaper's boot on my neck.

I met Edie in the dingy green hallway. I could almost smell the hope seeping from her skin.

I wrapped my arm around her shoulders. "Edie, we all come and go in this life, every one of us. We just forget about the going part."

She nodded and flung her arm around my waist. My phone

buzzed with a text from Annie asking me to meet for lunch on Saturday.

"Come on, Miss Cleary, let's go get some ice cream. I have some news for you that I know will make you smile."

EDIE DROPPED ME OFF at my place and sped off to get ready for a party. There was a boy, a straight one this time, and she was smitten. "So smart," she said. "Totally aligned with my world view and very hip to the feminist agenda"—something obviously highly desirable, given the way she prioritized it over his beauty. "Incidentally hot," was how she put it.

The minute we parted, my relief at her being caught up in something other than me quickly evaporated as I began to envision the various suitors who would eventually present themselves to her. Boys I would never get to cast my sly eye over and decide if they had what it took to be worthy of her. I knew the chances of her choosing wisely were good, but I also knew too well that a single moment of distraction could dim even the brightest of futures. I settled on optimism and laid my aching head on the pillow for the night.

In the morning, I had another seizure. Nothing as grand as the ones I'd had before, but with enough wallop to leave me with a smoke-filled kitchen littered with broken dishes and a face that looked like I'd gone a few rounds in a boxing ring. A red swollen cheek, a blast of purple and black around my eye. I was alone when it happened, and it was a wonder I hadn't finished myself off then and there, or set the whole building ablaze. I woke up on the floor and had to crawl to the living room to get to my phone.

When she arrived, Edie surveyed the kitchen and whistled. "Man," she said, "dying is dangerous business."

She did her best for my face with ice packs and a tube of ointment, then spent an hour clearing up the mess I'd made. She slept on my couch that night, and the next day, she decided I was in need of a little pampering.

Edie drove me to a spa, where a young woman spent an hour on my hands, massaging and soaking, trimming and filing until they looked smooth and refined. The skin was supple and free from any trace of toil. My nails were all the same length and shone with clear polish. Each time I moved my hands, they'd catch my eye and surprise me, stirring a foreign pride that they were indeed mine. Then the young woman went to work on my feet. She woke me from a deep sleep to tell me she'd finished.

By the time I got home, I was exhausted. I was still a bit wobbly from the seizure and had to lean on Edie as we climbed the stairs to my apartment. When we reached the top, she told me to close my eyes.

"What for?" I asked.

"Just do what I say and don't ask any questions."

"Edie, I'm dropping and half-starved to death."

"Trust me. Close your eyes."

I heard her fiddling with the stubborn door handle, then a rustle of movement.

"Okay, now you can look."

When I opened my eyes, she and Colin were standing in the doorway, grinning like two fools. They stepped back. Behind them stood a small, fully decorated Christmas tree where my television used to be. My table was draped in a red tablecloth, and a small feast was laid out on it.

Edie jumped up and down and shouted, "Merry Christmas in July!" and Colin pulled out a chair for me.

"The chicken is just one of those rotisserie ones from the grocery store, but Colin and I made the rest," Edie said. "I know how much you like Christmas. And you know . . ."

Oh, these kids. I was so overcome that I couldn't speak for fear of bursting into tears and ruining the whole thing. I sat and held up my plastic glass to receive some sparkling cider. They gave me a Santa hat to wear and made me up a plate. After dinner, I opened gifts. Fancy skin cream, a box of handmade truffles, and a pair of red cashmere socks from Colin. The last gift was a framed photo of Edie and me, one I'd never seen before. She would have been about twelve. We were sitting in her backyard at the picnic table, both of us squinting into the sun. She was wearing her school uniform, every bit of it askew after a day of being Edie. Her head rested against my shoulder, and my hand was wrapped under her chin, my fingertips pressed on her cheek. We looked like family. I had no memory of it being taken, yet there it was, the record of how far we'd come together.

"Nicely done, little girl," I said.

"Right back at you, old woman."

After they'd gone, I sat for a long time in the soft glow of the tree lights thinking about Edie's uncommon kindness, about what an important companion and ally she'd become. I was starting to second-guess my decision to leave her in the dark about how exactly this would end. I was starting to second-guess that and every other decision I'd ever made. How naive I'd been to think that going home for a day would bring me the peace I wanted to rest in. Instead, all I'd done was tear open old wounds, mine and the ones I'd inflicted on Annie. I thought it deeply unfair to come this far in life and still be so inept at living. Where was the wisdom that was supposed to rise up out of age and situation? To be on the brink of death and still not have a clue how to leave the world with all the knots untangled. I hadn't even worked out the details of my own passing, the where and the when and so on, and the clock was ticking. Perhaps it would be better to be struck down by a car, killed instantly in the street with nothing more on my mind than what to make for supper. My chest grew tight, and I took slow, deep belly breaths like Oliver taught me and put a tiny blue pill under my tongue—the ones Dr. Langley said were good for times like this. Neither was of any use. Within minutes, I was soaked in sweat and overwhelmed by the sense that the walls were closing in around me. I pushed my bare feet into my sandals and lurched out into the summer night.

I wandered aimlessly through the deserted streets of my neighbourhood, the cool and quiet of the night calming me enough to realize that I'd never actually seen them at this hour. How different and lovely the world seemed once powered down, like a sleeping child mercifully collapsed after a day of mischief. My head was pounding, but I just kept walking and breathing until I came to a bench. I lay down and begged the squid to settle.

I opened my eyes to the glare of the early morning sun and with no idea where I was or how I'd got there. The wooden slats of the bench had done me no favours through the night, and I rose slowly and unsteadily to try to get my bearings. A young man stopped to toss a paper coffee cup into a bin next to the bench.

"Hey," he said, "you all right?"

I nodded and took a few tentative steps away.

"You sure?" he called out.

I gave a small wave without turning around and made my way home. I opened the door to my silent, empty apartment, the safe and comforting space that I prized. It seemed suddenly wanting in my eyes, stark and altogether dreary. I went into the bedroom, the room where my life would end, and all I could think was that it looked like I felt—sad and rundown. I felt weary of how I lived, so desperately tired of being alone. I slumped down on the bed and wept until I felt dried out. Then I turned my thoughts to the day ahead. Tea and bread and milk needed replenishing, the sheets needed changing, the bathroom needed cleaning. *Minutiae.*

12

Edie groaned and stamped her foot. "If you don't hold still, I'll never get this right." She squeezed another dollop of beige cream onto a sponge and kept dabbing at my face until she was satisfied.

I leaned in toward the mirror. Even with my failing eyes, I could still see the faded purple of the bruises and the raised scabby welt along my right cheek. I ran my finger over it and shook my head. "I don't see the point. It just looks like a bashed-up face with makeup over it."

"Well, what do you expect?" she said. "There's not enough Maybelline on the planet to fix that mess. But it's still better, trust me. Anyway, the point is that Annie will see you made an effort."

She rummaged in my closet and laid out clothes, then drove me downtown.

"Nervous?" she asked when we pulled up to the hotel door.

"Yes."

"Ready?"

"No."

"I can stay and wait for you if you like."

"Edie, this might take five minutes or five hours. You go on, enjoy your day."

I stepped into the air-conditioned lobby of the Sheraton hotel, the same characterless lobby I imagined could be found in any other Sheraton on the continent. How much it had changed since the day I first walked in the door to start my career as a chambermaid, and not for the better. Cheap shiny woodwork and dime-a-dozen floor tiles, fake plants made waxy under the glare of harsh fluorescent lighting. I was early and went to the bathroom to check my face. The makeup had gone chalky and settled into the lines of my skin. I looked like a corpse. I wet a paper towel and rubbed it all away. When I came out, a house-keeping cart was parked in the hallway. I fished a ten-dollar bill from my bag and tucked it between the rolls of toilet paper.

Annie was standing by the front desk, scanning the lobby. I hung back out of sight watching her wait. My gaze shifted back and forth between her and the emergency exit located a few feet to my left. The squid broke the deadlock. "Coward," it hissed, and my feet carried me forward. I forced a smile and waved when she noticed me.

"Good Christ!" she said. "What happened to you?"

"A little mishap in the kitchen. It's nothing."

She frowned. "Doesn't look like nothing."

"You should see the kitchen."

I smiled; she did not.

"Okay if we just grab something here at the hotel?" she said.

I nodded and followed her to a wood-panelled lounge. I ordered a double whisky. Annie looked impressed and asked the waitress to bring two. We each took a sip and leaned back in our chairs. I had planned on letting her speak first, but several minutes of silence passed, and I cracked under the pressure.

"So you came in to do a bit of shopping, did you?"

"I did not. And I didn't come for a bit of idle chit-chat either."

The woman at the table next to us raised her eyes from her paper. I shifted in my chair and pulled my shirt away from my sticky back. The waitress returned and I ordered a plate of fish and chips I knew I wouldn't eat. Annie took a big gulp from her glass, and as soon as the waitress was out of earshot, she picked up the thread.

"I came to see you," she said. "I wasn't too pleased with how things got left."

"Me neither. Maybe we could start over?"

"I wouldn't even know where to start, Frances. Not a clue, maid."

"How about you ask me some questions and I'll do my best to answer."

"Good enough. Have you been here in town all this time?"

"Yes."

"Married?"

"No."

"Kids?"

"Just the one you know about."

"How long have you been at this housekeeping racket?"

"Since I last saw you."

"So what happened to becoming a teacher?"

She asked it so casually, as if I'd simply made a different choice. For years I'd thought about nothing but going for my teaching degree. Once, in my late twenties, I met up with a woman from the university. She laid it all out for me—the courses, the books, the fees. And for a brief, delirious time I thought it could actually happen, that some miracle mixture of cash and courage would appear, allowing me to be part of a class and one day have my own. But short of literally starving myself for an education, I was shut out. And even if I'd had the money, there'd be the doing of it—the crowded classrooms and study groups, presentations and oral exams, student socials. All things I knew my nerves would simply not allow. I kept the brochures and application forms for years, then finally tossed them in the garbage along with the soggy tea bags and eggshells and settled for the finest education a library card could buy. Convinced as I was that Annie's absence was the root of it all, my resentment had run bitter and deep. But now here she was, sitting across from me, radiant and lovely still, seeking me out and looking for answers, and I was surprised to find that any blame I'd held was gone.

"It just didn't work out, Annie."

"Well, I'll thank you not to lay that at my feet."

"I'm not doing anything of the sort."

"Seems like a terrible waste to me."

I bristled slightly. There was no end of disparagement and pity for the maids of the world, that I knew very well. People either treated us like the dirt we beat back every day or went too far the other way—doctors and lawyers feigning equality, talking loudly and often about the great importance of our contribution to the world. But then there were people like old Mrs. Heneghan. She respected my work, needed me as much as I needed her, and said so many a time. She was a dignified woman, and somehow there was dignity in cleaning her myriad messes.

"There's nothing wrong with cleaning for people. It's honest work," I said.

"But it's not the same as being a teacher."

"No, I'll grant you that."

The food came. We each ate a couple of French fries, but the fish sat untouched. We fell silent and the air between us grew heavier by the second. Annie downed the last of her drink.

"I can't take this. You got any smokes on you?" she asked.

I nodded.

She tossed a wad of bills on the table and stood up. "Let's go."

I followed her outside. She asked the doorman where we could find a place to smoke. He pointed to a small courtyard where he said no one would mind. We sat at either end of a bench. She took a long drag of her cigarette and swivelled to face me.

"Why did you come back?"

I took a long drag of my own cigarette before answering her. "Brain tumour. I have a couple of months, tops."

She blinked at me, a trace of confusion, then understanding. "Well, don't put any gloss on it now. Just give it to me straight."

The expression on her face, the tone of her voice, the long-lost Annie Malone. All I could do was laugh.

"Frances, if this is a joke, I swear to God, I'll friggin' smack you."

"No, it's true," I said. "It was the way you sounded just now. It took me back in time, that's all."

"But you don't look sick. Apart from that shiner."

"I had a seizure in the kitchen. Beat the crap out of myself and nearly burned the house down."

Her face fell. "Are you in a lot of pain?"

"Sometimes."

"Christ, nothing is halfway with you, is it? Back she comes with the bang of a cannon." She sat quietly for a few minutes. "I'm sorry. Truly I am. After all you've been through, hardly seems fair."

"You've got your own bone to pick with fairness, I'd say."

She finished her cigarette and ground the butt under her shoe. "You know I came to town right ready to receive my due, ready for you to own up to the past and serve it up to me on a silver platter, but the present seems to be upstaging me. That sounds a bit selfish now, doesn't it?"

"Maybe a smidge."

A tear slid down the side of her face. "I haven't changed much, have I?"

"I don't know yet."

She reached in her purse for a tissue and dabbed her eyes. She pointed a finger in the air. "Am I losing my mind or can you hear that too?"

"The music? That's the folk festival. It's on over at Bannerman Park this weekend."

"How close is it from here?"

"Close. A ten-minute walk, maybe."

"Up for a stroll?"

The park was packed, a sea of lawn chairs and blankets facing a large stage. We found a small patch of grass and sat down. People clapped and sang along and danced where there was room. We listened to the fiddles and whistles and accordions pump out the old standards of the island, the ditties and toe-tappers, the music of struggle and loss, of perseverance and triumph, the music of our youth. The festival had been running for years, but I had never come for fear of breaking into pieces at the first note of a song I grew up with. I looked around at the people clapping and singing along—and at Annie, who was doing the same—and let the guard fall away. I closed my eyes and let the music wash over me. I heard the singers' voices rising in harmony, singing, "Heave away, me jollies, heave away," a line from the tune Annie and I had always loved best.

Annie grabbed my hand and pulled me up. "Come on, Frances. Someone needs to show these goddamn townies how to have a proper scuff."

She led me through the crowd to an open space by the front gate. We stood shoulder to shoulder facing opposite directions, then linked elbows and circled around, clockwise, then counterclockwise, again and again until I was transported to the living room of my parents' house, the fire aglow, the boards vibrating beneath my feet from the stomp of boots as half the town danced away their cares. I could hear Annie singing in the distance, her voice clear and pure, and I knew I'd made it. I'd lived long enough to experience the happiest moment of my life. When the music stopped, I fell to the grass, dizzy and spent, and lay next to Annie Malone.

It was getting dark when we left. I was exhausted and unsteady on my feet, and Annie rode home with me in the taxi.

"I was going to invite myself in for a drink, maybe steal another smoke," she said. "But I expect you need your rest."

"No, no, I'll be fine. Come in. One for the road."

I made up a plate of fruit and cheese and poured us each a drink.

"Why is there a Christmas tree in your living room?" she asked.

"Ah, that's Edie's handiwork."

"Right. Because you won't be here in December." She teared up and reached for her glass.

"No need to be crying. It's been such a happy afternoon."

"Is there nothing they can do for you?"

"They want to cut it out, but it will only grow back."

"But wouldn't that give you more time?'

"A little. A few months, maybe."

"Why don't you want to fight it?"

Fight. Such a flat, ugly word. Why was everyone forever harping about fighting? I'd taken to reading the obituaries lately, paying close attention to the ones that read "lost her courageous battle with cancer" or some such nonsense. It seemed to me that mortality had somehow been made over as a character defect. My thoughts must have made their way to my face, and she let it be.

"So what now?" she said.

"I don't know. Take up line dancing. Do some nude modelling. Write a spy novel."

"Jesus, be serious."

"I'm going to let it play out, and when it's time, a nice doctor is going to come and put me down."

"Come where? Here?"

"What's wrong with here?"

"Nothing. I'm just trying to get my head around it. Put you down. You make it sound like you're some rickety old mutt."

"I've thought about this long and hard. This is what's right for me. I don't expect you to understand."

"You're right, I don't understand," she said, her tone veering toward anger. "And if you knew what it was to bury a child, you'd know the value of a few extra months."

A wave of heat flowed through me and the constant faint ringing in my ears rose up to a shrill pitch. "I've lost three people, including a child. Four, if I count you. So please don't lecture me on time and loss and all the rest of it. I haven't lived the life I wanted—I've lived the one that happened. So I'll bloody well be having the death I want, thank you."

She raised her hands in surrender. "Okay, okay. I'm talking like I know you. God knows it would take more than a bit of music for us to be friends again. It's just that sometimes I feel like I'm the only one in the world who's suffered the loss of a child. That's how big it is. It just blots out everything and everyone, and all I can see is my boy alone in a ditch. All I want is more time with him, minutes, seconds, anything. I guess it feels like a slap, like you're just throwing it away."

"To me it's the opposite, like I'm grabbing hold of something. I don't know how to explain it any better."

She tossed her head toward the Christmas tree. "What about Edie? Does she know?"

"She's knows I'm dying, but she doesn't know how it's going to happen."

Annie leaned back against the couch and stared up at the ceiling. "Christ, I hope you know what you're doing."

"You and me both."

We stood by the window and smoked. She yawned and I saw it was after eleven.

"I suppose you should get back to the hotel."

"How about I stay here tonight?"

"You'll waste your hotel room."

She shrugged and smiled. "No odds to me. I'm made of money."

"You can have the bed," I said. "I don't mind the couch."

"Frances, I might still be riled, but I don't think I'll be casting a woman with a brain tumour out of her own bed. I'll take the couch."

I was too tired to argue. I found her some bedding, a spare toothbrush, and a clean nightgown the likes of which she said she hadn't seen since she was a girl. I retreated to my room and listened while she settled herself. I woke up in the night to find her beside me, flat on her back on top of the covers, snoring softly. I rolled to face her and let my hand rest lightly on her shoulder. She stirred but didn't wake. I suddenly wished she hadn't come at all. I'd had a taste of her now, and how could I not ache for more. Tomorrow she'd be off, and I'd be left with a new gaping hole I knew I could never fill. I closed my eyes and listened to her whistling breaths until well after the sun had risen.

When we were up, I laid out a pot of strong tea, some toast, and two bowls of fruit. She sat and spread a thick layer of jam on a piece of bread, poured a generous stream of milk in her tea, and said good morning to me as if we'd been doing this every day of our lives. I'd never sat in my home with anyone other than Edie, and it was as unsettling as it was thrilling. Her presence made the space I'd lived in alone for so long seem ridiculously small, as if she were a giantess who'd crashed through the roof of my dollhouse with the heel of her huge foot. We ate in silence, then stood by the window smoking and watching for her taxi.

"I need to ask you something," she said. "And I need you to tell me the truth. Would you have come back to Safe Harbour if you hadn't got sick?"

"I don't know."

She scoffed and hung her head.

"Annie, look at me," I said. "Would you be here, lying on my bed, eating breakfast at my table, if I weren't?"

She turned back toward the window. "I don't know."

The taxi rounded the corner and I walked her to the door.

"Look after yourself, Frances."

"You too."

She patted my battered cheek and left. The apartment seemed hollowed out and eerily still. I took my pills, pulled down the shades, and went back to bed. When the phone rang at midnight, I knew it was her.

"Are you up?" Annie asked.

"I'm up."

"I'm not feeling too good about things. Truth be told, I'm sick over the lot of it." She drew in a shaky breath.

"You still there?"

"I've been on the computer all evening, reading about this death plan of yours."

"And?"

"And I called to tell you that I respect your decision. I don't know if it's right, but who am I to judge? Maybe I'd do the same. I don't know. I don't fucking know anything anymore."

"What's going—"

"Tell me about your friends."

"What?"

"Who do you have to help you besides Edie?"

"That's enough now. You sound like you've been drinking."

"That's what I thought. See, I do know you, Frances. I know you too well." Her voice started to break. "And yes, I'm drinking. I'm here with my bottle, thinking about you dying alone in that hovel."

"Annie, please."

"You're not going out like that. I'm not having it."

"So what are you saying?"

"I'm saying I think we can do better."

I sat up and switched on the lamp. I could see my reflection in the mirror over the dresser, the image of a woman at once familiar and strange, whose face was pale and drawn but dangerously hopeful.

"I'm listening."

13

nnie's proposal was an extraordinary one. At first, I'd chalked it up to the drinking and rejected it out of hand. But the more she talked, the more convinced I became that she had carefully wrung it out. It had come to her on the drive home from my place, she said, and once the idea took shape, she decided there was simply no other way forward for me, and for her. "It's a lovely room," she said. "Good light, a nice view of the backyard. I'll give it a coat of paint, buy you some pretty bedding. You'll have your own bathroom, whirlpool tub and all."

I warned her that a dying woman in her home was bound to be messy in every sense, but she wouldn't hear it. She'd guided her mother through cancer years before, and she believed that was training enough for anything I could throw at her. She also believed it was what her mother would have wanted, and for that I had no argument.

I told her I'd think about it and sat up half the night making a mental list of reasons to turn her down as the squid nattered in my ear. "Only a fool would say no," it whispered over and over, and by first light, I found I had no argument for that either.

DR. LANGLEY TOOK OFF her glasses and massaged the small red indents on either side of the bridge of her nose. "It's a fair way to travel and it would narrow down your choice of dates. I know we've talked about this before, but do you want to reconsider the option of taking the medication yourself?"

"No. I'd still rather you do it." I interlaced my fingers and laid my manicured hands on her desk. She must have been used to all sorts of lovely hands, as mine failed to catch her eye. I held my breath while she mulled it over.

"It'll take some doing from a scheduling point of view, but I'll make it happen."

I exhaled and unlocked my clammy hands. "Thank you. You have no idea what this means to me."

"Frances, I grew up in Twillingate. Bay girl through and through. I know exactly what it means."

When I called Annie to accept, she was already painting the bedroom.

"What if I'd said no?" I asked.

"You were coming one way or another, free will or brute force," she said. "At least this way, you're saving me the work of a kidnapping. Anyway, you're doing the right thing. You'll be comfortable and want for nothing, and maybe make some peace in the bargain. Plus, there's the added bonus of my company. What kind of fool would say no to that?"

It was a fresh, sunny morning, far too perfect a day for little ones to be inside, so the library was beautifully quiet. I'd come to return the last of my books, all unopened. I'd begun to accept that my library days were done, something I thought almost as lamentable as dying. I sat in my armchair trying one audiobook after another, but I couldn't adapt to having a story read to me. I kept trying to conjure a face to match the voice, and by the time I settled on one, the plot had unwound without me. I gave up on it and handed my last stack over to Hillary. I noticed her neck was bare.

"No scarf today," I said.

She groaned at the ceiling. "My youngest found his way into my closet this morning, and before I knew it, every scarf I own was covered in something sticky. God knows what. They're home soaking as we speak." She shrugged and smiled. "Kids, right?"

She started to check out two books she'd kept aside for me. I opened my mouth to tell her not to bother, then clamped it shut. I left the library and took a cab to the same store where I'd bought my suit. I laid out eighty-five dollars for a pale-blue-and-white scarf, soft silk that looked like a watercolour painting. The salesgirl wrapped it in pink tissue paper and placed it neatly in a shiny white box tied with a pink ribbon. I went back to the library and sat on the bench by the door. When it was almost closing time, I stood and caught my reflection in the glass. *Feeble.* I smoothed my hair and went inside. I found Hillary tidying up the back tables.

"Hi, Frances, did you forget something?"

I handed her the books she'd given me earlier. "I won't be needing these after all. I'm moving away."

"Oh. Where are you going?"

"Back home to Safe Harbour."

"Ah, seaside retirement. I'm much of your mind. All I want is a clear view of the ocean when I'm done. I can't imagine ever living in a place where I can't see the water every day of my life. Well, I'm happy for you, but you'll be missed."

I smiled. "Will I?"

"Are you kidding? My most loyal reader."

"Hillary, I want to give you something—a token for all your kindness to me over the years." I passed her the pretty box.

She pulled the scarf out and I could see that she loved it. She didn't say I shouldn't have or comment on how much it must have cost. She simply wrapped it around her neck, and it looked to have always been hers.

"Frances, how beautiful and how incredibly thoughtful of you. This one will be kept far from tiny hands. Thank you so much. Can I give you a hug?"

She didn't wait for my answer. Before I knew it, she was against me, her hands pressed on my upper back. She felt solid and strong and smelled of lavender. I'd hoped for a handshake, perhaps a squeeze of a shoulder, but this level of contact was a riot of sensations that threatened to topple me over. She stepped back and playfully modelled the scarf.

"Come on," she said. "Walk out with me."

She locked the door and wished me good luck. As she turned to go, I heard myself saying her name. All my lost chances with her, all the things I wished I could have found a way to say. Tell me about your childhood, the house you grew up in, the lessons your mother taught you. About how you met your husband. Is he loyal and kind and deserving of you, or does he disappoint you every day? About your children, who wreck your scarves and gobble your cakes. Tell me why Liz Cleary is the way she is and how someone like you is friends with someone like her. Tell me what you've seen of the world. Your favourite food, a movie that makes you cry every time you watch it, and what you do when you can't sleep. Are you as happy as you look in all those pictures on the computer, or is it all for show? Tell me everything.

"Maybe I'll send you a picture of my view of the sea."

"I wish you would," she said and walked away.

I watched her cross the street and get into her car. She made a quick phone call, then drove off.

When I got home, I could still smell Hillary's lavender scent on my clothes. I pressed my shirt to my face and breathed her in for the last time. I shed a few tears, then soaked in the tub with a shot of warm whisky. I thought about a poem tacked to the wall above the desk in Edie's room. I'd noticed it many times but only got around to reading it one rainy morning last summer. I thought it lovely until I got to the last line, which struck me like a slap to my face. The line asked what I planned to do with the one wild and precious life I'd been given. And while I often wanted to, I never could bring myself to read that poem a second time. I suspected if that venerable poet were to take stock of my cloistered, colourless time on the planet, the word *squandered* would be bandied about. But who was she to say what my life was worth?

I was worn out with wishing and wanting and scolding myself for what I had or hadn't done because of my nature. I was fed up with the visions of how I'd failed forever blocking any view of what I'd overcome. Against some pretty rough odds, I'd survived for almost sixty years, and that would have to be enough. Regrets at this late stage would be nothing more than waste upon waste. Tossing away a wild and precious present, however short, to live in a past that could never be made over right—that would be a waste. "Amen," the squid said, and I raised my glass in its honour.

EDIE STUFFED THE LAST of an apple turnover in her mouth. "Don't you want yours?" she said, spraying crumbs across my table.

"You eat like a longshoreman."

"What's a longshoreman?"

"Someone who eats like you."

"Actually, you don't look so hot. Have you taken your pills?"

"Listen, I want to talk to you." I reached for her sticky hand. "I hope you know how much help you've been to me over the last couple of months. Frankly, I'm not sure what I would've done without you."

She let out a low moan. "Oh my God, what is happening?"

"I'm going to Safe Harbour."

"Oh. Okay, cool. You just looked like you were about to roll out some drama."

"Annie's asked me to come stay at her house."

"For how long?"

"That's the thing. I won't be coming back."

She nodded, then pulled my hand up and inspected my nails. "They still look good."

I laid my palm against her cheek. She leaned into it and smiled, that heartbreaking wobbly smile she always made whenever she was trying not to cry.

"Can I come see you?"

"Absolutely. Any time. I'm sorry, Edie. I need to do it this way. I really do."

"No, I get it. I'm really happy for you. It's just, you know."

"I want you to remember something. I'm pretty sure that I never would have reached out to Annie. You made this happen for me. You. And it's not a small thing. It's a very big and special thing, and I'm so thankful." I sat quietly and let her sniffle it out. "What say you show me how to do those video calls? That way, you can see my ugly mug any time you like. Then we'll look at the calendar and pick a time for you to visit." I rubbed her back until she pulled out her phone.

She helped me pack up my books and a few odds and ends

that she offered to cart to the charity shop. She loaded the boxes into her blue car, then embraced me in the street.

"You're the big and special thing, Frances," she said. "I'm the one who's thankful."

I hung on tight and let her be the first to pull away. I walked to the end of the street with a plan to take a last look around the city I never really got to know, but my withering body had other plans. This town and I would remain strangers. It had sheltered me well enough, but it was never my home. Instead, I spent the rest of the day cleaning the toaster and the kettle and all the other everyday items that would now be someone else's collection of second-hand things. The good Mr. Heneghan said his next tenant was starting with nothing, and she'd gladly take whatever I could spare. I wiped down the kitchen table and placed a card and a bottle of wine for her and a letter of thanks for him. I had neither strength nor spirit to scour the place one last time, so I called a gal from my hotel days who was fierce with the bleach and in need of the work to come in once I'd gone.

I emptied my closet and dresser, stuffed my work clothes into a garbage bag, and whittled all my possessions down to the bare essentials. A pauper's pile that fit into a single suitcase. Then I laid my bones down one last time on the mattress I'd carried with me from place to place. I slept in fits and starts, too haunted by the sense of everything ending, and too fired up about what was beginning.

ANNIE ARRIVED AT NOON the next day. I'd been up and dressed for hours, perched on the edge of the couch, not sure what to do with myself. She waited in the living room while I peed and took my afternoon dose. When I came out, she was sitting on top of my suitcase.

"Where's the rest of your luggage?"

"That's it."

She looked around the bare, shabby room and smiled. "Sold off the heirloom silver, have you?"

"Ah yes, I believe *hovel* was the word you used to describe my lovely home. Very insulting that."

"Brace yourself, my dear, because the one who takes in the dying old bag gets to speak her mind at will."

"And will you be doing that for the rest of my life?"

"Maybe. I haven't decided yet. Come on, Frances, let's get it in gear. I want to be home by supper."

I opened the door, but the finality of stepping beyond it took my breath away. I turned to Annie and shook my head. "I can't."

"What do you mean you can't?"

"I can't move."

"Like you can't physically move or you're too scared to move?"

"The second one." I clutched at my chest and, thinking again of Oliver's teachings, started to count my breaths.

She went to the kitchen and came back with a glass of water. I tried to swallow, but my throat was closed up tight.

"Frances, I'm at a loss here. Tell me what to do."

I shook my head.

She leaned back against the wall and closed her eyes for a minute or two. Then she snapped her fingers. "Okay, I've got it. Think back to when you gave birth, right? When they're telling you one more push and it's all over? And you know you just can't do it, right? You don't care if you have to walk around forever with a baby half hanging out of you. There's just nothing left. Then the nurse tells you there's no choice. Come hell or high water, that baby is coming and somehow you find it. That's what this is. One last push and you're out."

I stood panting in her face, inspired but still rooted to the spot. She turned me toward the door, placed her hand on my lower back, and gave me a small shove over the threshold.

"Congratulations," she said and picked up my suitcase. "It's a woman."

We didn't speak again until we reached the highway. As we merged into the speeding traffic, Annie said, "Well, Frances, I'd say we're in it deep now."

I rested my head against the cool window. "Up to our goddamn eyes."

14

The car stopped and I snapped awake, slack-jawed with a trail of drool down my chin. Annie yanked the key out of the ignition and hopped out to get my bag from the trunk. I opened my door and stepped into the drizzle and fog that smelled of the sea. I breathed in and held it, letting it settle into my lungs.

Annie led me down a long hall to a room easily three times the size of any one I'd ever slept in. I wiggled my toes against the thick sand-coloured carpet. Two big windows faced me, and I could smell the fresh paint on the walls—soft blue, a spring sky. There was a high, wide bed covered by a white duvet and pale purple sheets and four massive pillows propped up against a pine headboard. A small white night table held a lamp and a crystal vase of yellow tulips. In the corner of the room sat a faded yellow armchair beside a low pine bookcase stacked full of paperbacks, and on the wall above hung a large flat television.

Annie opened a set of white doors. "Here's the closet. A little dresser in there for you as well."

Then she opened another door to show me a gleaming white bathroom with a small glass shower and a whirlpool bathtub, a set of new blue towels folded on its edge.

"I know it still stinks of paint," Annie said. "When the weather clears, we'll open the windows and give it an airing. But it's a good room."

"It's a perfect room. I don't know what to say."

"Say, 'Thank you, Annie.'"

"Thank you, Annie."

"Now get yourself settled, and if you're up for a drop of my famous pea soup and tea buns, I'll be in the kitchen."

I put away my things and tried out the bed, hard at first then yielding to my weight, slowly shaping itself to cradle my body. I got up for fear of drifting off and walked down the hall to see about that soup.

I sat in Annie Malone's kitchen and ate her delicious food. I listened to her talk about the house, how she and Anthony had it built just after Stephen was born. How they'd spent oodles of money renovating the kitchen a few years ago, then split up not long after it was finished. She also told me that Angela had been training to be a nurse in St. John's, then ran into her high school sweetheart, Ryan, in the hospital after he'd busted up his knee playing hockey. She gave up on her nursing course with only a year left and followed him back to Safe Harbour, a decision Annie was sure Angela would live to regret. Now they owned the restaurant where Annie had taken Edie and me for lunch. "They run a brisk trade in the summer," Annie said. "But the winters are lean. Not much different than making a living on the water, I suppose."

I watched her clear away the dishes, all my offers of help waved off. How surreal it all was. I felt weightless, as if I lifted my elbows from the table, I might float up to the ceiling like a balloon. Annie gave the counters a final swipe and poured us each a shot of whisky. She raised her glass and looked me in the eye.

"To the return of Frances Delaney."

I clinked my glass against hers and reached for my cigarettes. We stood on the back patio, the fog settling in our hair.

"What did Angela say about me being in her old bedroom?"

"I haven't told her yet. About the room or about you."

Her words caught me on a large drag of smoke. I coughed until tears poured down my cheeks. "Christ, Annie. When are you planning on telling her? When she finds me dead in her bed?"

"Frances, I've had this daughter for a while now. All information is released on a strict need-to-know basis. And you're not in her old room. You're in Stephen's."

"Now I really don't know what to say."

"It's high time that room got put to some purpose beyond gathering dust. You're as good a cause as any."

"Won't Angela be even more upset about me taking over his room?"

"You've enough to be thinking about. You leave her to me."

I rubbed my temples. "It's a good thing I'm half-dead. I don't have the wits or strength to argue with you."

"That will come in right handy." She flicked her cigarette butt into an empty clay flowerpot. "Why don't you go off to bed? The sun might shine tomorrow, and you won't want to miss a minute if it does."

I burrowed into the fine bed and was asleep within minutes, but in the wee hours, the pain broke through. I swallowed two pills at the sink and sat in the armchair to wait it out. My head slowly settled, and the worn spine of a small paperback in the bookcase caught my eye. I reached for it—a copy of *Anne of Green Gables,* its pages yellowed and wavy from damp. I squinted at the writing on the inside of the cover, my name spelled out in pencil. The book my mother had been given when she was a girl and passed on to me on a snowy Christmas morning. The rest of my girlhood trove was there too. Every book I'd foolishly left behind sitting on the shelves. I scooped up as many as I could carry and tossed them on the bed. I couldn't read the fine, faded type of a single one and instead placed the story of an orphan girl on an island under my pillow and slept with the others piled at my feet.

I woke to the sound of raised voices. It took me a minute to work out where I was. I recognized one of the voices as Annie's, and the where and the why came flooding back. Almost every day now, I'd wake and for a few blissful minutes the squid and I would be unacquainted. Then it would slowly sink in, a new death sentence handed down with every sunrise. I opened the door and poked my head out. Annie and Angela were in heated discussion, their harsh words flowing from the kitchen.

"Angela, stop overreacting."

"If you saw first-hand what smoking does to people, you'd know I'm not overreacting in the slightest."

"She's a grown woman. If she wants to smoke, what's it to you? If it's Stevie you're worried about, she smokes outside."

"How long is she staying?"

"As long as it takes."

"As long as what takes?'

I took a couple of light steps down the hall.

"Sit down. I need to talk to you."

I heard the scrape of a chair against the tile floor. Silence, then Annie's voice, softer and slower.

"She's not well."

"So double for the smoking."

"She's dying. She has a brain tumour. She has only a short time left."

"What about her treatment? How will she get that down here?"

"She's not having treatment. She's come here to die."

"Here in this house?" Angela's voice had shot up a few levels in volume and pitch.

"Keep your voice down. I made up Stephen's room for her. When the time comes, her doctor will come down and that will be that."

They fell quiet for a few moments, and I took another step toward the kitchen.

"You cannot be serious."

"Oh, I'm as serious as can be."

"You're making a big mistake."

Annie scoffed. "Oh, I am, am I? And on what authority do you come to that conclusion?"

"For God's sake, as someone who knows a bit about health-care, as a Catholic, as a person who values life. Take your pick."

My nightgown was growing damp with sweat, and I desperately needed to pee, but I couldn't tear myself away.

"You know you can't take part in this. Everyone in town will be talking about it within five minutes of it happening. And in Stephen's room to boot? Dad will lose his mind."

"I've long since stopped worrying about what your father or anyone else blessed with a wagging tongue thinks of me. You know, Angela, you surprise me with this. Why should she suffer any more than she has to? You had no issue putting the family dog out of his misery."

"She is not a dog."

"But she's had her share of misery, I can tell you that. You've no idea what that poor woman has been through."

"Everyone has their burdens, Mother."

I jumped at the sound of something shattering against the floor.

"Don't you talk to me of burdens," Annie said. "She lost her father, her mother, her home, her child, and now here she is, not a teacher like she wanted but a cleaning woman with a frigging tumour eating away at her brain—a brain far sharper than what you and I have under our skulls—and from what I can tell, no one but a teenage girl and me to help her out. Now get some goddamn perspective and get it right quick."

"All right, calm down."

"I will not calm down. I've carried this family on my back for nigh on twenty years. A bastard of a husband, a son ripped from me, a daughter who treats me like an idiot, and not once have I asked for something for me. And this is as much for me as it is for her. That woman and I were once each other's world, and there's a history between us that you couldn't possibly know or understand. Frances needs me and I need to help her, so either get with it or get the hell out of my way. And the Church and the good citizens of Safe Harbour and your sainted father can all go fuck themselves. And you can clean up that plate I broke."

I heard shards of glass being swept up, then the stomp of feet toward the hall. I made a beeline to my room and kept going through to the bathroom, my heart banging against my ribs as I sat on the edge of the tub. I heard a soft knocking on the bedroom door.

"Frances, you up?" Annie asked.

I flushed the toilet and turned on the sink taps full blast so she'd think I couldn't have heard them. "Be right out." As I was brushing my teeth, it occurred to me that I'd never once been a guest in a home where I wasn't on the payroll. I spit and rinsed and fought off a compulsion to bleach something.

I made my way to the kitchen, where I found Annie sitting at the table, arms and legs crossed, chewing on her lower lip. I sat across from her and reached for the teapot.

"I hope Angela and I didn't wake you with our first fight of the day."

"Not at all. And even if you had, it's your house. Carry on as you see fit."

"You missed that one, but stay tuned. There's bound to be another as soon as she walks back in the door. Honestly, I don't know where I went wrong with her."

"Where is she?"

"Tore out the door in a huff. What odds. There's cereal and bread and eggs. I think I might have some bacon."

"I'll just have some toast with the tea. But stay where you are, I'll make it. You want some?"

"No, I'm too bloody vexed to eat. You go ahead and hurry on so we can go outside and smoke. My nerves are rubbed raw."

"You don't have to wait for me. Go on out now."

"No, I'm after making a rule for myself. I'll only ever have one with you. That way I can convince myself that I'm not smoking—I'm supporting."

"Excellent logic."

"Isn't it, though. How's that bed for you?"

I spooned a great heap of partridgeberry jam on a piece of hot homemade bread and bit into the breakfast of my child-hood. "Annie, there are no words for me to convey just how good that bed is. Or how good this jam is. Did you make it?"

"No, that's from Mrs. Dillon. She'll give you some if you ask her. She's got a pantry full of everything under the sun, God love her."

I polished off another two pieces of jam-covered toast, washed them down with sweet tea, and grabbed the Rothmans.

The morning sun had chased the fog away, and the large swath of Annie's newly cut, impossibly green grass steamed and glistened. Her land extended into a wide tree line of white birches and spruces, and a yearling moose emerged from the forest and nibbled at the lawn. A pair of blue jays perched on the branch of a tree watched over us while we sat in silence at the patio table. The chilled island air was as pristine as it had always been, and blowing clouds of smoke into it seemed like sacrilege.

"Is Angela upset that I'm in Stephen's room?"

"Oh, I imagine so, but what isn't Angela upset about? Every day it's something new."

"I'm not keen on causing any tension here."

"The tension was here long before you. What she has to be unhappy about I'll never know. But I say the one with the brain tumour wins. And she can stuff any objections right up her backside. Years I've been kowtowing to her just to keep the peace and I've had enough. There's a new sheriff in town."

I laughed. "Annie, get your gun."

"I'm telling you, Frances, God help the next fool who crosses me." She made a pistol with her hand and took aim at the two blue jays. "So it's a beautiful day. Up for the water?"

When we arrived at the shore, I was pleased to see so few people about. I was also pleased that Annie had thought to bring two square cushions for the hard plank of the dory. We nestled our aging behinds and faced the sparkling sea.

"Annie, I forgot to mention it. My books."

"I was wondering how long it would take you to notice."

"But how did you come to have them?"

"After you left, Mom went down and boxed them up. They were in her attic for years, then in mine."

"Why did you keep them all this time?"

"I guess I hoped you'd be back for them someday."

"I'm very grateful to have them."

"As you should be." She reached into her bag and pulled out a small tube of sunscreen and spread a dollop over her face and neck. "So what's happening with young Edie?"

"She's worked up about a boy these days. She wants to come for a visit next weekend, if that's all right with you."

"Sure. She's a sweet little thing. She'll have a hard time with your passing."

"Edie is as strong as she is sweet. She'll be fine."

"And what about me?" Annie said. "Will I be fine? I don't know how strong I'll be when that doctor comes through my door. I don't know if I'm strong enough to sit and hold your hand and see you through. I hope I am, but I don't know."

"You don't need to know. Not yet, anyway."

She nodded and watched the water. "You know, I never grow tired of this shore. Not once has that ocean failed to impress me. I could never be away from it."

"I never thought I could be near it again. I'm just happy to be able to look at it without falling apart."

"You're easy to please, I'll say that for you."

"It's easy to be pleased when there's nothing left to lose. Believe me, I've never had it so easy."

She gave me a doubtful look.

"No, it's true," I said. "I find dying makes living easier. At least for me. I can't recall ever feeling this settled in myself. You must remember what I was like, nervous as a cornered cat."

"You were just shy is all."

"No, it was more than that. Like what you saw at my place yesterday. Oftentimes much worse. Being around people would set it off, so I did everything I could not to be around people, which only made it worse. And over the years, it just got wedged so far in me that there was no getting it out."

"Why didn't you find someone to help you? You can't throw a rock nowadays without hitting a shrink."

"I don't know. Back in the day, nobody talked about that kind of stuff. I was too ashamed and ignorant, I suppose. Too scared of someone calling me crazy and locking me away.

Too sad, too busy trying to scratch out a living. Anyway, it's got in the way my whole life. Stopped me from doing so many things."

"Like what?"

"Like everything. Like seeing you before now."

"We don't have to get into all that right now. You only just got here. There's time."

"I know, but just listen to me. I'm not sure you know just how much you helped me when we were young. How much easier my life was because of you. Just being near you always made me feel like a stronger person, a better person."

"That went both ways."

"But when I went away to the home, it was like my mind somehow locked everything in place. Like everything would be frozen in time exactly where I left it. But then Mom died, and everything seemed ruined. And then that awful fight we had. And when I called and you talked about getting married, it was like I realized for the first time that you'd carry on without me. That nothing was ever going to be the same again. And I couldn't bear it. So I just ran away, and then I couldn't seem to find my way back. I put it all aside and tried not to think about it just so I could keep moving forward, one day after another, until too many days had passed. I'm not making excuses. I'm just trying to explain myself. To you and to me, I guess. I know what I did was wrong. I've always known it. But I didn't know just how wrong until I woke up in that room this morning. Your clearing out your beautiful son's things to make way for me. I mean, the kindness in that, Annie. It's hard to take in. And then the books." I paused and drew in a few ragged breaths and let the tears I'd been holding flow. "I'm so sorry for those horrible things I said about you and your mother that night. And I'm so sorry for everything I put you through. I really am."

"It's all right, Frances. Come on, now. Don't go upsetting yourself. We'll hash it all out by and by. For now, let's just sit here and say nothing. Then we'll go back to the house and eat and drink too much and talk about stupid shit that doesn't matter. As for everything else, it's kept for this long, and it'll keep a little longer."

15

I stayed up with Annie later than was good for me and woke
with a thick head, gasping for a spot of tea. In the kitchen I
found Angela sitting at the table, nursing Stevie. I scanned
about for Annie and started to weigh the pros and cons of a
hasty retreat to my room.

"She's popped out for groceries. She shouldn't be too long,"
Angela said. She gently separated herself from the baby. "How
are you feeling?"

"Not bad, all things considered. You?"

The baby expelled a puff of gas and Angela almost smiled.
"Finally." She wiped his face with a washcloth and laid him in
his car seat on the floor. "I'm fine other than the fact that I hav-
en't slept more than two hours straight for six months."

"Can I fix you some tea?"

"Sure."

I rifled through the cupboards looking for cups.

"To the right of the fridge. No, the next one," she said.

"I guess I'll get the hang of it soon enough." I could feel the heat of her stare on my back as I boiled the water and reached for the bag of bread on the counter. "Would you like some toast?" I asked without turning around.

"Just tea is fine."

I joined her at the table. Neither of us spoke. She sipped, I sipped and chewed, and Stevie slept. I rose, dishes in hand, planning on going back to bed until Annie returned.

"So how do you like the bedroom?" she asked.

I laid my dishes in the sink and sat back down. "Very much. Your mother did a lovely job getting it ready for me."

"Did she? I haven't seen it." She looked toward the baby, then back at me, expressionless.

"You're welcome to have a look."

"No, thank you."

"I know it was your brother's room. I was so sorry to hear about his passing."

She nodded and drained her cup. "Sorry to hear about your illness."

She didn't look sorry. I got up and wiped the counter and considered my next move. I checked my hands, steady. Breaths, deep and even. Heartbeat, slow and strong. I walked back to the table and sat facing her.

"Angela, it seems like you've got something to say."

She offered me a thin smile. "Not really."

I tapped my middle finger lightly on the table and jutted my chin at her, a signal to get on with it.

"Fine. I don't agree with what you and Mom are doing here. All due respect," she said and raised her hand, her palm thrust toward me, a sign of respect yet to catch on with the masses. "I just think it's wrong."

"I see. What is it exactly that bothers you?'

"I just believe that all life is precious and it's wrong to take one under any circumstances."

"Hmm. Precious. Something of great value, not to be wasted or treated carelessly."

"My point exactly."

She folded her arms across her chest and kept talking, but I'd stopped listening. All I could hear was her tone, the same condescending tone I'd heard from people all my life. I looked at the face of this smug chippy and I saw every single person who'd ever hurt me or made me feel small. The kids at school, Michael Doyle, Sister Bernadette and Father O'Leary. The people of Safe Harbour who'd made me pay for the sins of my mother. The maids who'd shunned me, and the clients who'd looked down on me. I thought about the countless times I'd voiced clever retorts in the quiet of my bedroom or in the shower hours after the offending comments had been laid down. Then I saw that Angela's mouth had stopped moving.

"I can't speak for your mother," I said, "but I've known her for many years, and she's always been one to know her own mind. You've just met me and yet you feel free to speak to me this way about something so deeply personal. I wouldn't dream of telling you how to live your life, and for sure I wouldn't tell you how to die. I hope you never find yourself in my situation, but if you do, I also hope you never have to endure a conversation as rude and distasteful as this one."

Before she could respond, Annie walked into the kitchen loaded down with bags of groceries. "What's distasteful?"

"Oh, I was just explaining to Angela here my thoughts on dying."

"Ah," Annie said. "And how's that working out for you?"

"Quite well, I think."

Annie busied herself with putting the food away while Angela stood and slung the baby bag over her shoulder. She picked up her son, the weight of the car seat dragging her arm toward the floor, and turned to Annie.

"So you're really doing this?"

"Angela, I'm warning you, mind your own," Annie said.

"Mom, you have no idea what you've got yourself into here. You're still not over Stephen dying and you think you can handle having this woman die in his room? Are you cracked or what?"

"Enough." Annie's raised voice echoed through the kitchen. She took a few steps toward her daughter. "That's enough," she said quietly, and went back to her groceries. "Now who wants strawberries? You should see the size of them."

"Good luck to you both," Angela said. "You'll need it." She walked out and closed the front door with a loud bang.

"She'll come around," I said.

"Ha! Don't bet on it."

"Right," I said. "What's this I hear about strawberries?"

AFTER LUNCH ANNIE WANTED go see Stephen before the fog came in. "Why don't you come along and see your people?" she said.

At the cemetery, she kissed her fingertips and slapped her mother's headstone, then walked toward her son. I ambled over to my father, laid a bunch of stalky lupins on the grass above him, then made my way toward Stephen's grave. I hung back while Annie knelt and cleared away the dead flowers and swept a few stray leaves with her hands. She pressed her head against the black stone and left him. I followed a few steps behind. Suddenly, she stopped and her body stiffened. She turned around and her face was twisted with pain, every feature so wrenched and distorted that she was barely recognizable.

"Annie, what is it?"

"Oh, Christ. Oh, good Christ."

She sat on the grass and cried. I lowered myself down beside her. I wanted to hold her hand or rub her back like I did for Edie, but I wasn't sure if my touch would be welcome, so I settled on an awkward little pat on her shoulder.

"I don't know what to do about you and me. I look at you in my house and it's like you're some stranger who wandered in off the street. And I look at you now and it's like we're sixteen again." She caught her breath and lay on her back. "All those years of slapping you around in my head. Worrying about you, missing you, blaming you, damning you to hell. Easier to blame you than myself, I suppose. Making you come to that party down the shore that night. I was the one screwing my way through town. I was the one who should've got knocked up. And that day you called me asking me to come. And I should have."

"You were young."

"Not too young to be thinking of getting married. But maybe too young to know that between you and Anthony Rideout, you were the better bet. A million times I've thought if only I'd come. If only. You'd be a teacher and I'd be something better than that bastard's ex-wife. Maybe I would have been happy. And maybe I wouldn't have a child in the ground."

She started to cry again, and I lay down beside her.

"Annie, whatever has come before is gone. We're gonna have to figure out a way to let all this go or else we'll never make it through what I've come here for. We can't bring the past into that room when my time comes or we'll both die with it all hanging over us. And seeing as I'm going first, I get the last word."

"You're right. I know you're right." She reached into her purse and pulled out a wad of tissues to sop up her face. "Have you been to see your mother already?"

I shook my head.

"Go on. I'll wait here for you."

"I'm not going. I haven't been to that grave since the day she was lowered into it."

She snorted into her tissues. "So this talk about letting it all go—more preaching than practising, is it?"

"There's some things that are beyond forgiveness."

She heaved a long, heavy sigh and got to her feet. "Come on, there's something I need to show you."

I LAY ON THE bed while Annie flipped through the books in my room.

"Here it is," she said, and handed me a white envelope.

"What's this?"

"It's a letter from my mother. She wrote it not long before she died. One morning, she asked me to dig it out of her dresser and told me to put it in a box of old books in the attic, which was the first time I realized she'd kept them for you. It was an interesting day all around."

"And you didn't open it?"

"It's not addressed to me, now, is it? She made me promise to leave it be. All she said was that it was something you needed to know. I have my suspicions what it's about and I don't know if it will make you feel better or worse, but it's your letter. You decide what you want to do with it."

"I've only got one good eye these days. You'll have to read it to me."

"No, I can't. We need to find a way for you to do it on your own." She left and came back with a large magnifying glass. "Here, try this and see if you can make out her writing." She held up the envelope.

"Miss Frances Delaney. Confidential."

"See? She'd have never written that if she meant for me to see it. Come find me when you're done," she said, and closed the door.

All Mrs. Malone had done for me, and in return I'd given her my silence. Not a single phone call or letter over the years. Not even a goddamn Christmas card. I'd read somewhere that of all the human emotions, shame was one of the most difficult to bear. And holding that envelope, I felt coated in it. So much so that I considered not reading the letter. But I knew the least I could do for Mrs. Malone was let her have her say. With trembling hands, I pulled the letter from the envelope and smoothed out the pages, then sat in the armchair and held up the magnifying glass.

My dear Frances,

I don't know if you'll ever read this, so I may be writing it more for me than you, but I'm an old woman now and not long for this world, and I figure I'm long overdue to carry on as I please. I'll not be seeing you again, as I'd always hoped I would, and that weighs heavy on my heart. I'm not saying that to make you feel bad, only so that you'll know how much I cared for you. I never really got past the loss of you, but I know you must have had your reasons for staying away. I was never one to judge the motives of others, and I hope you'll not judge me now.

I remember it like it was yesterday, that day you and I sat in your mother's kitchen. She only days in the ground and you were blaming yourself for what she had done. Maybe I should have told you what I'm about to—maybe it would have made all the difference in the world—but things were so different then than they are now. There's so much you don't know about your mother.

I laid down the glass and rubbed my eyes. I put the paper down and went to the bathroom to splash cold water on my face. I didn't want to know what Mrs. Malone wanted to tell me. What use were any hard truths now? I thought. The squid begged to differ. "She's waiting," it said, and I found my way back to the chair.

Frances, you can't imagine the happiness you brought to your parents. Your mother had a rough go carrying you, sick as a dog every minute you were inside her. But once you were out, she told me that it was all worth it. For the first few weeks, she was tired and low, but it was put down to the stress of having a new baby. I told her she'd be right once she got the hang of it. But then your father went to sea for a couple of weeks, and by the time he got back, she was in a bad state. I was too busy with Annie just being born and the boys running around every which way to have noticed that she'd fallen so ill. He came racing down to my door, asking me to look in on her. When I got there, the house was a wreck and so was she. Barely able to speak. Hadn't eaten for days. You were in a bad state yourself, underfed and wailing non-stop. I had to put you to my own breast while your father dressed her and took her off to the doctor.

She ended up in the Waterford Hospital—you'll remember everyone used to call it the Mental before we knew better. Nowadays we'd call her suffering postpartum depression. I know because I'm after reading everything I can find on it over the years.

We kept it between us, your father and me, because as you know, she would have been judged unfairly for it. We told everyone she had bad gallstones and needed an operation and left it at that. It was your father who cared for you while she was gone, and he did well, God bless him. He was a good man. As soon as she was well again, she swore she'd never have another child, lest she have to go through that again. And that's why there was only you. She had another bout of it when you were around three—not as bad as the first one, but bad enough to send her into the Waterford again. Then she seemed to return to herself until your father died. I think he helped keep her steady, and without him she just couldn't rally back.

Now, in case you're going down the road of blaming yourself all over again, know this: not once did your mother ever regret having you. I know for a fact that had she known what she was to suffer, she'd have gladly gone through it ten times over to have you. She told me that it ran in the blood of her people. I wonder if you remember me hovering over you like a hawk after you had your child. Now you know why.

After you left, Annie told me what you said about how if we'd looked after your mother properly, she wouldn't have taken her life. Maybe there's some truth in that. After rolling it around in my head all these years, I'm no closer to working that out. All I can say is that I saw your mother the day before she died and there was not a sign to be seen that would have foretold what happened. And had there been anything off in the days or weeks before, I believe I would have noticed. I don't know what drove her away. I never will. But I do know she broke your heart, Frances. I know too well because she broke mine too. But my heart was not so broken that I couldn't find room in it to understand why she did what she did. I think she must have been in terrible pain to leave like that. It's as I told you on that day so long ago—sometimes people just have to lay it down. I guess she could find no other way.

I hope you've been able to make peace with it all, and if not, I hope this letter helps you move closer to it. You were a good girl, Frances, and I expect you've turned out to be a good woman.

All my love, Bridget Malone

I folded the letter, too stunned to feel much of anything. I had only thoughts about what I should feel. Anguish over the tragedy of it all. Bitterness for not having had this letter in my hands years ago. Rage over all the misguided punishment I'd doled out for so long, blaming first my mother and then myself, then later sweet Mrs. Malone. But all I could find in myself was an overwhelming sense of being released, like waking from a long and violent nightmare safe and sound in my bed. My whole life had been coloured by the legacy of this weak, spiteful woman whose spirit was tied to the loss of a man. A woman whose child wasn't enough to keep her in this world. I read the letter a second time, and by the end I felt a warm, almost joyful kinship with my mother that I'd never felt before. A sick, tortured woman who chose to end her suffering; how could I condemn her? We were kindred souls, hostages to some defect buried deep in our cells, and whatever was wrong with her was never her doing, which meant the same held true for me. I put the letter back in the envelope and went to find Annie.

Ten minutes later, we were back at the cemetery. The fog was well in and I was glad for the cool gloom of it. I handed Annie the letter. "Here, read this," I said and asked her to wait in the car. My mother's name was chiselled into the face of a white gravestone, a gift from Mrs. Malone, who couldn't bear her lying unmarked, convicted in absentia, then forgotten. I laid the flowers I'd bought on the way on the grass and asked her to forgive me. I heard the car door open and close behind me, then Annie was beside me.

"I knew that letter would have something to do with your mother, but I had no idea," she said. "Just now in the car, I had a flash of memory, of Gordie saying something less than kind about your mother and Mom going up one side of him and down the other. I'd never seen her so mad. Makes sense now."

"I don't know if what your mother said was true."

"Which part?"

"The part about me being a good woman. She said she didn't judge me, but how could she not?"

"Because she was the very best of women."

"Annie, maybe I've no right to ask and maybe we'd need more time than I have, but is there any chance we can find our way to a clean slate?"

She nodded and wrapped her arms around me, and I held on tight.

"You're your mother's child, Annie Malone."

"No," she said. "I'm just so fucking tired of being sad and angry."

AFTER DINNER, WE SAT outside and watched the birds flutter and loop over the grassy field. Annie talked about unimportant things—how the girls we went to school with had turned

out, what a cruise she'd taken two summers ago was like—
and as I listened, I felt a slow shift taking place throughout my
body, things softening and blooming, as if all the dried and
brittle bones and flagging muscles and organs were reviving
themselves, taking in great gulps of water and oxygen from the
blood as it flowed through them, soaking up the nutrients and
surging back to life.

When I lay in bed, I thought back to what Annie had said
before she gave me the letter—about how she didn't know if
I'd feel better or worse after reading it. I still wasn't entirely
sure. I did feel deeply changed by it, unburdened and raring
to try living beyond the grip of guilt and shame. In my mind, I
likened it to breaking through a dark cocoon and taking flight
as a butterfly, some short-lived species that knows better than
to waste a moment on anything other than finding the sweetest
flower for its feet.

I was surprised to find my head beautifully still. My thoughts
rolled out at an even pace, and for the first time since my father
died, the whirl of worries had disappeared. Somehow all the
senseless angst seemed to have been dismantled and discarded.
Good riddance and God bless. Better, I decided—infinitely
so—knowing full well that nothing was ever that simple. I
knew I'd die with a lingering sense of responsibility for being
born, for the pain my very existence had brought to my mother.
Nonetheless, I offered a final word of gratitude to Mrs. Malone
and eased into a long dreamless sleep.

16

I could hear Annie's voice, tinny and far-off like a bad phone connection, calling my name over and over. I could see nothing but white, and I slowly realized it was a ceiling. The left side of my face was wet, and my body felt like it was on fire.

"Frances, can you hear me?"

Thick carpet under my back. Annie on her knees, her face above mine. I was on the floor of my room. She hinged back and sat on her heels, then raised her trembling hand to her forehead and exhaled deeply.

"Don't move. I'll be right back." She ran to the bathroom and came back with a wet washcloth and wiped my face. "You're all right, you're all right. You had a seizure."

I closed my eyes and lay still until I felt the hardness begin to leave my body.

"Okay," Annie said. "We need to get you into bed. Think you can walk?"

I shook my head.

"Let's start with sitting."

She stood in front of me, then bent forward and reached for my hands. She started to pull me up, and searing pain ripped through my body. I let out a loud yelp, startling Annie enough that she let go of my hands. I fell back and felt my head bounce against the floor.

"Jesus, Mary, and Joseph!" Annie cried. "I'm so sorry. Are you hurt?"

I tried to speak, but my mouth was too dry.

Annie dropped to her knees beside me and began frantically inspecting my head. "Frances, please. Say something—anything—to let me know you're okay."

I croaked out, "Okay," and she heaved a sigh of relief.

She wiped my face with the cloth again, then wiped her own.

"Just give me a minute. I'll figure this out." She took a couple of deep breaths, then squatted beside me. She put one arm under my upper back, the other behind my knees, and hoisted me up. She lurched toward the bed and heaved me onto the mattress like a sack of potatoes. I lay in a twisted heap while she sat on the edge of the bed, panting from her efforts. Then she rolled me onto my back and tucked the duvet around me.

"What time is it?" I asked, my words thick and slurred.

"Early. Just after seven."

"Did I pee on your floor?"

"I don't think so. And who cares if you did."

She left and came back with a glass of water, then lifted my head and held the glass to my mouth. I swallowed two small sips, laid my head down, and everything went black. When I woke up, she was lying beside me, staring at the ceiling.

"What time is it?" My throat was dusty and raw, my voice a hard rasp.

"Almost nine. Want some water?"

I nodded and gulped down a full glass of Safe Harbour well water, still the best I'd ever tasted. "Annie, I'm sorry."

"No, I'm sorry. I was supposed to put a pillow under your head, and I forgot. I'll get better at this, I swear. Still, it was lucky I was here at all. I woke up about six and couldn't get back to sleep. I got up to find something to read and just happened to be walking past your room when I heard a loud thump. You going down. What are the odds?"

"At the rate I have seizures these days, pretty good I'd say."

"Are you taking your pills?"

"I can't remember if I took them last night. My guess is not."

"I'll buy one of those pill organizers for you."

"Small penance for almost killing me earlier." I shifted in the bed and winced from the pain of moving muscles that had been pushed to their limit. "Might be time to take that bath for a spin."

She hopped up off the bed. "Stay there."

I heard the water running and realized I wasn't going to be able to get in on my own. Annie would have to help me. She'd have to undress me, support my battered, naked body as I swung a blue-veined white leg over the side. She'd have ample time to inspect my dry, dimpled skin, my slack breasts and belly, my calloused, horny feet, and I would have no choice but to endure it. Aside from the partial and carefully calculated nudity required by doctors and Oliver, no one had ever seen my unclothed body. Sweet Jesus, the indignity of it all.

"Come on, Frances. Let's get you in."

She pulled back the covers and helped me out of the bed. We took slow steps toward the bathroom and into the humidity made by the tub of steaming water. I turned away from the mirror and kept my eyes closed while she pulled my nightgown over my head. She reached for my hand and supported me as I lifted my foot off the floor and lowered it into the water.

"That's it. Go slow," she said.

I stood in the tub and let her help me down into the soothing heat. I leaned my head back against the edge and exhaled. Annie turned a dial on the wall, and the jets rumbled to life. The water banged against me, pushing away the stiffness. I felt a wide smile form in spite of myself.

"It's something, isn't it? Old as the hills but still does the job," Annie said.

"It looks brand new."

"That's because it's been used only a handful of times. We had it put in for Stephen about a month before he died. He was forever getting beat around playing hockey, and my God, he loved it. I remember always being afraid that he'd doze off and drown in it." Sorrow dawned on her face and she turned away. She put the toilet lid down and sat on it. "I'll stay until you're done, if you don't mind. Just in case."

When she helped me out of the tub, there was no avoiding the mirror. Leaning against her healthy, ample body wrapped in a thick white robe, I looked shockingly thin and frail, my skeleton peering out at me through almost translucent skin, my flesh withered and hanging from the bones. It was worse than I had feared, and I was thankful for Annie's focus on my unsteady feet. I clutched at the towel on the hook and covered myself as quickly as I could.

Annie ordered me back to bed and I offered no protest. I could hear her clattering in the kitchen and a man's voice reading the news on the radio. Then Angela and Stevie arrived. Murmured voices, muffled music, cupboard doors opening and closing. The noise of life. This house was a living thing, an extension of Annie as much as any one of her limbs. Her presence could be felt in every corner of it. I could still feel the warmth of her in the bed, smell her in the sheets, see her footprints in the carpet—all the little signs that I was not alone.

Annie appeared in the doorway, still in her robe and carrying a tray of tea and toast. "What do you say to a day in bed? Junk food, shitty television, feet up, lolling about like two queens."

I patted the bed. "Your Majesty."

We spent the rest of the morning propped against the headboard, watching nervous brides fight with their mothers about dresses and industrious couples gut derelict houses. We dozed for an hour, then Annie rustled up a couple of sandwiches and bags of chips. We closed the door, opened the windows to the wet weather, and smoked without caring what Angela would have to say about it later.

Annie rested her ankle over mine. "God, this takes me back. All those nights stuffed into those kiddie beds, not an inch between us, happy as clams. Sadly, it also takes me back to when I was first married. Anthony and I used to spend whole weekends in the sheets. By Sunday night, the bed would be full of crumbs and everything else that went along with it."

"What happened to you two?"

She took a deep drag on her cigarette and blew out a long thin stream of smoke. "Well, we were too young to start with. And we hardly knew each other. Hijacked by hormones we were. Then the kids came along. Angela was a difficult child." She side-eyed me. "No shit, says you. Stephen was easier, but still. And with the store, and the second store, and the third, Anthony was gone more than he was home. Then he started up with his women, and by the time Stephen died, we were two hateful strangers standing over a grave."

"I'm sorry."

"Don't be. I should've listened to you and saved myself a world of heartache. What about you? Ever come close to the altar?"

"No, I'm not the marrying type."

"Torrid affairs, then?"

"I'm not the torrid kind either. I'm better on my own."

"I'm not sure you missed much. I think I liked being chased better than being caught. And over the years, there were a few who made a run at me and failed. Although I slowed down for one."

I shifted on my side to face her. "When?"

She slid down the bed and rested her head on the pillow. "About six months after Stephen. It was nothing, really. Fumbling about in his car. He was married too."

I pictured Annie ripping off her clothes in a steamy car parked in the dark shadows of a back road, her tear-filled eyes shut tightly as a large, faceless figure loomed above her. It made me sad and vaguely queasy. I wanted to respond to her in a way that any other woman would, say something clever or make a raunchy joke, but without anything to draw from I was stuck. I knew women talked to each other about sex and such. I overheard them in stores, saw it play out in films, read pages and pages of their thoughts and conversations in books, but in all cases, the women had rich experiences—good, bad, and downright ugly—to guide them. I had thirty seconds of Michael Doyle, and even that was thirty seconds too many.

"Did you love him?" I asked.

"Good God, no. I was just using him to feel something other than what I was feeling at the time. It was a bit of madness, really. It lasted a few weeks and then one day I just didn't show up to meet him and never spoke to him after. I see him now and I just nod hello like nothing happened. Now I wish I hadn't told you that."

"Why?"

"Because you'll think I'm an old tart.'

"I don't think you're old."

She laughed and tipped the empty chip bag toward her mouth, catching the last greasy crumbs. I got up to use the bathroom and take my pills. When I got back, she was gone. I lay down and closed my eyes.

Sometime later, I opened my eyes to Annie's face hovering inches above mine. She had showered and smelled of soap and something floral. Her robe had been replaced by a pair of crisp pink-and-white-striped pajamas. She held up a bottle of whisky.

"I figured it was time to break out the booze."

She sat cross-legged on the bed and poured me a small shot. I let the whisky burn down, then held my glass up for a refill.

"So," she said, "how are you feeling about it all? The letter, your mother?"

I thought about it for a few moments. *Unimpeded.* "I feel free."

"I'll drink to that." She took a sip and got back under the covers. "You know, I was thinking about your mother last night, wondering, if we could see the pain we'd go through later in life, would we still press on? Would we do something like she did, or would we slog it out anyway?"

"Who knows? Some people survive all sorts of hardship, don't they? One disaster after another and they just keep going. I don't think I'll ever understand what it is that makes one person decide to leave and the other to stay. Maybe no one does."

"If only she'd been born later. Who knows what they could do for her now? Or maybe she would have come to the same end. It makes my head spin a bit just thinking about it."

"And mine. What say we move on to something a touch lighter?"

"Okay, tell me about your baby."

I laughed. "Maybe suicide is easier."

"It's just that I can't remember us ever talking about it. It was like it never happened. And I think we can agree that I'm entitled to a few updates."

"Agreed. Ask away."

"What did you call her?"

"Georgina."

"Do you know what happened to her?"

"I do. She was adopted by professors and got better than what I could have given her."

"Yeah, but do you ever wish you'd just said to hell with the Church and everyone here and raised her yourself?"

"Sometimes. Many times, really. But after what happened with my mother, it would have been almost impossible."

"But say she hadn't died, would you have wanted to have the baby with you?"

"Too many 'what ifs' in that scenario to know. Do you still go to church?"

Annie shook her head. "I used to take the kids when they were young, for Christmas and Easter. But then when all the abuse reports started rolling out, I wouldn't let my kids near the place. What a racket they're running. When one of the priests down the shore was convicted, it nearly killed my mother. It took her ages even to admit it was true. If it were up to me, I'd shut the whole operation down."

"Me too. Burn it to the ground. So we've covered drowned mothers, lost babies, pedophile priests. What's next on the light-topic agenda?"

"Here's an easy one. What do you want for supper? Pizza or pizza?"

ANNIE SERVED UP SLICES of pepperoni-and-sausage pizza in bed while I chatted on the phone with Edie. She gave me a good grilling—pills, sleep, cigarette and alcohol consumption, seizure status. I told her fibs and turned the conversation to her upcoming visit. She'd read that the weather was going to be uncommonly warm—warm enough for us to swim in the ocean, she hoped. "No way I'm going in that water," I said. But she pressed me so hard that I finally promised that if the temperature hit a number above twenty-five degrees, I'd wade in, knowing full well that the chances of heat like that were slim to none.

"So what's the plan?" Annie asked when I hung up the phone.

"Edie's coming on Friday."

"No, I mean the big plan. What do you want to do with the time you have left?"

It struck me as an odd question, given that I was doing exactly what I wanted to do and doing it right before her eyes. "This," I said.

"This what?"

"I don't know. Some nice food. A chat at the shore. A smoke on the patio and a nip of whisky, then into this miracle of a bed."

"That's just sad. Think shopping spree, a roll around with a handsome stranger, a weekend in Paris. Anything."

"It's too late for silly wishes now."

"What do you wish you'd done?"

"Travel, mostly. I once saw a picture of this library—I think it was somewhere in Portugal. The most beautiful rooms I ever saw. Enormous carved white columns and a curved ceiling that would knock your eyes out. I would have liked that. Maybe see all the paintings and statues in Italy. Just silly stuff. Have you travelled?"

"Not really. Toronto, a few trips to Florida, that cruise I told you about. Never to anywhere good. Anthony always used to say that Europe was filthy, but I'd like to go someday."

"You should. You could go anywhere you like. You could even live somewhere else if you wanted to. Have you ever thought of leaving?"

"I used to. But then little Stevie came along. He's my joy, so as long as he's here, I am too. But never mind me, we're talking about you."

"Annie, honestly, a bit of company is all I'm after."

"You're a woman of simple needs."

"I'm a woman who needs the toilet." I pushed myself up in the bed, muscles screaming, and let out a loud groan and eased back down.

Annie wrapped her arms around me and hoisted me to standing. I inched my way to the bathroom. My head pulsed and my body felt impossibly stiff and heavy, as if every piece of tissue had been kitted together and turned to stone. I feared having to live out my remaining days on the toilet as facing the walk back felt like standing at the foot of a mountain. I rocked and weaved my way toward the bed with Annie guiding me along, clucking with sympathy until I was again safely reclined.

"I'll tell you what you need—a proper rubdown," Annie announced. She ducked out and returned with a white bottle and plunked it on the nightstand. She yanked back the bedding and pumped a great glob of lotion into her hand, then sat on the edge of the bed. "I used to do this for Anthony after hockey games. Trust me, I know what I'm doing."

She pulled up my nightgown and gently slapped her hand down on my right thigh. The cold of the lotion mixed with the heat of her hand sent a wave of tingling shocks along my leg down to my toes. She talked as she rubbed and kneaded my muscles. About how Gordie and the two other Malone boys had followed the trail of money west to the oil sands, where they'd found jobs with big paychecks and bought big houses and big trucks. How they would all be home for Christmas, brothers and wives, kids and dogs, bursting through the door, turning Annie's house into a rowdy circus tent for a week. How she loved it when they came and loved it more when they left.

She kept talking as she moved over me like a pro, her voice a comforting distraction from her eyes so intently fixed on my body. There were no memories this time, only the moment I was in. I tried to focus on her words, to bring her face into clear view, but with each passing moment, my senses were leaving me. I pictured the squid in a yellow hard hat standing before a tiny electrical panel in my head, slowly and methodically snapping off the switches, gleefully rerouting all the power to touch. I saw nothing, heard nothing, but I felt everything, every inch of skin alive and brimming with energy.

Annie's hands never came anywhere near the epicentre of sensation. It began as a flutter somewhere between my hip bones, then travelled down, a steady throb, lovely and thrilling, yet almost intolerable in its intensity. What a puzzling machine my body had become. The engine in full decline, but the gears still grinding. Spiky new hairs still sprouting under my arms and along my shins, toenails that needed clipping, bladder and bowels filling and emptying like clockwork, organs humming and blood flowing. And now the pulsing of a minuscule bud of flesh I'd long since forgotten I even had. If Annie sensed it in me, there was no sign of it on her face. I closed my eyes and let it ebb and flow of its own accord, but not without thought for what it might mean.

I'd always been an outlier when it came to sex. Alone in a world of creatures who seemed to be ruled by something I didn't understand. I always figured I came off the assembly line missing the pieces that fuelled the drives other people seemed to have. Anytime I'd ever brought pleasure to myself, it was simply a gesture of comfort inspired by nothing and no one in particular. And while longing for the touch of another was something with which I was far too familiar, the desire for a man in my bed was as foreign a thing as I could imagine. I suddenly recalled a particularly ignorant maid at one of the hotels, Darlene Something-or-other. She rode me incessantly about my lack of luck with the fellows. One day, with all the other maids sitting around the break table, she called me a queer one, hurled it at me as if it were something heinous and unholy. I had no way of knowing if what she said about me was true, as I had no experience with women either. But Annie Malone's touch was an initiation of my body, and a revelation of my heart. A long-overdue acknowledgement of what I'd always known. "Better late than never," the squid said. I thought it was only half right—earlier would have been far preferable—but I was too content to argue.

I woke to the glare of a white sun. Dank, humid air had drifted in through the open windows overnight and taken over the room. I was an oily mess, lotion and sweat slicked together from head to toe. Annie was sleeping soundly beside me, strands of black hair plastered to her forehead. I thought of lifting the hair away with my finger, but I didn't want to risk waking her. I needed a little time before I looked her in the eye again, just long enough to gird myself against betraying any or all of what I'd felt last night. I rose, almost supple and released from the seizure, and soaped myself under the cool spray of the shower until my skin squeaked.

Angela appeared with Stevie in tow just as we were finishing breakfast. We'd never be friends, she and I, but it appeared that we had wandered into a workable truce. She was not made more pleasant by the oppressive weather, though, and Annie saw refuge for us all in a day by the water.

The breeze off the ocean was enough to cut through the haze of heat. Annie and I skipped the dory and plopped down on two folding lawn chairs. Angela busied herself slathering sunscreen on Stevie. I quietly asked Annie if she was all right after her first real brush with caring for my broken-down body.

"Nothing to it. Easy-peasy," she said to the sea.

"Annie, look at me."

"I'll get used to it," she said as her eyes filled with tears.

Angela stopped tending to Stevie and turned toward her mother. "What's wrong with you?"

"Nothing. Menopause," Annie said.

"That's because you refuse to take any hormones. I've told you a hundred times to—"

"Angela, I don't need any bloody hormones. I'm growing this moustache on purpose. It makes me look powerful. Isn't that right, Frances?"

"Absolutely. You look like you could bench-press a truck," I said.

"Exactly," Annie said. "Christ, it's hot. I don't remember it ever being this hot here. It's supposed to be like this all weekend."

Angela walked with Stevie toward the water. I watched them frolic in the waves and realized that Edie might get her wish after all.

17

Annie and I had had a sleepless night, hers made fitful by the heat, mine made doubly so by the added misery of a blinding headache topped off with several bouts of vomiting. We were slumped at the kitchen table trying to revive ourselves with tall glasses of iced tea when Edie appeared in the doorway looking crisp and cool, a cheery daisy among the wilted weeds.

Annie managed a limp hand-flap for a greeting as I stood and drew Edie to me. She was buzzing with something, radiating an energy that was new. Ah yes, I thought, the boy.

"Hey, Frances," she whispered in my ear.

"Hey, sweet girl," I whispered back.

"Okay, I'm going to leave you two to catch up," Annie said. "A cold shower is the only way out of this mess."

"Nice to see you again, Annie."

"You too, kid," she called out over her shoulder as she shuffled off down the hall.

I pushed Edie back and looked her over. "You look wonderful. Sit. I'll make you some food."

"I'm fine, really."

"A smoothie, then. I have all the fruit you like just waiting for you."

Edie moaned about her mother as I gathered and washed the fruit, both of us slipping easily back into our old routine. I don't know what happened next, but I was suddenly standing in a sea of purple sludge. A huge glob fell from my hair and landed with a loud splat on the floor. Edie and Annie stood stupefied in the doorway. Annie was wearing different clothes and her hair was wet. I was completely confused. I knew something had gone horribly wrong in that kitchen, but I wasn't sure what exactly, or what it had to do with me.

Annie spoke first. "Jesus God alive. What fresh hell is this now?"

Edie turned to Annie. "I went to the bathroom for, like, two minutes."

I remembered. I was making a drink for Edie.

Annie picked up the lid for the blender off the counter and shook it at me. "You forgot the top, you fool." She laughed and began wiping down the counter. "Edie, in that closet behind you is a mop and a bucket. Sit her down, then make yourself useful."

I watched them deal with my mayhem. They were laughing together now, but I'd seen it, the brief look that passed between them, the alarm in Edie's eyes. I knew what they were thinking but would never say. Poor old Frances, her mind is gone. For anyone else it would've been a silly mistake, but for me, a typically meticulous woman with a head full of tumour and a bloodstream full of narcotics, it was an undeniable sign of what was coming. The squid in the room.

I cleaned myself up and Annie went off to sweet-talk Mrs. Dillon out of a few more jars of jam. Edie and I settled on the couch for a proper chat. There was no more mention of my mishap, only talk of Edie's boyfriend, Tareq. She showed me a picture of him on her phone. A dark, thin face, a halo of black curls, gleaming white teeth. He was unquestionably striking, but this was no boy—this was a full-grown man, with dark chest hair poking up from beneath his shirt, and my heart revved up a little.

"He's like a movie star," I said, then paused for a few seconds. "Now, he looks to be a bit older than you."

"He's only eighteen, well, nineteen next month. He's from Syria. He and his family came over a few years ago. He speaks four languages and he's going to study international development. He wants to focus on refugee issues."

"As long as he's treating you well, he's squared with me. Have your parents met him yet?"

"No. I'm waiting for the right moment, I guess. I'm worried Mom will start in on him, ask him all sorts of awkward questions. Then she'll start in on me about his age, you know what I mean?"

I knew very well, but from what I'd heard, she'd have a hard go finding fault with him. He'd left a war-torn country, adapted to a new one, excelled in school, and secured multiple scholarships for university. His family sounded warm and welcoming, and he appeared to be meeting my high standards of care for Edie. If that didn't impress Liz Cleary, there were always his good looks to fall back on. I knew he wouldn't be the One—there'd be a string of equally compelling fellows after him—but he was the one to whom Edie would turn for comfort when I died. I picked up her phone for another look. I stared at the handsome face with the bright smile and willed him to see her through.

Annie and I weren't up for much activity. Edie took pity on us and satisfied herself with lounging around with the two rundown housecats. We fed her and laughed at her stories of adolescent hijinks until the sun melted down below the horizon. Only then did we venture outdoors. The evening air was still thick and close, settling in my chest alongside the smoke I inhaled. Edie was unusually silent when the cigarettes came out. She stood at a safe distance as I lit a second, watching me closely but without judgment, and I knew she'd shifted into acceptance. Her phone rang and she strolled around barefoot in the grass, laughing and tossing her hair in a way I'd never seen before, an intricate reflex triggered by the sound of Tareq's voice.

I relented to Annie's limit of one whisky. If the weather held, Edie wouldn't rest until I was waist-deep in the ocean with her in the morning, and I couldn't afford another night like the one before. I went to bed early, took my pills, and waited for sleep, but all that came was a short medicinal doze and a hard snap back to heightened alertness. Death was all around me again, prodding me into a tailspin of terror. I turned on the lamp, sat on the edge of the bed, tried to breathe and slow my heart and settle the ruckus in my head. A splash of cold water on my face. Slow turns around the room. Television on, then off again. Another splash of cold water. When I felt I could take no more, I opened the door and went to Angela's old room. Edie was sitting up in the bed tapping away on her phone.

"Oh good, you're awake," I said.

"What's wrong? Are you sick?"

"No, just restless. Keep me company?"

"Sure." She typed out a final message and followed me down the hall.

We lay side by side under a single sheet, sweating while the fan in the corner whirred the humid air around the room.

"Edie, will you do me a favour?"

"Of course. Anything."

I reached under my pillow and pulled out the musty book. "Read this to me."

She edged a little closer and turned to page one. I breathed in the familiar scent of her skin and hair, listened to her soft, sweet voice as she delivered the words of my girlhood, and slept.

"FRANCES! FOR THE LOVE of God, come on. Edie is going to melt in that car." Annie was yelling from the porch, her patience dwindling by the second.

"I'm coming. One more minute."

"Time and tide, old woman."

I heard the front door close as I took a last spin in front of the mirror. I didn't own a bathing suit, hadn't owned one since I was a girl. The one I was wearing, a strappy hot-pink one-piece, was a cast-off of Angela's. Good Christ, what a sight I was. All knobs and gnarls and crepey skin. Jutting bones and sunken cavities. Flappy breasts hanging behind pink moulded cups. I pulled on a tank top and a tattered pair of white cotton shorts, also courtesy of Angela, that allowed my pink bum to come shining through.

I slid into the passenger seat, the car finally cooled from the blasting air-conditioning, and Annie looked me over.

"Your top is on backwards."

I looked down. So it was. And inside out to boot. I pulled it off and rested it on my lap, unsure of exactly how to get it on right.

"Well, I was rushing now, wasn't I? I'll put it on when we get there. Are we going or not?"

The shore was crowded, half the town drawn down to the water for relief from the remarkable heat. The old dory was overrun with youngsters, and it irritated me to see them climbing on it, dripping ice cream on the seat, rocking it with their sticky hands. I glared at them as we passed and got a grubby middle finger thrust at me in return. The sound of the crowd mixed with the crash of the surf was painfully amplified and overwhelming, and I made us trudge to the end of the rocky beach, as far away from the hordes as possible.

We set up our folding chairs, cracked open the small cooler filled with drinks and sandwiches, and took in the frenzied spectacle of an island summer. Soon enough the cold winds would rage, sleet would coat the trees of the surrounding woods, mammoth chunks of ice would break off glaciers and lodge just offshore, but today there was only sunscreen and bare feet and bodies on proud display.

"Just look at them, will you? Not a mark on them," Annie said as three lithe young women walked out of the water toward their admiring boyfriends. "Oh, I remember the power of that."

I turned toward Edie. "Annie was always the queen of the shore. She was the Raquel Welch of Safe Harbour."

"Who's Raquel Welch?" Edie asked.

Annie rolled her eyes. "Someone who wishes she was as gorgeous as I was back in the day. I was a knockout, Edie, and let me tell you, I knew it. I milked it for all it was worth and then some. Anyway, those days are long gone."

Not quite. Annie still looked every bit the bathing beauty. Her body had weathered time far better than mine. Apart from the softness of her middle and the faint silvery lines that came with childbearing, she looked much the same as I remembered. Sturdy limbs with muscles held tightly in place by smooth unblemished skin that easily took up the sun. Dainty feet and hands with perfectly shaped nails. I saw men looking at her with approving glances—that hadn't changed one bit. What had changed was that she didn't seem to care.

Edie pulled out her phone. "Yesss!" She pumped her fist for effect. "Ladies, the temperature is a balmy twenty-nine degrees. Frances, you're going in." She pulled off her T-shirt and stepped out of her shorts. She was wearing a sleek black swimsuit made more for athletes than pin-up girls, all business. "Come on, get up! A deal's a deal, right, Annie?"

"Go on, Frances. It'll do you good. I'll watch you both from the cheap seats and film the blessed event for the evening news. The Old Woman and the Sea." She gave me an abrupt nod of encouragement.

I uncovered my pink splendour and took Edie's hand. The stones burned under my feet until I felt the first rush of the cold Atlantic over my toes. I yanked down on Edie's hand hard. She turned to me, alarmed.

"You don't want to go in?"

"This water and I have a lot of history. Just give me a minute."

I took a few halting steps, my feet slipping and sliding over the rounded rocks. The sea pushed against my knees, and slimy tendrils of seaweed wrapped around my ankles. The squid leaned forward, an eyebrow arched in interest. I waded in up to my waist. Another step and a wave against my chest. A splash of salt against my lips. When the next wave rushed toward me, I let go of Edie's hand, inhaled deeply, and surrendered. I tumbled under and over, limp and powerless until my body remembered the movements needed to propel me forward through the green murk, past the rocky shoal, and into the clear, deep water. I raised my arms above my head and sank down into the cool silence, waiting and listening until the last second of breath was spent, then burst up through the surface gasping for air. I faced the horizon, closed my eyes, and listened once again for the call from the deep to join the dead. I heard nothing but my panting breaths, the wailing gulls, and a gentle round of applause from the squid.

I was overcome with the beauty of it all—the bracing cold, the shimmering sunlight, the rhythmic rocking to and fro as I lay on my back smiling at the sky. All around me water quenching an unbelievable thirst I didn't even know I had. I'd faced it down and won, my prize this homecoming I now knew I deserved. I couldn't recall a moment in my life when I'd felt more alive—blissfully, intensely so. I was carefree and bound by nothing. *Buoyant*.

I drifted along until I felt the sun and salt burning my face, then I paddled toward the shore, where two women—one young and thin and fair-haired, the other older, shapely with dark curls—stood laughing and waving and calling my name. They looked happy, whoever they were.

18

It was the heat, they said. The heat and the exertion. The shock of the sea. Painkillers, fatigue, dehydration—every remotely plausible excuse was offered up for why it had taken me a few minutes to recognize Annie and Edie, every explanation save the obvious one.

I had stumbled toward them in a state of near ecstasy after my reunion with the ocean. They looked friendly, but beyond that I knew nothing of them. I introduced myself, and a great deal of chaos ensued. The girl looked terrified and the woman vexed. They said their names over and over, asked me to say mine as well as the name of the town. They led me to a chair, wrapped me in a towel, rubbed my shoulders, and gave me water to drink. At no point had I shared their concern, at least not that I recall. It was while they were hovering that it all came back to me. Annie and Edie. All was well, although you would never have known it judging by the state of those two. At the time, despite their opinions and some pretty compelling evidence to the contrary, I thought my mind was clearer than it had ever been, unfettered by worry, all my nervous energy dissolved and dispelled. True, I was worked up—breathless, heart racing, flushed and distracted—though to me it was nothing more than joy run amok.

The car ride home was a silent affair. I sat in the back seat, not perturbed in the slightest. In fact, quite the opposite. The squid would have to hiccup harder than that to knock loose what I'd found. Even the sight of the church did nothing to dent my mood. It occurred to me that other people felt like this all the time. They spent days, months, even years awash with contentment. I'm not sure I would have known what to do with myself had it come before now. All I knew for sure was the sun on my face, the voices of my friends in the car, the comforts waiting for me at Annie's house, and a whole ocean with nothing to say to me but "Welcome home."

Edie headed off to the shower, and I'd started down the hall to do the same when Annie laid her hand on my forearm.

"We need to talk about what happened."

"I told you, I'm fine."

"Frances, you didn't know who we were."

"For five minutes. Look, I had just had a big moment out there in the water. Some sort of healing experience or whatever."

She gave me a quizzical look and pointed two fingers at her head. "As in healing your cancer?"

"No, not that. Like a healing of the soul. Oh, I don't know how to describe it." I raised my hands in the air, closed my eyes, and swayed. "I saw the face of God."

"You need to see the face of the doctor."

I dropped my arms and took her hands in mine. "Annie, I'm joking."

"You're calling the doctor."

"To say what exactly? That I'm forgetful? To which she will say, 'Well, that's what you get for growing a big tumour in your head.'"

"Maybe there's another pill or something. What do I know?" She leaned in and lowered her voice. "Frances, she was scared to death."

"All right, I'll talk to her later."

"And maybe you need to lie down for a bit, hey?"

"That's what I don't need. I couldn't sleep if you paid me. I feel too good. Honestly, I do." I grabbed her by the shoulders. "Did you see me in that water today? I'm telling you, I can't remember when I ever felt this good."

"Okay, okay," she laughed. "Far be it from me to go up against that. But you'll talk to Edie, right?"

"Yes, as I said only seconds ago. Now may I go shower?"

She tossed her head toward my bedroom door and wagged a finger in my face. "But no whisky tonight."

I turned away from her and walked down the hall smiling. Good luck with that one, Mother Malone.

BY SUPPERTIME, THE TWO of them appeared to have fretted it out. Edie was her usual chatty self as we sat at the outside table, me with a whisky in one hand, a smoke in the other, Annie with her hands in the air, resigned to letting me be as she went inside to tackle the dishes.

"Edie, about today," I said.

"Yeah, that was pretty weird, right?" She smiled weakly and twisted at the waist slightly, as if she were trying to lean out of an unwanted touch.

"I know you were scared. I know I forgot your name, but I remember the look on your face."

"I was just worried, that's all."

"What were you worried about?"

She didn't answer.

"There's no way around this. You know that."

"It's just that you seem fine. You don't even look sick."

A thick tear slid down her face and dripped from her jaw onto the table. I reached over and swept my fingertips across her cheek.

"Well, I take a lot of drugs. A lot."

"And maybe that's what happened. Maybe you took too many."

"You're right, it could have been the drugs or the heat—all those things you and Annie said may very well have played a role in it. But the most likely cause is this thing in my head." I knocked against my skull. "Edie, love, my eyesight is failing, my legs are weak, my balance comes and goes. I'm exhausted all the time, plus the seizures, and now my memory. This is the evolution of it. The natural course of things."

"I don't like it."

"You and me both. But if I put all the problems aside, I can tell you this: I have never felt better than I did today. Being out in that water—my God, it was something. And you gave me that. You took my hand and led me to it. That's quite a gift. I'll never forget it. And you shouldn't either."

"Frances, trust me, I won't forget any of this."

She passed me a cigarette and lit it for me, then stepped out into the grass. She did three perfect cartwheels, then stood grinning with the setting sun aglow behind her. I'd never seen her look so lovely, this half-child, half-woman living in harmony in one body. Surely she'd been blessed with the stuff that money could and couldn't buy, her destiny laid out long before I came around, but I indulged myself with the knowledge that, however small and insignificant, I'd had a hand in moulding this magnificent creature, and going to the great beyond with that in my heart was what I'd been blessed with.

Edie's phone rang. She raced back to the table to answer her call. She mouthed "Tareq" at me and strolled back out to the centre of the lawn.

Annie plopped down into the chair across from me. "My Jesus, I'm worn out. Pour me one too. A big one." She downed a glug and smacked her lips. "Oh, that's the stuff. Look at herself, will you? I assume by the riot of giggling and hair flipping that she's talking to the boyfriend. Christ, she's all in, poor trout. No idea that the takeoff won't be worth the crash landing. Ah well, so it goes. You know, people always say, 'If I knew then,' and all that, but I bet I still would've leapt off all the cliffs I did."

"You can't fight your nature," I said. "But do you really regret leaping at Anthony?"

"Ah, I don't know. Regrets like that are hard once children are in the mix."

"I was thinking about that day by the car when you said you thought you got married to rub the stain of me off you."

She winced and swirled her whisky before raising the glass to her lips for another large, loud swallow. "That was a stupid, cruel thing to say, and a bloody lie. The truth of it is, I think you were some sort of compass for me, someone who would always stop me from straying too far off course. I never knew how much I relied on you until you were gone, although I expect not even you could've talked me out of that wedding dress. Maybe my life would have been wildly different or maybe it would've played out exactly the same. At any rate, I've come to see it was nobody's doing but my own." She reached for a cigarette, took a deep drag, and watched Edie pace around the grass for a few moments. "What's that saying? The heart wants what it wants or something like that."

"Think you'll get married again?"

She scoffed. "Married? Good God, Frances, I'm not sure I'll even get laid again."

"What are you getting on with? Sure look at you. You're prettier than half the women on television."

She tossed her hair and smiled. "You'll find no argument from me on that one, but there's no one around here worth my time, that's for damn sure. Truthfully, I just can't be bothered. The whole song and dance of it, you know?"

"How do you mean?"

"Well, it's all a big show, isn't it? All the primping and posing. Look at Angela. Fake suntan, fake eyelashes. All her friends are the same. Walking around Safe Harbour with bald pussies, the lot of them. If you ask any one of them, they'll say they do it for themselves. But who in God's name gets scalding wax spread over their hoo-ha just for themselves?"

"Do you?"

"Do I what?'

"Wax your hoo-ha?"

"Frances, you couldn't pay me enough. But I've done my share of foolishness. I've got more lingerie than I know what to do with. God knows how much money I've spent on hair dye and makeup over the years. And how many times I opened my legs just to try to keep Anthony from straying. I'd be run ragged with the kids and he'd come home half in the bag looking for a bit, and I'd let him have it and fake my way through it. He'd lie back like he'd just given me the world, and I'd lie and tell him he was marvellous. I'm making it sound like the problem with us was all about the sex, but that was the least of it. I just don't think he was ever interested in me. As a person, I mean."

I had no idea what to say to her, no point of reference to speak about the nuances of marriage. All I could think to say was one thing I knew for sure. "Well, he's an idiot."

"Yeah, but it's not just him, though, is it? Remember Sharon Gulliver? She was two years behind us in school. She and I were great friends for years and then she moved to Toronto. Her husband died a while back, and last year I went up to see her. She'd just started seeing this man, and wasn't she doing all the same shit, including the waxing. Fifty-odd years old and talking about getting breast implants. And I thought, At what age does all that end? I asked her what they talked about, and she couldn't come up with a single worthwhile conversation they'd ever had. Anyway, she decided to set me up with her boyfriend's buddy. Nice enough guy, good-looking, successful, and I think, What the hell, right? We have a lovely dinner, he seems keen on getting to know me, asking me all about my past, what I want in life now, and so on. We go back to his place, have a few drinks, fall into bed. And then doesn't he tell me that he needs a porn flick on to get off. Not before, mind you—during. And what do I do? I smile and say fine. He finishes in three minutes flat, and before his dick is dry, he starts talking about an early meeting and next thing I'm in a cab. Never heard from him after. I mean, if that's what's next for me, I'd rather go to bed with a cheese-and-bacon sandwich and a bottle of wine."

I laughed. "I'm sorry, it's not funny. You just haven't found the right person yet. Someone you can just be yourself with."

"Nah, I'm done with it. I like me better without a man around. Although I am thinking of getting a new vibrator. One that loves me for me. Anyway, I feel like I'm always talking about myself. How are you doing?"

"Dizzy, weak, tired, constant headache. All in all, not too bad for being half-dead."

"Did you talk to Edie?"

"Yeah, she's okay." I looked in Edie's direction. She was still on the phone. "Tareq heals all wounds, as you can see."

"What say we go out tomorrow night? Edie leaves in the morning, right? We'll have a lazy day, get you rested up, then we'll head down to the pub for a drink. There'll be a bit of music on the go."

"Tear up the town?"

"Exactly. Come on, it'll do you good."

"All right. But I want to do up a bit. Not for anyone else, just for me. But no waxing. I'll let the old hoo-ha run free."

"That's the spirit."

EDIE DECIDED WHAT I would wear for my night out, then she read me to sleep again. She was still next to me in the bed in the morning, her clothes rumpled, her hair matted to the side of her head. I watched her sleep, marvelling at her kindness in choosing me over Tareq for a weekend—an eternity for two kids just discovering each other. A few hours later, we stood hugging in the driveway and again I let Edie pull away first.

"So you're sure you've got the FaceTime down, right?" she asked.

"Yes. We'll try it out tomorrow night. Don't forget to send me a picture of you and Tareq together. And be careful. You know what I mean."

"Don't worry about me. Just look after yourself. I'll be back in a few weeks, okay?"

I managed not to cry when she left, but I almost bit clear through the side of my cheek holding it in. I figured it might be her last sight of me, so I smiled and waved and stood up straight, doing my best to look serene and elegant. I spent the rest of the day in bed, where in between naps the tears flowed.

By early evening, the heat and humidity had broken, the air cleansed and cool and fresh once again. Annie made us a light supper, then disappeared into her bedroom to get ready. She strutted into my room, a ghost from my youth in her tight jeans and a fitted pink T-shirt, lip gloss and shiny hair.

"Annie Malone, the gods have smiled upon you."

She was holding a small red makeup bag. She cupped my chin in her hand, swept soft brushes over my cheeks and eyelids, coated my eyelashes with mascara, and dabbed fruity balm on my lips with her fingertips.

"There. That's better," she said and led me toward the mirror.

From what I could see, she was right. It was better, but still only a thin veneer over a truth that no amount of makeup could conceal. The hollowed cheeks and the sallow skin fighting against the vibrant powders. I briefly wondered if I was grotesque. Then realized I didn't care.

The Seahorse Tavern was an old whitewashed house near the shore. In my youth it was someone's home, but it had been made over into the local watering hole. There was a painted wooden sign that swung in the wind and a door the colour of candy apples. Inside, the hanging glass globes cast a warm yellow glow over the distressed wooden floors and panelled walls. High stools with cognac-coloured leather stretched over the seats were lined up in front of a dark wooden bar lacquered to a mirror shine. I suspected all of it was a calling card of some city slicker. If not for the southern shore accents I heard all around me and the smell of ale and battered fish, I never would have known I was home.

As we passed, Annie waved and nodded to folks, a few of whom looked familiar to me, but she didn't stop until we reached the bar. I could feel the eyes of the patrons on me, and for a fleeting moment my nerves started to spark, a brief jolt that flickered and extinguished before it could catch and do any damage. A young man with gingery hair and freckled forearms was pulling drafts.

"Hiya, Mrs. Rideout. What's your pleasure tonight?"

"Christopher, I'm not Mrs. Rideout anymore, and you're old enough to be calling me Annie now. Two whisky sours, please. This is my friend Frances. She grew up here once upon a time."

"Ah, welcome back," he said and extended a meaty hand for me to shake.

Behind us, two men sat by a stone fireplace, one on the fiddle, the other on the accordion, pumping out the old standards. I turned around so I could see them. No one was paying much attention, but I couldn't take my eyes off them. They weren't the best I'd ever heard, but it didn't matter. Their songs were memory; my mother and father were alive and breathing in every note they played. I closed my eyes and the music flowed through me like a lovely cool breeze.

Annie elbowed me in the ribs, handed me another drink, and nodded at a short, paunchy man coming toward us. His hair hung in dry thin wisps that brushed the collar of his shirt. He teetered slightly as he walked, clearly a few drinks ahead of us. His skin was ruddy and thickened, and he smiled, showing his sharp yellowed teeth.

Annie dropped her head and muttered, "Oh, Jesus, here he comes. Safe Harbour's most eligible bachelor."

"Annie, Annie, Annie," he said. "Gorgeous as always, I see."

"Half-cut already, I see," Annie said.

"Ah, go on, I'm only having a bit of fun. Who's this with you now?"

Annie turned away from him and kept her eyes on me. "Frances, this is Donny Doyle."

I gave him a nod and turned back toward the players. Donny called out for the bartender to bring us two drinks on him, but Annie said we were all right. I got up and asked Christopher to point me toward the bathroom, then I walked to the back of the tavern. I lingered in the stall, wondering if I'd been gone long enough for Donny to take his leave. When I got back to the bar, he'd taken my stool.

"Up you get now, Donny," Annie said. "Give the lady her seat back."

He stood but didn't move far enough away that I could sit down without brushing against him. Annie handed me a fresh drink, and I turned my back to Donny.

"Where's she from?" he asked Annie.

"That's Frances Delaney, you old fart. From school. The smart one."

"Ah, right. Turn around so I has a better look at you."

I gave him a brief glance over my shoulder, and he nodded.

"Right on. I got you now," he said.

I jumped when he put his hand on my arm.

"Weren't you the one that went with my cousin Michael that time? That night out at the old shed?"

"All right, Donny," Annie said. "Frances and I got some lady business to chat about, so best move on now, hey?"

"Oh, Annie, remember that night? Now that was a good time."

He clamped his hands down on Annie's thighs, made a thrusting motion with his pelvis, and leaned in to kiss her. Annie raised her hand to push him away, and before I knew what was happening, I'd thrown my drink in his face, cherry and all.

"Jesus, woman," he shouted and staggered back. "What the fuck is wrong with you?"

Annie stared at me, mouth agape, as Donny stomped toward the bathroom. Then she burst out laughing and slung her arm around my shoulder. I reached for some napkins to wipe down the bar and stammered an apology to Christopher for the mess I'd made.

"Proper thing, missus. The man's a bloody menace," he said and mixed me another drink. "This one's on the house."

WE GOT HOME JUST after eleven. Annie was right about the night out doing me good. My body was done in, but my spirits were high. I had just climbed into bed when she appeared in the doorway with a tub of chocolate ice cream and two spoons. We lay in silence, watching an old black-and-white movie that we both loved but couldn't remember the name of, and I knew that everything wrong between us had finally loosened and separated, the last of the clogging silt and sticky muck of the past washed away. We're clean, I thought, as my eyelids grew heavy. I had just begun to slip under when she rolled me onto my side. She slowly brought her face toward mine and kissed me. Her lips were soft and cold, and she tasted of whisky and chocolate. She drew back and scanned my face carefully, then moved toward me again. She brought her lips to mine and opened her mouth, then parted my lips with her tongue and moved it slowly into my mouth. She made a small sound, a breathy sigh, and suddenly I was wide awake, every cell in my body flipping and turning. My heart raced as I was engulfed by a wave of heat.

I laid my hand against the centre of her chest. "Annie, wait. What are you doing?"

She pulled off her nightgown and tossed it on the floor. "Leaping off a cliff."

I closed my eyes and tumbled after her.

19

Through the window I could see the milky pink dawn and I hadn't yet had a moment of sleep. I spent the night reliving what had passed between us, which bore no likeness to anything I'd ever seen on a page or screen. No throwing back of heads or gnashing of teeth. No daring skills had been put into play. Just two girls locked in older women's bodies fumbling about in the dark without a map. Glorious, nonetheless. When we'd finally unwound from each other, I lay on my back, weak and spent, so free it felt like flying.

Now Annie was sleeping soundly beside me. I reached out and held a clump of her black curls in my hand and wondered what she'd think of it all once the light of the sun shone on us both. I wondered if she would see it as I did, a sort of primitive ritual that served a deeply evolved purpose. How, if only for a few hours, she'd taken my grief and I hers, and somewhere in the tangle of hands and feet and everything in between, it all got cancelled out. I also wondered if I'd gambled with the larger purpose—that she'd wake to repulsion and shame, deem it a last-minute act of madness and mercy, then be relieved to be rid of me.

She stirred beside me and I quietly left the bed in search of my overdue pills. When I came back, she stretched like a lazy cat and smiled, and I exhaled the breath I hadn't realized I'd been holding.

"Frances, I'd say we've crossed the Rubicon. Crossed it and burned every bridge behind us."

She held out her hand and I held it loosely in mine. I tried to speak and failed.

She raised her other hand and rested it against my cheek. "You don't need to say anything. Just breathe. Just sit and breathe, okay? And I'll go rustle up some food."

I sat and breathed for a while, then joined Annie outside, where she'd laid out the breakfast. She wolfed down a mound of fluffy scrambled eggs, tossed her fork against her plate, and laughed to herself.

"I'm telling you, I can't get the vision of Donny Doyle dripping in whisky out of my head. For the rest of my days, whenever I'm feeling low, I'll think of that and smile. God knows he had it coming."

"He hasn't aged well. I'd say you were lucky to have dodged that bullet."

"I dodged nothing. That arsehole was never in the running. Can't hold down a job. His looks are long gone, and still he's out grabbing on to any woman in his way. All balls and no brains. I suppose he's more to be pitied than blamed." She swigged her tea and reached for the cigarettes. "Jesus, look at me, smoking like a tilt. Once you're gone, I'm going to have to quit this mess all over again." Her face fell. "Oh, Frances, I'm sorry. Oh my God. Just smack me. I didn't mean it the way—"

"It's nothing," I said. And I meant it. It was nothing. Not so much what she said, but death itself. Nothing but a uniquely dependable thing in this life that inexplicably blindsided us every time. And the closer I came to joining all those who'd gone before me, the more I knew how completely mundane it was. I would've liked to talk to her of such things, but what use was deathbed philosophy to a woman whose child had been smashed to bits? I waved away her concern. "Please don't worry about saying stuff like that."

"I didn't mean to come off so insensitive, especially after last night."

My skin began to sear. Oh, Annie, Annie, please let us return to the far more comfortable matter of my death. I had no idea of how to carry on after such intimacy. Was one expected to chat casually about goosebumps and nipples held gently between teeth, about fleshy wet recesses and the slipping in of fingers and tongues? Was it rude to speak of it, or ruder still to say nothing at all? My head began to spin, and I settled on politesse and gratitude.

"Yes, last night. I wanted to thank you for such a lovely time," I said.

"Listen to you. So formal. I can't say I've ever had anyone thank me for sex before. At any rate, you're welcome. It *was* lovely, wasn't it?"

"You've no regrets, then?"

"My dear Frances," she said, "I've had many a morning after filled with regret, but trust me, this is not one of them."

I picked at my breakfast and kept my eyes on my plate. "Tell me something, and be honest. Did you do those things with me out of pity?"

She took a sip of tea and lowered her cup to the table. "Yeah, I think I did."

Getting the answer I knew was coming did nothing to lessen the sting of it. Still, I smiled. "Well, don't put any gloss on it now. Give it to me straight."

She smiled back. "It sounds bad, but it's not. I'm the one who started it, and yes, I did so because I felt sorry for you. But thinking on it now, I also felt sorry for me." Her expression took a turn toward wistful, and she finished her tea before speaking again. "I don't believe I've ever once shared my body with someone who loved me. I mean really loved me. Not Anthony or any other fool I've rolled around with. And I guess I just wanted to see what that felt like. But now you tell me something—this thing you have for me, is it new or has it always been there?"

"What do you mean?"

"This love for me."

I looked at her face and every moment I ever spent with her spooled out in my mind. I thought of the years with her, the years without her, how she'd always been with me in some form or another. "Of course I love you. I always have."

"No, I mean exactly how long have you been *in* love with me?"

The tea in my cup rippled from the trembling of my hand. The squid leaned in, impatiently tapping a tentacle. I closed my eyes. "I can't remember a time when I wasn't."

I don't know what I expected—astonishment, anger, disgust—but when I opened my eyes, I got none of it. If anything, she looked flattered and hugely satisfied with herself.

"You're not even remotely surprised, are you?"

"Why should I be? Half the men in this town are crazy about me, and now I'm wondering if half the women might be dreaming of a night in my bed. I first twigged it the other day, when you said something about not fighting your nature. Then I thought back to how the minute I told you Anthony was talking about marriage, that was it—you were gone. Then last night at the pub. You defending my honour like a lover. Pieces of the great puzzle snapping together all over the place. Anyway, I love you too, Frances. Maybe not in quite the same way, but love all the same. And pity or no, I wanted to do what we did last night, and I bloody well enjoyed myself. I've been lonely and miserable for years, and today I feel reborn. I really do."

She leaned back in her chair and raised her face to the sun. "It was so different from what I've had with men. Softer, slower. None of the grunting and jackhammering they're so fond of. And how is it that they all seem to have no idea whatsoever how to touch a breast? Odds are you'd find at least one who didn't go in for the grab and twist."

"I wouldn't know."

"Not if you're sleeping with women, I suppose."

"I wouldn't know anything about that either."

She snapped upright. "Surely there've been other women before me?"

I shook my head. "Don't make fun now."

"No, no, I would never. I just can't imagine a whole life without it. I suppose the good news is that makes me the best you've ever had."

Angela walked through the patio door with Stevie in her arms. "What are you two laughing about?"

"You're just in time," Annie said. "We're talking about sex."

"Mother, please."

"Frances, as you can see, my daughter is quite the prude. Never mind that she's holding the by-product of sex in her arms."

"I'm not a prude. I just wonder how good a topic it is for the breakfast table."

Annie shook her head. "Here, pass me my grandson before he gets infected by your Victorian ways." She rested Stevie flat on her thighs and rocked him back and forth.

"How are you, Frances?" Angela said.

"Not bad, thanks."

"Not bad!" Annie said. "You should have seen her down at the Seahorse last night. Didn't she toss a drink right in Donny Doyle's face. Him standing there soaked with a maraschino cherry stuck to his head."

"Annie," I said, "don't be telling Angela that."

"I won't be the only one telling her. You've been away in the city too long, Frances. Everyone in town will know about that by lunchtime. I bet she's heard that story twice already today."

"Only once," Angela said. "Grocery store."

"Ha, what did I tell you?" Annie laughed and made goofy faces at Stevie.

"Well," I sniffed, "he deserved it. Grabbing at your mother."

"I'm sure my mother probably had something to do with that."

"Easy, Angela," I said. "Your mother was just minding her own business."

"Don't pay any attention to her. She just likes to get a rise out of me, which she will fail miserably at today. Isn't that right, Stevie?" She held the baby above her head and made kissing sounds at him.

"Mom, don't hold him high like that. He'll spit up."

Annie handed Stevie back to her daughter and gave me a weary glance. "Angela, what can I do for you today?"

"I was hoping you'd watch him for a couple of hours. I'm going to get my hair and nails done."

"Off you go. I'll try not to corrupt him in your absence."

Angela turned and left without so much as a word of thanks, and I thought maybe she needed a drink thrown at her as well. That poor youngster having to grow up with the likes of Angela, and poor Annie having to love her. If she were mine, I doubted the ability to summon my heart toward her. Then again, who was I to have any say on the skills required for mothering.

◇◇◇◇◇◇

THAT NIGHT, I HAD a dream about my daughter, a teenage version of her. We were sitting together in the Sisters of Mercy Home. She made me a grilled cheese sandwich, then cartwheeled out of the kitchen. I woke in the middle of the night whispering her name, then stiffened into another seizure. It came and went faster than the others but left me with a searing headache that eclipsed the ones before it. I had to call out for Annie to bring me my pills.

She slept beside me once again, and as the pain began to recede, I could feel the squid gathering strength, stretching and growing in length and girth, its suckers clamping down on the pulpy ridges of my brain. No longer a whispering cartoon character in cute costumes but a growling monster bred for destruction. I squeezed my eyes shut, put my hands over my ears, and pressed my lips together just to keep it from bursting into the room. My chest grew tight and the little air I drew in felt dry and dusty. I got up and stumbled around looking for clothes, then made my way down the hall and out the back door into the cool, windless night. I stood under the black sky, the uncountable stars, the sliver of yellow moon, then limped around the grass in my bare feet, damp blades poking up between my toes. I spied my cigarettes on the table but had no appetite for them. I went back into the house and squinted at the clock on the kitchen wall. Quarter to twelve. My arms and legs were rubbery, and I sat on one of the wooden chairs wondering what to do with myself. I was freezing one minute and burning up the next. My skin itched and stung as if I'd been baking in the sun. Water. I needed water. I walked to the front door, pushed my feet into my sneakers, and stepped outside. I started walking, using the edge of the pavement to guide me along through the dark night. I don't know how much time passed before a car pulled up alongside me. I heard the whirr of the window going down.

"Now where might you be headed this time of night?"

The taxi driver. Name begins with a C. He was leaning across the seat and smiling at me through the passenger window.

"The water."

"Hop in. I'll run you down. It's as black as tar out here." He pushed the door open.

"I don't have money."

"No odds. It's only five minutes down the road."

I hesitated for a moment, then got in beside him. The car smelled like beer and men's cologne.

"Frances, right? Annie Rideout's friend. Don't mind the stench. I'm just after dropping off the young fellas from the tavern. What a state they were in. They'll have fine heads on 'em come morning. Anyway, what's down at that water that you need to go this time of night?"

I shrugged and turned toward the window.

"Not the talkative sort, I see. All right, nothing wrong with that. Me, I talk too much—at least that's what my missus says. Of course, you want to hear her once she gets going. Talk the paint off a house, that one." He laughed. "Still, she's a good woman. She'd have to be to put up with the likes of me now, wouldn't she?"

The car moved at what seemed to be light speed, and my stomach lurched. I lowered the window and gulped down the night air. He stopped the car as close to the water as he could. I thanked him and closed the door. He backed the car up and pointed the headlights toward the path as he said he would, and I stumbled slowly, pitching and weaving on the rocks toward the sound of the waves. Once I reached the water's edge, I saw a flickering of orange light, a bonfire down the beach. I stood and listened. The surf against the stones and the sound of my own heavy breaths. The distant voices of the kids around the fire. Three hard barks of a dog. Then it came, muffled at first and then increasing in clarity and intensity—my father's bow across the strings, drawn-out notes scaling upwards, the low humming of my mother's voice. I closed my eyes, letting myself yield to their lure, then stepped out of my shoes, pulled off my clothes, and walked slowly into the waves. The shock of the water numbed my burning skin. I walked forward until the water flowed above my head, the cold soothing away the ache. I floated down and then I heard her calling my name. I surfaced, shivering and sputtering. "Frances," she called, her voice strong and clear. I spun my head around, scanning the darkness for her face. "Frances, I'm here."

Suddenly I was facing a blinding white light, a flurry of movement and splashing in the water. Over and over she called my name. Then she was wrapped around me, pulling me toward her. I clung to my life for a few desperate seconds, kicked and flailed against her, then gave over. I was done.

I was in a moving car again, covered with something heavy, something that scratched and scraped against the skin on my shoulders. I felt a warm weight against my left side. Annie Malone speaking.

"Now, Cyril, not a word of this to anyone. I hear so much as a whisper of it and I'm sharpening my scissors to hack off anything that dangles from your body. Do you hear me?"

"Not a peep, Annie. Swear to God," the man in the front seat said.

She opened the car door. "Come on, Frances. In we go. Take my hand."

She led me into a yellow house, tossed a pile of clothes on the floor, and then pulled the scratchy thing off me and threw that on the floor as well. A blanket. It was an old grey camp blanket. I looked down and saw that I was naked except for my shoes. Curious, that. Not like me to be out and about without clothes on. Annie walked me straight to a blue-and-white bathroom and pushed me into a hot shower. She sprayed me down with a nozzle, dried me off, put a nightgown on me, and helped me into a warm bed. Then she handed me two white pills and a glass of water.

"Here, take these."

I swallowed the pills. "Annie, did you hear it?"

"Did I hear what?"

"My father playing and my mother singing. They were in the water."

She walked to the other side of the bed, lay down beside me, and placed her hand across my forehead. "Shush. Quiet yourself. Go to sleep now. You're all right."

"I just wanted to see the water one more time."

"It will still be there tomorrow. Go to sleep."

"Thank you, Annie."

She was panting softly and slowly as she looked up to the ceiling. "You're welcome. Now close your eyes."

20

I opened my eyes and looked around the room. I recognized the faded floral sleeve of my old nightgown. I believed the bed to be my own but the blue walls to be someone else's. I knew there was no need to rise for work, but why exactly escaped me. My pillow was damp, puzzling until the memory of my jaunt to the ocean came flooding back, a memory so vivid yet so incomplete. Logistics, mostly—how I got there and how I got here. Then I knew everything. This brain of mine, slipping so spectacularly, then snapping back into action to deliver the hard truth of things so clearly.

The walk to the bathroom felt like a marathon. I startled Annie, who was sitting on the toilet, fully dressed and blowing smoke out the open window.

"Jesus, you nearly gave me a heart attack." She opened her legs and dropped the cigarette into the bowl. "I was afraid

Angela would show up and catch me, and I'm in no mood for a lecture. How are you?"

"Fading fast, apparently."

I brushed my teeth while she kept a close eye.

"Listen, I asked my doctor to come and give you a quick check."

"Annie," I pleaded.

"Don't you whine at me. You're lucky I didn't cart your naked carcass straight to the hospital last night."

"You're right, I'm sorry. Thank you for looking after me."

"You can thank me by letting Dr. Patel have a run at you."

Annie's doctor gave me the once-over. She was concerned about my blood pressure, too low. Pulse, thready and jumpy. Arms and legs, weak. Memory, patchy. In other words, nothing new to report. As she was leaving, I asked her to pass me my phone and I called my own doctor. I left a message for her to ring me back as soon as possible. I hung up and Annie stepped into the room.

"Who were you calling?"

"My doctor. How did I get back here last night?"

"Cyril thought you were a bit off. He called me to come down and see to you. The one time I'm thankful for big mouths in a small town." She sat on the edge of the bed and looked around the room. "I was thinking about setting up a table there by the armchair so we can have meals in here."

I nodded. "Good plan."

She brought me tea and toast in bed. I napped until my phone rang. Dr. Langley. I waited until the last second to answer. She told me that Annie had called her earlier that morning and filled her in on my latest adventure. She laid out a plan and I agreed. I got up, dressed, double-checked that everything was on right side out, then found Annie in the kitchen, washing a frying pan in the sink.

"Was that your doctor on the phone?" she said without turning around.

I sat at the table. "Yes."

"What did she have to say for herself?"

"The thirtieth. Ten days' time. Seven o'clock in the evening. She'll be bringing a nurse with her."

She rinsed the pan and laid it in the drainer, wiped her hands with a towel, then rested them on her hips. She stood like that for long moments, facing the window, saying nothing.

"Annie, it has to be done soon or I'll lose my ability to consent," I said. "And then where would we be?"

She turned around. "Okay," she said.

"Okay."

We sat outside in the cool fog and kept an easy silence. At first, I found a peculiar delight in knowing the exact moment of my death, a privilege not afforded to others. How many people in the world would die at that exact moment and not see it coming, all their unfinished business left dangling? I would plan my day, say my farewells, and make my tidy exit, all my affairs in order. I'd tapped the date into my calendar with a sense of cool detachment, no more feeling than if it had been an appointment for a teeth cleaning. But looking at that date on a calendar for a few fascinating moments was one thing. Living through ten days of it looming—now there was the rub.

"So what now?" Annie asked.

"More of the same, I expect."

"This is a rough business, isn't it?" she said, her voice breaking.

"Could be a lot rougher."

"You go lie down. I'll bring you some lunch in a bit."

She came with a tray of food that I left untouched while we watched television. Through the window I saw that the sky had grown dark and threatened rain. Summer's days were as numbered as my own, and I had a sudden hankering for one snowy hour before I left, sixty minutes of sparkly flakes that floated down, coating everything in sight.

Annie spent the rest of the day organizing my room. A card table with a white cloth, a portable CD player, and a thick stack of music she thought I would like. A vase of field flowers, a white plastic chair for the shower dug out from the basement (a holdover from when she'd broken her leg after a fall in the icy driveway years before), and a worn photo album filled with pictures from our glory days.

"My God, look at you. That was the day you won the English essay prize, remember that, Frances? And they made you read it at the assembly. I thought you were going to pass out you were so pale."

She flipped the pages laughing and shrieking at her outfits and hairdos. I looked back through my life and saw the happiness in it. All the Christmases and birthdays Annie and I had celebrated together. The class photos, the ones of us at school concerts and dances—all documenting the ascending stages of our growth, with Annie blossoming like a wild rose and me doing my best to grab any leftover sunlight. And in every photo, either up front and centre or lurking somewhere in the background, a priest, a nun, a hanging crucifix. The reminders of the faith we'd once been ruled by.

Annie got up and walked to the bookcase and pulled out a small blue binder. "Here. I've been saving this one."

She handed it to me, then left me alone. I opened it and gasped at the black-and-white picture of my mother and father standing side by side, squinting at the sun and smiling. It was the photo that had sat on the table beside their bed, the one taken moments after they were married. She wore a simple knee-length dress and a small round hat on her head. He wore a dark suit that hung loosely on his narrow frame, the same suit his brother had worn at his own wedding a year before. I ran my hand over the image. They were plain, the pair of them, but made beautiful by love and hope. I pulled the photo out of the binder and turned it over—"Georgina and Patrick Delaney, Wedding Day," written in my mother's hand. There were a couple more pictures of the two of them, a few of me as a baby, several more of the three of us together. Only about a dozen or so in total, but still a worthy collection for a family that didn't even own a camera. I took the wedding day photo and another of me—age four, according to the back—sitting between them on a blanket near the shoreline. I propped them up against the vase on my nightstand, then limped down the hall to the kitchen.

"How long have you had those photos?"

"Years. They were in the box with your books."

"Years?"

"Frances, why are you shouting?"

"When were you going to show them to me?"

"I was saving them for you to have when your time was winding down."

"Cutting it a bit close, aren't you? What if I'd died before you showed them to me?"

"But you didn't."

"But I could have."

"Then I'd have to get 'World's Worst Friend' tattooed across my forehead, wouldn't I? But you're still alive, so stop yelling your damn head off and say thank you."

I was too tired to continue with my pout. "Fine. Thank you."

"Much nicer. I believe this dying is playing havoc with your manners."

"I'm not doing manners anymore," I said and went back to bed. I was still sleeping when Edie called.

"You look tired, Frances. Are you getting enough sleep?"

"All I do is sleep, it seems. But you look great. Tell me what's happening in Edieland."

"Mom met Tareq and she was sweet as pie to him, so points for that, but the minute he left, she was in my face about how I was in over my head with a guy who had no business being interested in a sixteen-year-old, blah, blah. Then she starts in on how terrified she is of me getting pregnant, which you and I both know is a colossal joke. So now we're not speaking. It's a mess, but I figure I just ride her out, right?"

"She'll find her way over to your side. What choice does she have?"

"Exactly. It's not like she's putting me off him. I mean, how does she see this playing out? Me climbing out my bedroom window at midnight and her chasing me down the driveway with a rolling pin? I'm telling you, she's doing me in. I'm hoping Hillary will talk some sense into her. She was here last night, and I could tell she was already over to my side. Oh, she said to say hello to you, and that she misses you at the library."

"Ah, Hillary. She's a good soul. Tell her I miss her too."

"I emailed Annie to ask her how you were doing. Like, really doing. But she said I had to ask you."

"I think things are winding down for me, Edie."

"How do you know?"

"I can just feel it."

"What does it feel like? Sorry, maybe I shouldn't ask."

"No, no, it's fine. Physically, it's just more of what you've already seen, but otherwise it's not all bad. It's like everything is clear and sharp, like the faces on the screen at the movie theatre. Or how everything looks after the sun burns through fog. I don't know how to explain it. I guess it's that life has a way of coating things and death has a way of scrubbing them clean. I don't know if that makes any sense."

"No, I get it. I guess it's that there's nothing competing for your attention anymore, right? Like there's only one thing to focus on."

"There you go. Smart girl."

"Yeah, tell my mother that, will you? She thinks I'm throwing my life away."

"You'll prove her wrong. Of that, I have no doubt."

"You'll still be here for me to visit again, right?"

"I can't promise you that, love."

She welled up but rallied quickly. "Just do what you can, all right?"

"I will."

"I guess I better go. I'm supposed to be tidying my room." She moved her phone around to show me the disaster zone I remembered so well.

"Edie Cleary, I swear one of these days they're going to find Jimmy Hoffa under your bed."

"Who's Jimmy Hoffa?"

"Good night, Edie."

"Later, Frances."

I held my phone in my hand long after she'd disappeared from the screen. I knew she'd eventually find out how I died. But I also knew she'd make peace with it. It was just her way.

Annie came in with a plate of supper for me, but I had no desire for it. "I'm sorry for being cranky earlier," I said.

"Please, you've met my daughter. You're an amateur crank."

She got in the bed and spooned in behind me. At the four o'clock alarm, she got up, fed me my medicine, and stroked my hair until I fell asleep again.

⬦⬦⬦⬦⬦

THE NEXT DAY, SHE took me down to the shore and slowly led me to the dory. Nine more days. When we stopped at the store on the way home, every item seemed to be ninety-nine cents or nine ninety-nine—nines everywhere I looked. As we drove, the squid pressed play on the loop: cloud nine, the back nine, a stitch in time saves nine, the whole nine yards, dressed to the nines, nine lives. I had to turn on the radio to drown it out.

"I feel like we're wasting time on some sort of massive scale," Annie said.

"How do you mean?"

"Like we should be doing something more important than sitting in an old boat and eating macaroni and cheese and watching movies we've seen before, you know?"

"What's more important than that?"

"I don't know. I've been racking my brain to come up with some flashy send-off and I'm stumped."

"I'm hardly the flashy send-off type."

"Still."

We pulled into the driveway and Annie shut off the car.

"I just don't want you to get to the last day and feel like you missed the chance to do something you'll never forget. Something truly spectacular."

"Annie, believe me, I'm doing that every minute of every day."

I pictured her carefully packing away Stephen's possessions and rolling the paint on the bedroom walls. I thought of the boxes of books and pictures gathering dust in attics for decades. The lash of her voice against Angela's indignation, the sound of her laughter at the tavern. The taste of her mouth and the gift of her touch. Her coarse demand for Cyril's silence. The flowers beside my bed, the weight of her foot on mine, and the warmth of her breath on my neck as we slept. *Spectacular.*

21

I suppose had anyone been curious enough about me to ask, they might have been surprised, even disappointed, to learn that many of my last hours were spent sleeping. I bet if I took a poll, a random sample of passersby on Water Street, every last one of them would list off all the marvellous activities they would engage in as the clock ticked down. But they couldn't know what taxing, tedious work dying is, more than any task I'd ever faced, including New Year's Day hotel rooms and Mrs. Heneghan's infuriating collection of antique silver. Sleep had become equal parts relief and torment. My body eased into it as if it were a warm, fragrant bath while my mind scrabbled at the edge of the cliff, frantic with the possibility of missing a single minute of consciousness. Mind over matter, Annie would say as I fought desperately to stay awake. But the matter won every time.

Any time I spent awake was filled with trips to the shore and movies and chatting with Annie, and nine remaining days rapidly dwindled to four, cherished time now passing at the speed of light. When the calendar showed the twenty-eighth, the same day I dozed off in the middle of a call with Edie, I asked Annie to cut back my medication.

"Just take it down a little," I said. "Imagine chit-chatting away and seeing a dying woman's face smack down on a screen. Poor Edie almost had a seizure herself."

Annie laughed. "I would've paid good money to see that."

"She failed to see any humour in it. Besides, I have something to do today, and I need my wits about me."

"What are you doing today?"

"I need to write Edie a little letter, a few final words."

"Here, then. Take a half-dose. Can you see well enough to write or do you need me to help you?"

"I think I can manage, but I need paper. Nice paper, if you have it."

"I do. Are you up for the shore today or no?"

"Maybe later. I want to get this done first."

Annie left and came back with a few sheets of thick cream paper and a matching envelope. I sat in the armchair and picked up a pen. The first draft was stiff and formal and didn't sound like me at all. I took some deep breaths, then began again, writing the words from my heart. I thanked Edie for the joyful noise she'd brought to my sombre life and told her how privileged I was to have had her to look forward to every day for so many years. I told her that I respected and admired her, and that my only real sadness was that my time with her had ended too soon.

I wasn't pleased with how shaky my writing looked, but I didn't want my last words to her written by someone else's hand. When I came to the most important part, I gripped the pen tightly and used my left hand to steady my right.

*Edie, here's what I really want you to know, what I
need you to remember as my parting words to you.
Not long ago, you made a very big decision. Afterward, you wondered if you had done the right thing.
Now I've made a very big decision, and I know for
sure I've done the right thing. I hope you'll understand why I chose to go this way. I also hope that
you live a long and happy life. But what I truly want
for you is a life of your own choosing, one lived only
on your own terms. No questions asked. The other
thing I want for you is a tidy bedroom.*

> *I love you as if you were my own,*
> Frances

I asked Annie to check it over for mistakes.

"It's a lovely letter, Frances. Come on, let's get your saggy arse down to the water before the wind picks up."

We sat in lawn chairs next to the dory and sipped tea laced with whisky. The weather had decidedly turned, and I could smell the fall coming. The sun shone brightly in the blue sky, but its heat had been bled out, trapped in the peeling pink shoulders and knees of children and tucked away until next year. Three days. Three musketeers, three's a crowd, three sheets to the wind, six and two threes, best of three, three strikes you're out.

"Annie, what about your friends?"

"What about them?"

"They've not been around."

"They know I've got some stuff on the go."

"Do they know about the thirtieth?"

"Not from me, they don't. Mind you, I can't vouch for Angela's tongue. I asked her to respect your privacy, and since half the town hasn't called me to give me their humble opinion on it, it's entirely possible she listened to me for once."

"Tell me about them."

"They're a great bunch. You know Tammy Douglas from school. She's on her second husband and he's halfway out the door. Mary Simpson, she's a very good friend. When I think back to when I almost knocked her block off for stealing Donny Doyle away from me. They were together for years after we left school. Thank God she didn't marry him. Her husband is as good as gold. The others are women I only see here and there."

"What do you all do together?"

"In the winter we curl . . . well, we play one game and drink for the rest of the night. Or we go cross-country skiing, stuff like that. And we go into town for the odd weekend and poke around. We're talking about going on another cruise next year, but we're waiting out Tammy's marriage, so we'll see. Mostly we just eat and talk and get each other through. I never would have made it through Stephen without them. And they'll get me through you."

"You're lucky."

"I am. What about you, Frances?" she asked. "I haven't really wanted to talk about this in case it was too sore a point for you, but I think your life has been so lonely. Maybe I'm wrong to say it now."

"No, you're not wrong in thinking it or saying it. I've had long stretches of too much time on my own, but it was mostly my own doing and I've no desire to dwell on it anymore. The main thing is I'm not alone now."

In another life, I would've curled and skied and cruised and been carried through. Maybe the Buddhists and the Hindus and all those other religions I'd read about in a thick red book years ago were right. In a few days I'd find out, and if my soul happened to find its way inside another body, I vowed to lead it straight toward any and all who'd care to call me friend.

Annie dumped the cold tea from the thermos over the rocks, then climbed out of her chair. "Okay, old bag, it's time for your pills."

I grabbed her arm. "Annie, wait. Look." I pointed to an enormous eagle circling high above the wheeling gulls. I'd once worked with a Mi'kmaq woman who'd taught me that the eagle is a special creature. I couldn't remember all she'd said, but it was mostly about courage and wisdom and communicating with the Creator. That the feathers could help ease the fear of moving on to the spirit world. It flew toward us and hovered high above our heads, circled three times, then flew off toward the woods. I shielded my eyes with my hand and searched the sky, but it was gone.

All day I couldn't get that eagle out of my mind. When I called Edie, I asked her to look up the significance of it, and sure enough all things positive were associated with them.

"I think it's a good omen," she said.

"I'm sure it's just a coincidence."

"Why not see it as a sign of peace or strength or whatever?"

"I suppose you're right. No harm in seeing it as a sign of something."

Later that evening, I stood in the grass out back, hoping to see it against the darkening sky, but all I got for my effort was a pair of crows digging for slugs and cawing at each other like a couple of angry spouses. Annie stepped through the door and shooed them away.

"What are you doing out here?"

"I was watching for the eagle."

"Listen, I want to know what you want in the way of food. Anything special you want me to make for you?"

"Last meal request?"

"Yeah, I guess that's what I'm asking."

I thought about it and was disappointed to find that I could think of nothing specific I wanted. I chalked it up to the sense of detachment that had settled on me in the last day or so. It wasn't that I'd lost the thread of what was happening—it just didn't feel like it was happening to me. I was a character playing a part, that poor woman in the movie of the week who had only two days to live. Two left feet, takes two to tango, two wrongs don't make a right, two peas in a pod, two shakes of a lamb's tail.

"How about a chocolate cake? With strawberry jam in the middle?" she asked. "I remember that used to be your favourite."

"Sure. That would be just the thing."

She whipped around the kitchen, and soon the glazed cake sat proudly on a crystal stand. I didn't have the heart to tell her I'd likely eat no more than a forkful of it. We went to bed and lay in the dark, breathing and staring at the ceiling until we both drifted off. Sometime in the middle of the night, I woke to the sound of her crying softly, maybe for Stephen, maybe for me. I didn't know, and I didn't ask. I just laid my hand on her head until she stopped. She rolled onto her side to face the wall and I moved in behind her, wrapped my arm around her waist, and closed my eyes.

THE NEXT DAY WAS dull and cool, and the sea was grey and dotted with foamy whitecaps. We were well set up by the shore with the thermos and smokes, slices of cake in Tupperware containers, and plastic forks. The wind whipped my hair around and stung my eyes and cheeks. Annie had wrapped me in a thick wool cardigan and grabbed a hat and gloves as we went through the door—a maternal reflex, I assumed. I left them in her bag, wanting to feel the island's wrath against my skin one last time. I lit two cigarettes and passed one to her.

A young mother and son appeared at the shoreline. She was teaching him how to get a kite airborne. He held the spool while she ran and flung the bright yellow diamond into the wind. It soared above them, and they jumped and hollered wildly. The woman waved and smiled at us, well pleased with her success.

"That's Tammy's daughter, Jeannie, and Tammy's grandson, Matthew," Annie said. "He's deaf. Tammy's teaching me how to sign with him. You should see how fast he can do it. The father up and left, bloody bastard. So now they live with Tammy. He's a sweet little boy." She sighed and stubbed out her cigarette. "Jesus, she's after seeing me smoking now. She'll tell Tammy and I'll never hear the end of it."

"Annie, we need to talk about some details before tomorrow."

She looked out toward the water, toward Matthew with his kite. "Five more minutes and I promise we'll lay it all out."

I sat and waited patiently as a thick clot of mental clouds began to form in my head. Once the pain set in, all hope of a straight path through thought would be gone. I'd written everything down for that very reason. I pulled the paper out of the pocket of the cardigan. My bank account information and the direction for the remaining pittance to go to the homeless shelter in the city. The cremation paid for in full. A request for my ashes to be sprinkled in the sea. And a final favour to ask of Annie: an obituary. Nothing exalting or self-serving, just a few lines to say I had come and gone.

Little Matthew grew tired of his kite and took off running down the shore with Jeannie at his heels. The abandoned kite pitched and weaved on a gust, then dove sharply nose first into the rocks, where it flapped back and forth until finally a wave claimed it. I handed my list to Annie. Long minutes passed with it balled in her fist.

"Annie, please."

She smoothed the paper against her thighs. "An obituary? You're trusting me with that now, are you?"

"I'll be a pile of soot in a jar. Tell all the lies you like."

"Do you want Edie to help with the ashes?"

"If she wants to. And can you call her tomorrow night and send her that letter?"

"No, Frances, I'm not calling her. I'll drive into town and tell her face to face. I'll put my arms around her and put the letter in her hand. I'll do it right. Don't you worry about that for a second." She watched the waves for a few moments, then stood and held out her hand. "Shall we?"

I nodded and rose up into the bracing wind. Annie led me to the water, where I stood in the North Atlantic until I couldn't feel my feet anymore. I left my socks and shoes among the cold wet stones and didn't look back.

22

I did everything I could think of to stay alert that night, my last night. Black coffee, two cups after dinner. I chain-smoked, added Coke to my whisky, gulped down great breaths of cool night air, skipped the seizure meds altogether, and yet there I was in the armchair, head bobbing and snapping hard enough to break my neck. Not ten minutes before, I'd hung up from Edie for the last time and sat wondering if I'd split in two from the sorrow of it.

An hour before Edie was set to ring, Annie had helped me shower. She'd dried my hair with a towel, then set it in rollers before waving a hot hair dryer at me. She rubbed cream all over my face, then broke out every bit of makeup she owned. She unwound the rollers, carefully brushed my hair, gave me a final dab of lipstick, and buttoned up my good lavender blouse, letting the hem fall loosely over my pajama pants. She propped me up in the chair, then picked up her phone and aimed it at me.

"Okay, Frances. One for posterity."

I sat up straight. "Make sure you don't get my pajamas."

"Cross your hands and lay them on the table. Tilt your head a little to the side. No, the other side. That's it. Now smile. No, that's too hard, too forced. Softer, like you've got a secret to tell."

"For God's sake, it's not the cover of *Vogue*. Just give me a second." I swiped through my phone and found the picture Edie had taken of us at the hair salon. I liked how I looked in that one. I studied it for a moment and tried to copy the smile.

"There you go, perfect. Hold that," Annie said. She took three shots and decided the second was the best. "Oh, that's lovely," she said as she thrust the screen at me.

"I don't know about lovely, but it'll do. You'll send it to her tomorrow night?"

"Right after. Just like you said." She laid my drink and an ashtray on the table and closed the door.

I sipped and smoked until the chime, then forced the corners of my mouth upwards and tapped the button.

"Whoa, Frances, you look fantastic."

"Thank you. You look pretty fantastic yourself." Her hair had been cut to her chin, and it suited her beautifully. She was wearing silver hoop earrings I'd never seen before and her pale eyelashes were curled and blackened.

"Tareq is on his way over. We're going to a fundraiser for Syrian newcomers. How are you feeling?"

"Fine. I feel fine."

"Really? Oh, I'm so glad to hear that. If the weather holds, maybe we can go swimming again the next time I'm out there."

I nodded and gripped my knees as hard as I could. "So Tareq is still the man of the hour, then?"

She got up and closed her bedroom door. "Oh my God, Frances, so get this. Last night we were out eating dinner, and just as I jammed a giant piece of pizza in my mouth, he blurts out, 'I'm falling in love with you.' I almost choked to death."

"Well, now, that's a big moment, right?"

She closed her eyes and gave a little shiver. "I felt like I was levitating."

"How do you feel about him?"

"Same."

"And did you tell him so?"

"I did, despite having a chin dripping with pepperoni grease. The height of romance, I tell you." She rolled her eyes and laughed.

"Good for you, even better for him. Your love is a gift, Edie. Remember that."

"Yeah, yeah, I know, I'm a precious jewel. What do you think about bringing him with me next time? I'd love for him to meet you."

"And I would love to meet him."

"Awesome. I'll email Annie in the morning and ask her. Listen, Frances, I'm so sorry, but I really should go. Mom is home and the minute he shows up it'll be like the Spanish Inquisition down there. I'll call tomorrow night and we can talk longer?"

"You enjoy yourself tonight. Edie, you look so beautiful, so grown-up and ready for the world. It's really something to see."

"Aw, thanks. I feel ready for the world. Okay, I'm off. To be continued." She blew me a kiss and then she was gone, off to love with abandon and to block interference from her mother, just as nature intended.

I sat and stared out the window, heartbroken and mired in distrust of my decision to leave Edie out of this. She'd been excluded for her own protection, and for mine. But maybe I'd got this wrong. Having her with me at the end might have been a blessing. A blessing to whom? Me? Edie? Both of us? I was still trying to work it out when I nodded off.

It was after ten when Annie tapped me on the shoulder to wake me. She startled me and I stood up too quickly. Within seconds I went down hard, a flopping fish once more. When it was over, I felt the warm puddle on the carpet beneath me, and I was overcome with relief, the last shred of doubt carried away by a stream of urine. I knew with a certainty that hadn't fully solidified until that very moment that I could no longer abide. The deed was righteous, and the time was most definitely at hand. A convenient revelation, I thought, given that the good doctor would be locked and loaded in less than twenty-four hours.

Annie stood above me holding a medication bottle in one hand, a glass of water in the other. "You need to take your seizure pills."

I shook my head.

"I'm not asking, I'm telling. I'd like to sleep beside my friend on her last night on earth, and as much as I care for you, I'm not interested in being whacked in the face or pissed on, so open your mouth."

I did as I was told—swallowed my pills, leaned against the shower wall while she cleaned me up, sat on the edge of the bed as she dressed me in a pair of freshly laundered pajamas, then watched as she sopped up my mess on her expensive carpet. I was mortified to be sure, yet there was a comfort in it unlike anything I'd ever known, a feeling of unparalleled closeness to this woman who was caring for me as if I were one of her own, a woman laughing as she blotted and scrubbed and told me to stick my croaked-out cleaning advice right up my arse.

"Pipe down. Two kids, two dogs over the years, and one man. I've cleaned up more piss and shit and whatever else a body can shoot out than you have in a lifetime. I know how to get a bit of lady pee out of this carpet."

"Yes, but have you ever had to pull a used condom off a ceiling? Because I've done that more than once. Two in the same hotel room."

"Jesus, what's wrong with people at all? I expect that gives you some talking room. Although washing a teenaged boy's sheets is worth a prize or two, let me tell you. There. Good as new. Now how are you? How's your pain?"

"Not too bad, but I'll pay for this tomorrow." How casually the word rolled off my tongue. *Tomorrow*. If tomorrow never comes. Here today, gone tomorrow. Eat, drink, and be merry, for tomorrow we die. Christ, that squid never knew when to let up. I spoke softly to it. "Can't you see I've got the upper hand?"

"What?" Annie asked.

"Nothing. I was just talking to myself."

She narrowed her eyes and walked toward me. She bent over me and gave me a soft tap on the side of the cheek. "Pull yourself together."

"Ah, you know you've got a good friend when she can make you laugh the night before you die."

"I think the better measure is in that bucket over there, but whatever you say."

She sat on the bed and put her hand on my cheek again. I pushed my face against her palm and closed my eyes.

"You know you can still back out of this if you want," I said, knowing full well that wasn't true.

"I want what you want. It's you who needs to be sure."

"I'm sure."

"Good, because I'm not cleaning that carpet again." She gathered up her cleaning gear and left me to rest.

I dozed again, then woke to the sound of soft fiddle music. The room glowed from the light of candles placed all around. Annie was next to me, sitting up against the headboard with her eyes closed. I gingerly lifted my aching arm and let it rest across the tops of her legs. Above the music I could hear rain driven by a howling wind pelting against the windowpanes. I made a move to sit up, but my muscles revolted, and I abandoned the effort. Annie kneeled on the bed and hoisted me up against the headboard. She reached down to the floor and pulled up the whisky bottle.

"Can I interest you in a drop?"

"You can indeed." I raised my glass to her and managed a small swallow.

She got up and walked to the window. "Some storm. I hope the power holds."

"Maybe God is giving the place a good going over before I come."

She climbed back in beside me. "Do you still believe in God?"

"I'm not sure I've ever really been a believer."

"I figured those nuns would've drilled it into you."

"If anything, they drove me away. What about you?"

"Depends on the day. I look at the state of the world and I can't imagine how any God would allow it. And when Stephen died, I was sure there was nothing but sky above me. But then I hold little Stevie and I see how perfect he is, or I see something silly like a rainbow and I think, Maybe. Maybe."

"It's a nice idea, heaven and angels and the like, but I can't get my head around the notion of God, not the one we were told about anyway. Some old man sitting out in space somewhere, judging and condemning and selecting who's good enough and who's not good enough to enter the kingdom. Sounds too much like Santa Claus to me."

"So where do you think you're going tomorrow?"

"I haven't thought about it."

"Not once since you found out about the cancer?"

"I was pretty sure there was nowhere to go but into an urn, so I didn't spend any time on it. But now you've got me thinking."

"Okay, just say there was something, some heaven or after-life or whatever. What would you hope for?"

I tried to construct my version of paradise, but my head was too muddy to build anything beyond fleeting visions. I saw water and my parents, old and wrinkled. Edie and Annie. A classroom with my name on the door, a pretty house filled with books, and me coming home to it after a day of teaching, smartly dressed, weary but placid and self-assured.

"I'd hope for a do-over, a chance to be who I always thought I'd be."

"You and me both. Well, I don't know what the hell is out there, but if you do find yourself at the Pearly Gates, I need you to do me a favour: find my boy and tell him I'll be along soon enough."

"Goddamn it, Annie. Don't be saying sweet stuff like that or I'll spend our last night bawling on your shoulder. Besides, for all you know I might end up down below."

"True. When Anthony shows up, tell him I said to go fuck himself."

"I will. And there's something I need to tell you. I was planning to wait to the last moment, but I'm afraid I won't remember tomorrow. I'm thinking about the time I first came back to Safe Harbour, about the day you tore into me for disappearing on you. I went back to town and thought that was it. I'll never see her again. She'll never forgive me. And I had no idea how to die with that hanging over me. But you turned it around. And to find myself here with you now . . . I mean, I don't even have words for it."

"I dare say we both turned it around. It's funny because I was thinking just this morning how proud I am of us for this, for just deciding we were worth the effort. Packing away all the old shit and making it happen."

"I'm proud of us too."

"You know, you make it sound like it was hard for me, Frances, but it wasn't. And you make it sound like it was all for you, but it wasn't. I didn't really know how much I was suffering until I saw you that first day you came back, and somehow going through this with you has really healed me. I wasn't going to tell you this because I'm pretty sure it's a shitty thing to say, but I feel like you've given me my life back."

"What do you mean you weren't going to tell me that? What's shitty about it?"

"Because, dummy, you're dying and here I am talking about a new lease on life. And because you won't be here to live it with me."

"Do you have any idea what that means to me? How happy that makes me? Don't you see? That makes this whole dying thing worthwhile for me. Imagine me going off without knowing that. Good Christ."

"All right, settle down. I told you while you're still alive to hear it. You keep this up and for sure you're going to hell."

"Don't make me laugh. My head is bursting."

I slowly shimmied my way down the headboard and she fed me my pills, then nestled in behind me.

"I'm going to miss you, Frances. More than you know."

I was in too much pain to answer. I reached for her hand and gripped it until I felt the morphine start to kick in, then floated away.

23

I woke to the sound of birdsong. One by one, my systems slowly switched on until I was fully awake and more alert than I'd been for weeks. A soft beam of sunshine streamed through the window, and I turned my face into its path to soak up the warmth penetrating the thick glass. There was no muddled grasping for my bearings, no sudden flood of details lost in the night. No longer did anything seem surreal, and no longer did I feel conveniently disconnected from my own circumstances. Only hours remained—about nine, to be exact—and I figured it didn't get any more real than that. I'd made neither plan nor request for this last day, nothing special to be squeezed in before the sun began to set, mostly because I still couldn't think of anything I wanted over and above what I already had. A brief thought passed through my mind of all the prisoners who'd ever been led to the gallows, like those I'd seen in the movies, those dramatic depictions of the repentant, the defiant, and the odd innocent. What did they do in their last hours? When the time came, did they flail and twist and cry out? Or did they walk gracefully from their cells, straight-backed and reconciled?

My phone chimed and I reached for it to see a calendar reminder on the screen: "Dr. Langley. 7:00 p.m." Seven-year itch, Seven Wonders of the World, seven deadly sins, seventh heaven. I made a last plea to that thing in my head to be still for once and show some bloody respect. I rocked and rolled my way out of bed, body as rigid as a tree trunk. Annie appeared in the doorway as I limped along. She put the tray of breakfast on the table and turned on the tub faucet.

"Food, then a bath and a rub. We're not having you go off like that."

"Yes, ma'am."

I ate half of a sweet juicy orange and a few bites of fresh pineapple, washed down my pain pills with a cup of perfectly brewed tea, and topped it off with a final cigarette that I didn't really want, though the symbolism of it was just too powerful to pass up. Annie lowered me into the bath and placed the CD player on the floor. She lit a candle that smelled like Christmas cookies baking. Then she washed my hair. I sat in the armchair while she dried and brushed, but I put up my hand when she reached for the makeup.

"No, I'm leaving with the face I came with."

She helped me into bed and went off to shower herself. She returned with the big bottle of lotion and rubbed her hands together to warm them. She started at the top of my right leg, currents of electricity zapping under my skin with every stroke. She made the full tour around my body, leaving only my hands and feet untouched, then knelt at the end of the bed and made slow, deep circles with her thumbs on the bottom of each foot and spoke for the first time she she'd started.

"Frances, close your eyes and think back. Back to when it was just you and me. Before nuns and babies and coffins and graveyards. Back to the time before we knew of anything beyond that old dory. I can remember it all now. Can you?"

"I can."

"When you leave tonight, promise me that you'll remember only the good."

"I promise."

She finished my feet and sat on the edge of the bed. She pulled a wrinkled piece of paper from the pocket of her jeans, laid it on her lap, and reached for my right hand. She massaged my palm and kept her eyes down on her words.

"Frances Delaney, fifty-eight, my first and most loyal friend, passed away today—peacefully, willingly, and with dignity. She was a shy woman but a strong one. A kind, clever, and forgiving soul who loved books and music, as did her loving parents, both gone long before her. While the twists and turns of life separated us for many years, she returned to this shore to live out her final days in my house, leaving me forever in her debt." She turned the paper over and picked up my left hand. "Frances leaves behind a legacy of proud service as a house-keeper—the best in town, says her young friend, Edie, who joins me in mourning Frances today and celebrating her for all the days that follow. Few knew her well, but those of us who did respected and loved her more than she could ever know. Please raise a parting glass with me in her honour. Safe journey, my beautiful friend."

I interlaced my fingers with hers and raised her hand to my lips, then brought it to the side of my face. "No mention of my sexual prowess, then?"

She laughed and dug her knuckles gently into my cheek. "I'll work that in after you're gone."

"And maybe thank Dr. Langley."

"I'll see if she's deserving of it first."

"It's as fine an obituary as I've ever heard."

"It is fine, isn't it?" She released my hand and laid the paper on the nightstand.

I thought about gussying up in an outfit, but in the end, I chose to slip back into my blue pajamas, thinking Edie would've likely approved. Annie and I lay outside on wooden loungers soaking up the last of summer. I ate a few bites of a ham sandwich, washed it down with sips of lemonade (a splash of whisky and a plump cherry), and worried down a morsel of Annie's chocolate cake. A whole hour was lost to sleep under the sun that left my face and neck pink. Annie talked and I listened. Once more about our childhood together, about Stephen, about Edie and Tareq, about everything and nothing, like every other day. The shadows grew long, and she grew quiet. I checked my phone. Five forty-five.

I looked at Annie's face in the slanted sunlight and I could see all our years apart in the lines etched into her skin. I found it didn't matter to me anymore. She was my beginning and my ending, and the middle I'd thought so terrible was now nothing more than a collection of tedious moments that had somehow brought me to the only one that mattered.

At six, I asked her to take me to the bedroom. She settled me against two thick pillows, then stood looking at me with a pained expression on her face and her arms wrapped around herself.

"Oh my God, Frances, I don't know about this."

I patted the bed. "Come sit down."

She sat on the edge of the bed with her back to me and leaned forward with her face in her hands.

"Annie, you don't have to stay if you don't want to."

"And what? Sit in the kitchen while you're in here alone? Just give me a minute. I'll be fine." She took a couple of deep breaths, turned the music on low, and lay down beside me.

And God help me, I dozed off. Down to the very wire and still a martyr to sleep. The doorbell woke me. Annie bolted off the bed and turned to me, wide-eyed and alarmed.

"That's her, isn't it?"

"Go open the door. I'm ready."

The doorbell rang a second time, and she backed out of the room slowly. I heard the introductions, the offer of tea and their polite refusals, then footsteps down the hall.

Annie stood in the doorway. "Will I bring them in?"

I nodded.

Dr. Langley stepped in the room, smiling softly, another woman trailing behind her. "Hello, Frances. It's good to see you again. This is Claire James."

She was young, sandy-haired, and so reminiscent of Edie that I almost wept at the sight of her. I expected white coats, but they were both wearing pretty summer shirts and jeans. They looked calm and humbly confident in what they were up to. Dr. Langley sat on the edge of the bed and took my hand in hers. Her eyes moved toward the flowers on the nightstand, then back to me.

"What a lovely room you have and what a beautiful day it's been. Tell me, how's your memory today?"

"I don't know, but I think it's a good day."

"I'm going to ask you a few questions. Just do your best."

The date, the time, the season. Annie's last name, the names of my parents. Seven minus two is what. Where are we now. What is about to happen. She nodded and made notes, then laid her paper down.

"Now just because we're here doesn't mean we have to continue. Do you understand?"

"I do."

"So I'll ask you one final time. Is it your wish to proceed?"

"It is." *Irrevocable. Absolute.*

She nodded solemnly. "If you'd like some more private time, Claire and I will step out. If not, we'll set up there on the table."

"You can start. Annie can stay, right?"

"Yes, of course. Whatever you need."

"Can I lie next to her?" Annie asked.

"Whatever is most comfortable for you both," Claire said.

Annie lay down on top of the covers and held my hand. Claire came to my side of the bed.

"Frances, I'm going to start an IV in your arm, okay?"

I gave Annie's hand a squeeze. "Love you."

"Love you too."

Claire walked back to the table, then Dr. Langley came and laid out the filled syringes on the nightstand.

"The first drug is a sedative that will send you off into a lovely sleep. The second and third will send you into a much deeper sleep and finally bring your life to an end. You won't feel any pain. You won't feel anything at all." She wrapped her hand around my shoulder. "Frances, I want to thank you for your trust in me, especially today. It was my pleasure to care for you all these years."

I nodded, then looked at Annie. She was staring at the ceiling, tears running down the side of her face. She turned toward me and tried to smile, a wobbled effort that she gave up on. I tried to speak, to clearly utter the phrases that would be my last, but I couldn't make my thoughts turn into sound. All those bloody words rattling around in my head for over half a century now suddenly sucked down into the dark and rotting recesses, never to be found again. No words to speak to her one last time, this woman whose uncommon mercy would be known by so few. No way to ask if her memories of me would ever again be coloured by anger and sadness. No words to tell her that I did my best. That I gave to this life what I could. That I was leaving happy. And I wanted to tell her that I remembered the good. All of it. Every minute, every single second locked away in my heart.

Annie held my face in her hands. "I was so afraid of this. So afraid that I couldn't see you through. But I'm not afraid now. All I am is grateful." She leaned in and laid her lips on mine and whispered into my mouth. "Thank you, Frances. Thank you for coming home."

She pressed the side of her face against mine, then slowly pulled back. I held the photo of my parents and my obituary in my right hand, gripped Annie's hand in my left, and nodded the go-ahead to Dr. Langley.

"I'm about to inject the first medication now."

Annie rested her hand on my chest. "You go on now, my love. Go in peace."

Suddenly the room falls away. I hear nothing but the beating of my heart, slow and strong, feel nothing but the weight of Annie's hand as my chest moves up and down with my last steady breaths. My mind is hushed, a clean white chamber where the squid is bowed in silent surrender. I wrap my fingers loosely around Annie's wrist and press my fingertips against her pulse as Dr. Langley slowly pushes the plunger on the syringe. I close my eyes and draw in a deep breath, and I am in the sea once again, rolling on the crest of a great wave. And as I feel myself being drawn under, every cell in my brain discharges a final flare, a flash of energy that instantly takes the form of an image—a woman with pale skin and strawberry-blond hair, a blue-and-white watercolour scarf wound loosely about her neck, a small stack of books held between her thin hands. I feel my mouth fall open as the final word breaks the surface. "*Georgina*." I exhale and let the tide take me.

Acknowledgements

Writing a book can be a lonely endeavour at times, but nobody writes one alone. In my case, I was surrounded and supported by many incredibly gifted people who gave of themselves so freely and completely that it often made my head spin. People like my superb, endlessly enthusiastic agent, Hilary McMahon (Westwood Creative Artists), who embraced this book so warmly, as did Meg Wheeler, International Rights Director (Westwood Creative Artists), who championed my book around the world; my equally enthusiastic and brilliant editor, Jennifer Lambert, whose skill and sensitivity made for very good care of Frances and me; the highly talented and dedicated team at HarperCollins Canada, especially Iris Tupholme, Canaan Chu, Janice Weaver, Allegra Robinson and Alan Jones; Bethany Gibson, whose invaluable expertise helped me steer this story in the right direction (writers, please seek her out—she's a lovely wonder); my dear friend and fellow author, Damhnait Monaghan, whose generosity, thoughtfulness, good humour, and intelligence know no bounds; Jennifer French, Joan Langevin Levack, Lori Shortall, Amy Gesenhues, and Geeta Kameth, who each offered a gentle critique of an early (and very rough) draft; Vivian Swift, who often sends me warmth and guidance from afar; Betsy Lerner, who has inspired and encouraged me for years, just as she has done for so many writers (*merci beaucoup, madame*); my family and friends, who show continued faith in this new work of mine; and of course, Neil McCulloch, with his unwavering support and steady supply of freshly baked cookies. If it takes a village to raise a book, then these people are my villagers. Without them, this novel would never have come to be, and I am so very grateful.

Lastly, I offer my deepest thanks to those who so kindly shared their journeys toward dying on their own terms. Their grace and courage have changed me in ways that are still unfolding.

A light-hearted disclaimer for historians, map-gazers, and sticklers for detail: I know, I know. There is indeed a real place called Safe Harbour on the island of Newfoundland—an abandoned fishing outport located on the northeast coast. However, this is a work of fiction, and the Safe Harbour depicted in these pages is entirely a figment of my imagination.